A slender Ami
usual black bo
reaching back **n.**

The boy pressed himself to his mother as she scanned her surroundings, her gaze stopping on Daniel in what he thought he read as alarm.

He straightened on a jolt of anger. One side of her face was discolored and swollen; the eye on that side opened only a slit. And something about him clearly triggered fear in her. Was it because, like most Amish, she was unwilling to report an assault and he was clearly a law enforcement officer?

The driver unloaded the last piece of luggage from under the bus and got back on board. With a deep sigh, the bus started down the street. None of the buggy horses so much as flapped an ear. It took something much stranger than that to bother them.

Daniel ambled forward, greeting folks he knew, stopping when he reached the Grabers and a cluster of Yoders who were enveloping the two newcomers.

Looking him in the eye, Samuel Graber stepped away from the group.

Protecting the woman and child? Daniel wondered.

"Sheriff." Samuel's greeting was pleasant but he didn't smile. Behind Samuel, his wife was hugging the woman from the bus, while the blond boy gripped her skirts. His straw hat fell to the sidewalk. One of the many relatives picked it up.

Samuel's message was not subtle: *this is none of your business.* But Daniel thought Samuel was wrong. Chances were the woman was escaping trouble of one kind or another. In his experience, trouble had a way of following people.

And the Amish were defenseless.

Dear Reader,

I confess: I'm a longtime fan of Marta Perry's and Karen Harper's romantic suspense novels set among the Amish. And then there's the movie *Witness*, with Harrison Ford dancing in the barn. Temptation came my way. I became even more intrigued once I started reading nonfiction about the Amish, notably Donald Kraybill's collaborations *The Amish* and *Amish Grace*. I found a whole lot to admire in beliefs that are very different than what we see in our typical lives. Forgiveness is not a concept we practice nearly often enough, for example. Their sense of community is extraordinary. Keeping their elderly close and caring for them through the end especially struck home with me, as I'm dealing with my mother's sharp decline into dementia.

Plus I have always loved the clash of cultures (my two historical novels explore this). In this book, both Daniel and Rebecca are steeped in Amish culture because of their childhoods, yet as adults are thoroughly modern Americans. Raised to turn his other cheek, Daniel now carries a gun. Talk about internal conflict! Yet Rebecca's need to save her son drives her to do what she thinks she must, even if it betrays her deepest beliefs.

No, sad to say, they don't slip out late at night to dance in a barn. What they get up to out *behind* the barn, though...

Janice

USA TODAY Bestselling Author

JANICE KAY JOHNSON

Plain Refuge

———

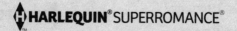

Recycling programs
for this product may
not exist in your area.

ISBN-13: 978-0-373-64021-8

Plain Refuge

Copyright © 2017 by Janice Kay Johnson

www.Harlequin.com

Printed in U.S.A.

An author of more than ninety books for children and adults, **Janice Kay Johnson** writes about love and family—about the way generations connect and the power our earliest experiences have on us throughout life. A *USA TODAY* bestselling author and an eight-time finalist for a Romance Writers of America RITA® Award, she won a RITA® Award in 2008 for her Harlequin Superromance novel *Snowbound*. A former librarian, Janice raised two daughters in a small town north of Seattle, Washington.

Books by Janice Kay Johnson

HARLEQUIN SUPERROMANCE

Visit the Author Profile page at Harlequin.com for more titles.

CHAPTER ONE

"DECIDED TO BOLT with your cut of the money, did you?" asked Detective Ray Estevez, his manner as insulting as his words.

Rebecca Gregory stared in disbelief at the man she had allowed into her apartment. Had he just accused her of being complicit in a crime? Thank goodness Matthew wasn't home! At five, her son was too young to understand the accusation, but he'd have picked up on the tone. Would Detective Estevez have bothered to restrain himself with a child in earshot?

"Or do you and Stowe plan to hook up once the investigation goes cold?" he continued, dark eyes flat and mouth curling in what she took for contempt.

Rebecca stiffened. What a creep. Steven Stowe, her former husband's business partner, had disappeared after embezzling millions of dollars from their construction firm. Why would this detective imagine for a minute that she had conspired with Steven, or had anything but the most distant relationship with him?

"I have never so much as had lunch with Steven Stowe without Tim present," she said icily.

"Yeah? Then why'd you leave your husband?"

Managing to meet his stare, she said, "That is between Tim and me." And, really, her marriage was irrelevant to any investigation, even though the separation had been precipitated by the tension surrounding the embezzlement.

In retrospect, she knew their marriage had already been in trouble when, several months ago, Tim's behavior changed. She knew now that he'd been hit by mysterious and crippling financial problems in the construction firm he had founded with Steven and another partner, Josh Griffen. Then, all she'd known was that the ridiculous hours he worked stretched even longer. He seldom bothered to spend time with his wife and son and brushed off her concern. Worried, frustrated, occasionally angry, he refused to even acknowledge there *was* a problem, not to her. What sex life they had left her feeling used. In fact, he'd shut her out so completely it became obvious she held no meaningful role in his life. Increasingly, she saw that he had never really talked to her, not the way her parents had to each other.

Rebecca had taken her wedding vows seriously. She had sworn to stick with him through these troubles. So she'd kept quiet and made excuses to their five-year-old son when he asked why Daddy was mad or never home.

Except then one of the three partners vanished and it came out that he'd embezzled a great deal of money. Tim's reaction? Not grief at the betrayal committed by a friend. Oh, no. The day after the news of Steven's disappearance hit the *San Francisco Chronicle*, Tim had bounded into the house in a great mood, swung her in a circle and ebulliently told her they wouldn't have to worry about money ever again.

She had looked at him and thought, *I don't understand or know who you are, this man who is relieved, even joyous, because his partner and friend has fled with millions of dollars.* As if that solved all his problems.

She could no longer love a stranger whose ethics she doubted.

But she didn't *know* anything. And she couldn't understand what had precipitated the lead investigator to grill *her*.

"Funny timing to leave your husband," he shot back.

She had to say something. "Tim had been under stress for months while he and Josh and Steven tried to understand what was wrong. That…exacerbated our issues." Wonderful. She sounded like a marriage counselor or a self-help book.

Estevez tipped the chair back, letting her know not so subtly that he had settled in and would stay as long as he felt inclined. "When did he explain the problems at work?"

"The day after Steven disappeared."

He let out a bark of laughter. "You expect me to believe that? You were living with the guy!"

She had been, and it still hurt, remembering how unimportant she'd been to the man who was supposed to love her. Rebecca would be ashamed of herself for staying as long as she had with him, given the way he treated her, but she had been raised to believe marriage was forever. Despite the months of estrangement, if she had been sure he really loved her, she could have forgiven a lot.

Now, she raised her eyebrows. "Believe me or not, it's the truth."

"You're a cool one, aren't you?" He did not sound admiring.

Detective Estevez was of average height, but he was built like a bull, his neck thick, his shoulders powerful. He kept asking questions to which she had no answers. His temper heated. He slammed the legs of the chair back on the floor and planted his forearms on the table so he could lean forward until his sneering face filled her field of vision. He shouted. He wondered aloud what would happen to her kid when she went to prison.

But she couldn't tell him what she didn't know. She didn't have the money; she had never felt close to either of Tim's partners, even though one or the other had dined at the house every few weeks until those last months, when she scarcely saw them.

"You're wasting your time," she said.

He snapped, "*I'll* decide that."

When he ran out of questions, he glared at her for what had to be a full minute. Rebecca laced her trembling fingers on her lap and stared back at him with the pretense of composure.

At last he shoved himself to his feet, eyes narrowed. After flinging a business card on the table, he said, "I'll be watching you."

She didn't respond—didn't move—until she heard the apartment door close behind him.

And then she hugged herself and tried to understand why Detective Estevez *had* wasted time on her when Steven Stowe was the embezzler.

FOUR MONTHS LATER, Rebecca let herself into this house for what she prayed would be the last time. Their house—Tim's house now. No, she'd be here to drop off Matthew for visits or pick him up, but that would be different.

And visits were all that Matthew's stays with his father would be. With resolve, she buried the whiff of fear that she would lose their custody battle.

Once she closed and locked the front door behind her, the silence was so complete that her footsteps on the marble floor of the foyer seemed to echo. Something about that silence gave her goose bumps, even though she had expected the house to be empty. Housekeeping staff had always been part-time.

As Rebecca walked from room to room, she marveled that she'd ever called this place home. Tim had been so excited about building it for them that she'd had to be careful about what she said. He'd ignored her gentle suggestions. An architectural magazine had run a feature on it because the design and function were cutting-edge. Naturally, the finest materials were used. It had just never come to feel homey to her. How could it, with six bedrooms, five bathrooms? To her, it felt like living in a hotel.

Would Tim have listened if she'd spoken out more strongly from the beginning? Rebecca smiled sadly. She could only imagine his expression if she'd said, *"For God resisteth the proud, and giveth grace to the humble."* She had strayed so far from her roots that she couldn't remember the whole quote, but knew there was something about clothing yourself in humility, too.

Pride, Tim understood. Humility wouldn't be a virtue in his eyes.

There was so much she hadn't let herself see when she'd foolishly fallen in love.

In the most recent meeting held at a law firm with both their attorneys present, Tim had told her to take anything from the house she wanted. Typical, she'd thought, feeling a mix of amusement and annoyance. He couldn't look stingy in front of the attorneys. Once he had understood really, truly, that reconciliation wasn't an option—something which had taken months— he'd been generous with financial settlements, as well as the small things.

His generosity had ended when it came to their son. Tim's father, Robert Gregory, was a cold man who too often expressed astonishment that his son had made anything of himself. Whatever had happened between Tim and her, she still detested her father-in-law for what his disdain had done to his own child. Unfortunately, Robert thought Tim had done one thing right—he'd sired a handsome, smart son to carry on the family name. *Divorce* wasn't a word Robert wanted to hear. He couldn't have a dynasty if he didn't have a firm grip on his grandson.

Rebecca had a very bad feeling that Tim's demand for joint custody was only the beginning. Her attorney supported her decision to fight for primary custody. No reasonable person could think a five-year-old boy should live half the time with a parent who routinely worked seventy- to eighty-hour weeks and rarely took a weekend off.

Her gut feeling was that Tim agreed, but he couldn't back down without facing his father's contempt. And so their current standoff continued.

Temporarily blocking her worries, she focused on her current task. She was here, so she should get this over with.

She walked quickly through the ground floor, surveying the ultramodern furniture, which had never been to her taste. Even though the apartment she had rented was still scantily furnished, she didn't want anything from here.

She did miss her exceptionally well-equipped kitchen, so she might raid the cupboards. The fine china or crystal goblets and wineglasses had mostly been given as wedding gifts, and she couldn't imagine using any of them.

Cooking utensils were another matter. She selected a couple of favorite pans and tools and carried them to the box she had left in the foyer. She didn't bother with Tim's office, where she had rarely been invited. Thanks to staff, she hadn't even entered it to clean.

A quick scan of Matthew's bedroom assured her that she'd left only enough toys and books to allow him to feel at home during his weekends with his father. Everything important had already been packed up and brought to her new apartment.

The master bedroom was last. Rebecca was confident she had taken all her clothes and shoes. She had left behind most of the jewelry Tim had given her. She would never wear it again.

There was only one piece she would like to keep—the necklace that had been Tim's gift their first Christmas together. The pendant was simple and lovely, an eighteen-karat gold heart studded with sapphires. They were the color of her eyes, he had told her before gently kissing her. It wouldn't have been cheap, but neither was it extravagant and ostentatious like his later gifts. It would give her one memory to hold on to.

Tim had had a small safe built into his walk-in closet, hidden by stacked hemp storage boxes. Mostly, her jewelry had been kept in this safe rather than the larger one in his office. He'd always insisted on getting the jewelry out for her, but she had seen him dial the combination and remembered it. She doubted he would even notice that she had taken one necklace.

She moved a few boxes and dialed, and a moment later the safe door opened silently. She looked for the small blue box she kept the pendant in, but a surprising flash of red caught her eye. This was a ring, but massive and clearly masculine. Tim never wore rings. Stranger yet, a black leather wallet sat next to it.

Puzzled, she reached for the ring, lifting it out into better light.

Harvard University.

Steven Stowe, embezzler, had worn a ring just like this. An irritated Tim had claimed his partner wore it to flaunt his Ivy League education. Tim and the third partner, Josh Griffen, had graduated from a state university. She had thought they were being unfair. Steven didn't talk about his past much, but she'd heard enough to know he had grown up in lousy circumstances. Making it to Harvard had to have been hugely symbolic to him. The sad part was that his mother had walked out when he was only a kid, and his dad had died of cirrhosis of the liver something like ten years ago. With no siblings, there wasn't anyone left to be awed at his accomplishment.

Rebecca had wondered before whether his background explained why he'd been so desperate for wealth that he had been willing to betray his partners.

Her forehead crinkled as she set the ring back down.

What was she thinking? Of course this couldn't be Steven's! When he'd taken off with the money he'd stolen, he wouldn't have left his treasured class ring behind. And they knew he wasn't dead, because he'd been using his debit and credit cards on occasion, staying constantly on the move. Tim had told her the police hadn't blocked his accounts so that they could trace his movements.

But dread formed anyway, making Rebecca reluctant to pick up the slim billfold. Her hands had become blocks of wood and her chest felt compressed, as if there was something wrong with the air in here. *I don't want to open this.*

But the glow of the ruby was impossible to ignore. *Just do it*, she told herself, and flipped the wallet open.

Steven A. Stowe's face looked at her from his driver's license. His *current* driver's license. One by one, she pulled the debit card and four credit cards from their slots. None of them had passed their expiration dates, either.

But…he was *using* his cards. That was how the police knew—

A whimper escaped her before she could sti-

fle it. Steven wasn't using them at all—Tim
was. He traveled enough for business that it
had never occurred to her to associate his trips
with the times Steven had supposedly cropped
up in Southern California. But maybe the investigators had.

Aghast, she thought about the huge risk Tim
had been taking when he'd used someone else's
credit card for cash advances and large purchases. Except… She gazed at the driver's-
license photo. Tim and Steven did look a lot
alike. People had always thought so. No one
glancing at the awful driver's-license photo
would have questioned his identity, especially
not when the man presenting it dressed well and
had a smile that said he was trustworthy. And,
of course, he could present other ID.

Rebecca dropped the billfold onto a shelf as
if the leather had singed her fingers.

Her almost ex-husband wouldn't have the
wallet, credit cards and, most of all, that ring
if Steven was still alive. So Tim knew he was
dead…and had a stake in keeping the police
chasing a man they believed to be alive and on
the run.

And Tim was *happy* that Steven was dead.
She couldn't forget that.

Panting, Rebecca ran head-on into a terrible dilemma. Did she ensure Matthew's father

went to prison by giving these to that horrible detective? Tim might not have had anything to do with the death. *Knowing* Steven was dead wasn't the same thing. It could have been an accident. And his first instinct would be to protect the company.

She wished as she hadn't in years that she could talk to her mother. But she knew what *Mamm* would expect of her. *"Pray,"* she would have said. *"Ask God what the right course is for you to take."*

Only, Rebecca's faith had been worn down by life with a nonbeliever, by the modernity surrounding her. What her mother, raised Amish, really assumed was that prayer would open her heart, where God's will would be revealed to her.

She wasn't sure she'd recognize God's will if it appeared in letters of fire in front of her, not anymore.

What if she pretended she had never opened the safe? Tim would never know.

Billfold still in her hand, Rebecca was already shaking her head. At least if none of the cards were ever used again, the police would start looking harder at the possibility Steven was dead, wouldn't they? So, in a way, if she took these things she'd be doing the right thing while not betraying a man she'd once loved.

Who *was* a good father, when he found time to spend with his son.

Heart hammering in her chest, Rebecca made her decision. She took the ring out of the safe again and replaced the hemp organizers. Then she rushed downstairs to stow the wallet and ring in her purse, and hurried for the front door.

Which opened just before she reached it.

"Shopping?" her husband said snidely.

A WEEK LATER, Tim arrived at the apartment to pick up Matthew. Playground and burgers, he'd promised.

The moment Rebecca let him in, she recoiled and took a couple of cautious steps back. He was waxen beneath his tan, his eyes wild and his forehead beaded with sweat.

"Dad!" Matthew yelled, and came galloping down the hall.

Taking a couple strides inside, Tim snarled at him. "I need to talk to your mother. Go to your room and shut the door."

Vibrating with shock, Matthew stared at his father. Then, with a muffled sob, he whirled and ran.

"Don't talk to him like that!"

Tim turned his turbulent glare on her. "Why did you have to go snooping?"

She opened her mouth to lie, but couldn't. "I

wanted the sapphire necklace." Which, in the shock of what she'd found, she had forgotten to take. She no longer wanted it. Why cling to a memory of this man's tenderness?

"You don't understand what you stole."

Rebecca stared at him. "Really? I'm pretty sure I do." She searched his face. "Tim, tell me you wouldn't hurt anyone."

"Of course it wasn't me!" He turned away and, with a jerky motion, swung back. "Misleading the cops a little, that's not so awful. It was the only way to save the company. Don't you understand?" he begged. When she didn't respond, his face darkened. "You like your financial settlement, don't you? What if I couldn't keep paying child support? You might have to actually work for a living."

The scathing tone and flushed face pushed her over the edge. "It was your pride that kept me from working during our marriage, and you know it. As it happens, I have a job." Assisting in an elementary classroom would give her an in with the school district when she applied for a teacher's position starting in the fall.

He rocked back. "What?"

"You heard me. And here's something else you need to hear. I haven't gone to Detective Estevez. I know, whatever happened, you *think* you're doing the right thing. And, for better or worse, you're Matthew's father. I did hide the wallet and ring somewhere you'll never find them."

"You can't do this to me."

She crossed her arms. "What exactly am I doing to you?"

"You're holding them over my head." He shook his head, baffled. "Why? You're the one who left *me*. I loved you."

The fury she'd been suppressing swelled inside her. "So much so that I felt like a ghost in your house. One of the few times I tried to make you really see me, talk to me, you shoved me into the kitchen cabinet. I had to hide for days after that so nobody would see the bruises. But you weren't around to notice. You were never around."

"I told you I was sorry!" he yelled back.

"Sorry isn't good enough!" Rebecca struggled to calm herself. She had forgiven him, hadn't she? She wasn't acting like it. "Tim, whatever you believe, my taking Steven's wallet and ring had nothing to do with our history. I just...couldn't let you keep fooling the police. It's *wrong*. Whatever you did or didn't have to do with Steven's death—"

"I told you. I didn't have anything to do with it. And it was an accident, anyway. We just..." He swallowed. "Him dying would have complicated everything. He took the money, he ran. That's all anyone has to know."

Hating what was staring her in the face, Rebecca whispered, "Why?"

"You don't need to know. You need to quit interfering with something you don't understand!" Teeth showing, the muscles in his shoulders bunching, he leaned in. *"Give me back everything you took."*

Rebecca took a prudent step back. "No." Groping behind herself, she found the knob and opened the front door. "You need to leave. I'll make your excuses to Matthew."

He didn't move. "You're blackmailing me."

"No!"

"It's the custody issue, isn't it?" He gave an incredulous laugh. "You've got me over a barrel, and you know it. If I back off, you'll give me what I need."

The possibility had never crossed her mind. She wasn't devious enough. But now that he'd laid it out…heaven help her, she was tempted. Her pulse raced. Matthew would stay with her, and he'd be safe from his critical, domineering grandfather.

What she was contemplating was a lousy way to protect her son, but she'd use anything or anyone for him.

"No," she heard herself say. "I won't give it

back. But you have my promise that I'll keep quiet. No one else will ever see what I found."

Her pulse raced as she waited. His eyes narrowed in a way that told her he was thinking, and hard.

Finally he grunted, said a foul word and agreed.

THREE WEEKS LATER, she had her divorce and primary custody of Matthew, subject to the usual visitation schedule and swapping of holidays.

Detective Estevez might still be watching her, but, thank heavens, he hadn't been back. She hated the idea of lying to his face.

Rebecca already felt tainted enough by a decision she knew wasn't morally defensible. She imagined her mother shaking her head and chiding Rebecca with a gentleness that could still sting.

Yet, her mother had never shed her discomfiture regarding law enforcement. A fear of authority was bred into any Amish man's or woman's very bones by their bloody heritage. Throughout their history, the Amish had been driven out of one place after another by men in uniforms. Burned at the stake, tortured, imprisoned.

To go to the police about a family member's behavior? No, *Mamm* would never have chosen that path. She would help that person see the error of his ways, guide him back to making godly choices. Punishing a wrongdoer wasn't the aim of the Amish, and they never willingly went to the law.

Rebecca shook her head.

Her mother wasn't here anymore. Rebecca was willing to live with a stain on her character if that was the only way to save Matthew from a life of being alternately shamed and molded by his grandfather.

THE DEAL HELD, although Matthew noticed the coolness between his parents. Worse, a couple of months after the divorce, he returned puffy eyed from a weekend with his father. Lower lip protruding, he stayed stiff when Tim hugged him.

Tim gave her an angry look, as if whatever had happened was her fault, then left. Rebecca followed Matthew to his bedroom and coaxed the story out of him.

Grandfather Gregory said some bad things about Mommy, and when Matthew objected, he had spanked him. Hard. And Daddy let him!

Furious, Rebecca hugged him. "Did he use his hand, or a belt, or…?"

Her little boy gaped at her. "A belt? Don't people always spank with their hand?"

Well, that was something. "Is your bottom sore?"

He wriggled on his bed. "Uh-huh."

She gave him another squeeze. "I'll talk to your dad. Sometimes I think he's a little afraid of your grandfather. He may have thought a spanking wasn't that terrible. Especially if you were rude."

"I wasn't rude!" he exclaimed. "I just said my mom wasn't a—" He sneaked a peek up at her. "He said a word you told me I can't."

She could imagine what Robert had called her. What she wondered was why. How much did he know about Tim's part in Steven's disappearance? And the leverage she held over Tim?

"Never mind," she said. "Remember, 'sticks and stones can break my bones, but words can never hurt me.'" Even so, he shouldn't *have* to listen to her being vilified.

Together, she and Matthew decided the best thing was for him to say with dignity, *Grandfather, I don't want to listen when you use bad words about my mom*, and then walk out of the room.

Forehead crinkling, Matthew repeated the line several times, then nodded firmly. "That's what I'll say."

As far as she knew, he wasn't spanked again. Perhaps Tim had confronted his father when Matthew wasn't there. She wanted to think so.

Two months after her confrontation with Tim over the ring, he attended Matthew's graduation ceremony from kindergarten. The three of them even went out afterward for pizza and had fun. At least, she thought they had, but when Tim drove them back to the apartment, he insisted on walking them up, where he asked Matthew to go to his bedroom.

He did it nicely enough, and Matthew shrugged and obeyed. Six now, he was growing like a weed and occasionally giving her glimpses of what he'd look like a few years down the road. That shrug was *almost* teenage. Rebecca wondered if he'd learned it from his fifteen-year-old babysitter.

She quit wondering when she glanced back at her ex-husband and saw the way his expression had tightened.

Feeling a little wary, she said, "What did you want to talk about?"

"Rebecca, you have to give me Steven's things." Tim kept his voice low, but urgency threaded every word. "Josh is pissed about this arrangement. He feels threatened, too."

"Too?" she echoed.

"You don't know what it's like." Hostility darkened his eyes. "Josh is after me, and Dad is angry because I gave in and let you have my kid. Sometimes I feel like that guy in the movie. I'm walking a tightrope between two skyscrapers. The only way off is to fall. That's a shitty way to live."

He was right. It was.

"I'd…like to think I can trust you, but I don't trust your father," she admitted. "Or Josh. And I've kept my word. I haven't told anyone."

"You know Josh is my best friend."

She did know. Josh and Tim had met during orientation for their freshman year of college and had been roommates. Steven Stowe had been a much later addition, needed for his financial acumen. Because Josh had spent his summers working construction, he supervised the job sites. Tim's gift had been convincing clients to choose G, G & S over other contractors. It was because of Tim that half the architects in the city recommended G, G & S to *their* clients. And when the company needed financing, Tim worked his magic on bankers.

"He's leaning hard on me. You need to bend a little, Bec." He hadn't called her that in a long time. But then he said, "I don't know how long I can keep protecting you. Be smart and think about it."

She was speechless, and he departed without saying anything else. Rebecca almost lunged to

flip the dead bolt on the door. Had he been telling her she needed to be *afraid*?

She tried to reason through the cloud of fear.
Even if she returned the ring and the wallet
and cards, she knew about them—about Steven.
Even if she gave Tim the benefit of the doubt,
what if *Josh* had killed Steven during an argument? Would he kill again to protect his secret?
But there was the chance she'd given them to
someone else as insurance.

Whatever he said to the contrary, keeping that
proof might be the only way she could protect
herself.

She put her back to the door and shuddered.

A COUPLE OF weeks later, Rebecca lay sprawled
on the sidewalk, grit stinging her cheek. Dazed,
she knew only that she was the near victim of
a drive-by shooting, and that some man had
tackled her to the pavement right after the first
crack of gunfire.

I would have stood there frozen, like an idiot,
she thought.

She groaned and pushed herself to a sitting
position. People all around were babbling in excitement and alarm. The middle-aged man who
had knocked her down was picking himself up,
too. She heard an approaching siren.

Her phone rang and she groped in her handbag for it. She had to be sure someone from Matthew's day camp wasn't calling. Rattled, she stared at the strange number displayed on the screen. Even the area code was unfamiliar.

"Hello?"

A metallic voice said, "Call that a warning. You have something we need. Return it, or next time we won't miss. And if you go to the cops? Your son is dead."

Knowing the caller was gone, Rebecca began to shake.

CHAPTER TWO

DANIEL BYLER PULLED his squad car to the curb to let a bus pass. Having already noticed several buggies and horses lining the street, he assumed an Amish visitor was expected. Come to think of it, weren't Roy and Nancy Schwartz supposed to be arriving about now from Iowa?

Roy was a cousin of his, although Daniel had lost track of whether they were second cousins or first once removed or… It didn't matter. The Amish tended to have a lot of children, and family networks sprawled and frequently tangled. Daniel and Roy had played together as boys. Too much had passed for them to reconnect as friends, but he did hope his parents would invite him to dinner sometime during the visit so he could say hello.

The bus groaned to a stop in front of the general store. Daniel got out of his car, careful not to jostle the people exiting the bus. He didn't see anyone from his direct family among those waiting on the sidewalk. Apparently, this wasn't the day Roy and his wife and children would

arrive. Emma and Samuel Graber, members of
his parents' church district and their contempo-
raries in age, stood in front of this group. Leaning a shoulder against the brick building, Daniel
exchanged nods with them.

As usual, it was the *Englisch* passengers who
got off first. They had a way of assuming it
was their right. That wasn't fair, Daniel realized, thinking of his good friends among the
non-Amish in his county. There was no way
around it, though—they had a different way of
thinking.

And me? How do I think? he asked himself,
as he did daily. Betwixt and between, that was
him.

Finally a slender Amish woman wearing the
usual black bonnet stepped off, reaching back
to help a young boy down. Looking tired and
shy, the boy pressed himself to his mother. The
woman lifted her head to scan her surroundings, her gaze stopping on Daniel in what he
thought was alarm.

He straightened on a jolt of anger, followed
by curiosity. One side of her face was discolored
and swollen. The eye on that side opened only
a slit. Had she been in an accident? Or was she
a victim of spousal abuse?

Her scan had been wary, and something about
him triggered her fear. Was it because, like most

Amish, she was unwilling to report the assault and thought he might press her to do so?

The driver unloaded the last piece of luggage from under the bus and got back on board. With a deep sigh, the bus started down the street. None of the buggy horses so much as flapped an ear. It took something much stranger than a noisy bus to bother them.

Daniel ambled forward, the picture of congeniality. After all, as county sheriff, he was an elected official. He greeted folks he knew and nodded at strangers while assessing them, until he reached the Grabers and a cluster of Yoders, all enveloping the two newcomers.

Looking him in the eye, Samuel Graber stepped away from the group.

Protecting the woman and child by distracting me? Daniel wondered.

"Sheriff." Samuel's greeting was pleasant, but he didn't smile. The Amish trusted Daniel as a person, but they were wary of everything he represented. Behind Samuel, his wife was hugging the woman from the bus, while the blond boy gripped her skirts. His summer straw hat fell to the sidewalk. One of the many relatives picked it up.

"Family?" Daniel asked easily.

"Ja." Samuel cleared his throat as he made a mental switch to English from the Deitsch

language the Amish used among themselves. "Rebecca is the daughter of one of my sisters. Here for a visit."

His gaze resting on the slim back clothed in a dark blue dress and apron, he said, "You know I'm only here to help."

"You saw she has been injured."

"I did."

"She was hit by a car and thrown over the hood of another. A miracle it is she was not hurt worse."

Daniel nodded. "I hope her little boy didn't see it happen. That would have been frightening."

"*Ja*, but I don't think he did. She will tell us more once we get her home." Without another word, Samuel returned to the group, his broad frame hiding the newcomers.

The message was not subtle: *this is none of your business*. But Daniel thought Samuel was wrong. The sight of a police uniform made many of the Amish wary, and accidents happened every day. But an accident did not leave a woman afraid of who might be waiting for her when she stepped off a bus.

Chances were that she was escaping trouble of one kind or another. In his experience, trouble had a way of following people, and the Amish were defenseless.

He often stopped to say hello to folks in his small county. He'd give the Grabers a day or two and then drive out to their farm, just to say he hoped their niece was recovering and enjoying her visit.

He was opening the door to the café, where he'd been headed for lunch, when he glanced back to catch Rebecca watching him, her expression now unreadable. With her high forehead, fine bones and sharp chin, she'd be a pretty woman once the swelling subsided. Between the bonnet and the prayer *kapp*, he couldn't tell what color hair she had, but she shared her son's blue eyes.

He smiled. She looked startled and quickly climbed into one of the buggies. Her *onkel* Samuel closed the door, and she was lost from Daniel's view. Thoughtful, he went into the café, taking a seat at the window.

As he watched the buggies drive away, he wondered how long the Grabers' guest intended to stay.

THE DRONE OF the metal wheels on the paved road, the sway of the buggy and the clip-clop of the horses' hooves would quickly make her drowsy, Rebecca feared. At least she didn't have to strain to understand Deitsch, often called Pennsylvania Dutch, which was actually a Germanic dialect. *Aenti* Emma and the others had spoken English from the moment she stepped off the bus. Or maybe they were doing so for Matthew's sake. Rebecca suspected the language would come back to her quickly. She had been reasonably fluent once upon a time— as a child, she had spent her summers with her Amish grandparents. She had loved those visits until she became a snotty thirteen-year-old with the same preoccupations as her other San Francisco friends. Boys, the right clothes, boys, how unfair their parents were, boys. The plain life had suddenly held no appeal. Her mother's disappointment in her wasn't enough to combat peer pressure.

That, she thought now, was when her foolishness had begun.

"Your *aenti* Mary gave you clothes, I see," *Aenti* Emma said approvingly. Her round face was as cheerful as always, but she had become considerably stouter since Rebecca had last seen her.

"Yes." Rebecca plucked at the fabric of her apron. They had gone first to her *aenti* Mary and *onkel* Abe's farm to confuse anyone trying to find them. "It feels strange, I have to admit." She kissed the top of her son's head. "Matthew doesn't know what to make of the suspenders."

Sarah, the younger cousin she scarcely re-

membered, chuckled. "They suit him fine! We
are so pleased to meet Matthew at last."

Matthew buried his face against Rebecca. His
hat fell off once again. The two other women
laughed. *Onkel* Samuel, in the driver's seat, either couldn't hear or was ignoring the women-
folk.

Sarah said, "He will be less shy once he sees
the horses and cows and chickens, ain't so?"

Matthew sneaked a peek Sarah's way.

Rebecca would have smiled if it hadn't hurt.
"He was fascinated by *Onkel* Abe's horse. I
don't think he's ever been close enough to pet
one before. He went to a birthday party this
spring that included pony rides, but that's it."

Aenti Emma beamed at Matthew. "He will
like our horses."

Rebecca let out a breath that seemed to drain
her, mostly in a good way. She wouldn't be able
to stay here forever, but for now she and Matthew were safe. She couldn't imagine Tim or
Josh would think to look for her among the
Amish, or succeed if they tried. She'd told Tim
that her mother had grown up Amish, had mentioned summers with her grandparents, but
would he remember? Would he know *Mamm's*
maiden name? Or that those summers had been
spent in Missouri? He'd rolled his eyes at the
idea she had been happy even temporarily in

what he considered a backward, restricted life, and she doubted he'd really listened when she talked about family. Because of his lack of interest, she hadn't mentioned her Amish roots in a very long time. And where the Amish were concerned, most people thought Pennsylvania or Ohio. An investigator could find her mother's maiden name on her marriage certificate, but no one from her family had attended the wedding or signed as a witness.

Graber wasn't quite as common a surname as some among the Amish, but there were Grabers in many settlements, so tracing her wouldn't be easy. In many ways, the Amish lived off the grid. They weren't in any phone directory unless their business was listed. They didn't need driver's licenses, and they didn't contribute to federal social security or draw from it. Living on a cash basis, none of the Amish Grabers would be found in a credit-agency search, either. They did have Social Security numbers, or at least many of them did, because they paid federal income taxes and state and local taxes. Still, would a private investigator have access to income-tax records?

She had done her best to complicate any pursuit by initially flying to Chicago, then backtracking by bus to Des Moines, where she and Matthew had switched to various local buses, paying cash. They finally wended their way to Kalona, Iowa, where more of Rebecca's relatives lived. Having received a note from *Aenti* Emma, *Aenti* Mary and *Onkel* Abe Yoder had kept her arrival and departure as quiet as possible. Their bishop and some members of their church district knew that their niece and her child had fled something bad and needed help. If an outsider came asking questions, she had confidence they'd pretend ignorance. Staying reserved was their way even when they had nothing to hide.

The unquestioning generosity still shook her. Even though *Mamm* had jumped the fence—left her faith—to marry Dad, the family considered Rebecca and now her son their own. She'd never even met the Iowa relatives, and yet they'd welcomed her with open arms.

Once she and Matthew were appropriately garbed, another cousin had driven them several towns away, where they caught yet another bus. They had meandered south into Missouri, changing buses frequently. By this time, Rebecca's entire body ached until she could hardly pick out the new pains from the places that already hurt when they set out from San Francisco. But at last they were here.

Aenti Emma leaned forward and patted Rebecca's knee with her work-worn hand. "*Ach,* here we are, talking and talking, when I can see you close to collapsing! Lunch and some sleep is what you need."

"That sounds wonderful," she admitted. A glance told her Matthew was nodding off already.

She was grateful when her aunt and cousin lapsed into silence and let her do the same.

She found herself thinking about the cop who had talked to *Onkel* Samuel just before they left town. A sudden certainty that someone was watching her had felt like icy fingertips brushing her nape. She'd known she should keep her head down so as not to draw attention, but she hadn't been able to stop herself from looking around. If Tim was already here, waiting for her... But then she'd seen the uniformed police officer, instead, as broad-shouldered and strong as the farmers and woodworkers she knew among the Amish, men who labored hard. His face was too hard to be handsome, too inexpressive, his eyes too steely. His cold scrutiny reminded her of the way Detective Estevez had looked at her. She guessed this police officer to be older than she was, perhaps in his midthirties. His hair was a sun-streaked maple brown that probably darkened in the cold Missouri winters.

Rebecca looked down to see that her hands were clenched together hard enough to turn the tips of her fingers white. With an effort, she loosened her grip. Yes, that man made her anxious. Had he only been interested in her because he'd noticed the bruises? But why had he been leaning against the building watching people get off the bus in the first place? Did he check out new arrivals every time the bus stopped in Hadburg? Was that one of his duties? In this rural county, she wouldn't have thought the local police force would have the personnel to be so vigilant—unless they were watching for someone in particular. Could Detective Estevez have figured out where she'd gone already?

A bump in her pulse rate left her light-headed. She was being stupid. Estevez hadn't bothered her since their one interview. Tim shouldn't notice her disappearance until tomorrow, after he arrived to pick up Matthew for his scheduled visit. And violating the custody agreement wasn't an offense that would draw police attention, certainly not at first. Would Tim even dare file a missing-person's report on her or accuse her of custodial interference?

No, the last thing he wanted was to attract more attention from the police. That didn't mean he wouldn't hire a private investigator to find her, if he didn't set out to do so himself. She wondered what he'd tell his father. Tim wouldn't want the man to know his grandson was out of his reach.

And Josh. What would Tim tell the partner who'd been pressuring him? Would he try to protect her, as she was protecting him?

She feared not, given the results after she had gone to him about the shooting and the phone threat.

Aenti Emma swayed gently with the motion of the carriage, her gaze resting on Rebecca and Matthew.

"I saw *Onkel* Samuel talking to that police officer," Rebecca blurted, not sounding as casual as she wanted. "Does he know him?"

"We all know Sheriff Byler. His family moved here when he was, oh, sixteen or so, you see." An odd hint of discomfiture in her voice caught Rebecca's attention, but *Aenti* Emma continued, "He went away and nobody knew for a long time what he was up to, but he became a police officer, of all things! And in the big city." She shook her head, scandalized by the mere idea. *Aenti* Emma had probably never been as far as St. Joseph, let alone Kansas City. Why would a local boy want to leave placid Henness County for a place that was all concrete and towers of glass and steel and noise? Sirens and car horns and people shouting. So much noise.

"What city?" Rebecca asked, as if it made any difference.

"I heard he went to St. Louis. I guess he didn't like it, because he came back three years ago and got the *Englisch* to vote for him to be sheriff. That Gerald Warren, who was sheriff before, nobody liked him. He was lazy, and he looked down on the people."

The *Leit*, she meant. The Amish. Lazy Sheriff Warren wouldn't have been alone. Even tourists equated plain with simpleminded and gullible. Rebecca's mother used to talk about how much resentment was caused by the slow, horse-drawn buggies with metal wheels that wore ruts in roads, even though the Amish paid road taxes like everyone else.

"So you like this Sheriff Byler?"

"He's a good man," *Aenti* Emma said, although a hint of ambivalence remained. "He listens and understands why we won't go to the law most of the time."

Rebecca nodded her understanding. Would that "good man" poke his nose in her problems? Perhaps she should take advantage of the opportunity if he did. It wouldn't be a bad thing if he knew to watch for anyone asking about her. Even if she didn't tell him about the unholy bargain she'd made with Tim, if the sheriff thought she was running from her ex-husband because he was stalking her, he might form another line of protection.

But of course that would mean telling him she wasn't Amish. Almost instantly she shook her head. What if he went looking for police records concerning the alleged abuse? Or even searched online for information about Tim? It might be the modern equivalent of yelling, *Here she is.* No, it would be better to stay away from Sheriff Byler, however good his intentions were.

She had to grab the seat as the buggy turned sharply. The wheels made a crunching sound that told her they were no longer on a paved road. Peering out the small window, she saw fields of corn growing high in the August heat. Oh—and sunflowers, an entire field of them! A minute later, the crops were replaced in her view by grazing cattle. A sign for a produce stand caught her eye. This was all so familiar. Comforted, she sat back and gently stroked her now-sleeping son's hair.

Finally they turned into a narrow lane. Corn grew on one side, while to the other was pasture. Enormous, dappled silver horses grazed. Rebecca smiled. *Onkel* Samuel still bred and raised Percherons, as his father had before him. As a child, she'd been awed by the gentle giants with velvety lips and stiff whiskers and big brown eyes. They had seemed magical to her. She hoped they would to Matthew, too. He didn't understand why they were making this trip or who these people were, but she had confidence he'd enjoy himself as much here as she had as a girl.

Another bonus of staying here—she didn't have to worry about Matthew getting to a phone and calling his father. She had left her cell phone behind for fear it could be used to trace them, and Sarah was the last of *Aenti* Emma and *Onkel* Samuel's children left at home. Some Amish teenagers did have cell phones during their running-around time, but Sarah looked to be past that. Rebecca had no intention of telling Matthew about the phone in the shanty that used to be halfway between the Graber farm and the neighbors.

The buggy swayed to a stop and *Onkel* Samuel got down and came around to let them out. She carried her sleeping son in her arms, though he began to awaken with the movement.

The large farmhouse was just as she remembered it, painted a crisp white, the wide porch still holding a swing and several comfortable chairs. A small wing attached to one side of the house, the *grossdawdi haus* where her grandparents now lived, had its own porch. Two dogs raced toward them from the huge barn.

"Down, down," *Onkel* Samuel said, intercepting them. The dogs spun around in excitement, barking.

Matthew tightened his grip on her neck and lifted his feet out of reach. "Mom! Do they bite?"

Onkel Samuel set a gentle hand on his head and ruffled his hair. "No, they will be your best friends before you know it. Especially if you sneak them some treats."

His wife turned a look on him. "Don't suggest he waste my good cooking on dogs!"

He only laughed, his face creasing above the distinctive Amish beard that reached his chest. It was the clean-shaven upper lip that made it different from facial hair among the *Englisch*. "Boys will be boys," he declared. "I will bring your bags once I stable Molly," he added, and got back into the buggy. The dogs hesitated, then bolted after him as he drove toward the barn.

"It's so good to be here." Rebecca's eyes burned. She tried to smile. "Thank you for having us."

"You're family," *Aenti* Emma said simply.

Sarah hugged her.

"We can't know God's purpose," *Aenti* Emma murmured, "but the bad things that happened brought you and Matthew to us, which is reason to rejoice. *Grossmammi* especially has worried about you. Letters aren't the same."

"No. I wish…" Rebecca didn't finish the thought, and saw in the two women's kind faces that she didn't need to.

Just then the front door in the *grossdawdi haus* opened and her grandmother hurried across the lawn to envelop her in more hugs. Her grandfather followed more slowly, every breath a rasp. In the eighteen years since she'd seen them, they'd aged more than she had anticipated. Both had white hair now and looked frail. Guilt stabbed Rebecca. Why hadn't she managed to visit? Brought Matthew sooner for them to meet?

But her grandmother showed no hint of accusation. It would not be her way. "How often I have prayed to have you restored to us!" Her wide smile included Matthew. "And now to be able to get to know your son, as well! Such a blessing."

The entire family ushered her and Matthew into the house. In no time, Sarah had poured glasses of lemonade while Rebecca's aunt and grandmother set out home-baked bread, different cheeses and cold cuts, as well as a special peanut butter sweetened with marshmallow cream. There were at least two kinds of cookies and fudge besides. Matthew's eyes grew wide, while Rebecca knew this was a modest meal by her aunt's standards. There would be a much greater variety at dinner.

Matthew was initially suspicious, but he tried the strange peanut butter and grinned his approval, exposing the gaps where he'd lost baby teeth. Before she knew it, lunch was over and they were upstairs, ushered into a typically bare room with two twin beds. Sarah helped Rebecca out of her clothes, drew the curtains and left them to lay their aching bodies down to rest.

Safe, Rebecca thought, and then sleep claimed her.

DANIEL THOUGHT OF the strange woman on Sunday, and even drove by Reuben Gingerich's house where church was being held. The every-other-Sunday Amish services were held in homes or barns, the privilege of hosting it rotating among the families in each church district. A dozen or more buggies lined the fence at the top of the lane. The horses stood hipshot and lazy in the shade from a grove of old black walnut trees that Daniel suspected were quite profitable for Reuben.

Daniel usually attended a service at the Congregational Church in Hadburg, which he had joined on his return to Henness County. The occasional Sundays he missed were understood as part of his job. Sometimes that was even true. Sometimes, he parked out of sight and walked across a field to where he could hear the Amish singing hymns, so much a part of his childhood. He never went near enough to a barn or house to chance being seen or to hear the sermons, but the singing quieted something in him even as it reawakened his sense of loss.

It was very different from hymns sung in the Congregational and Baptist churches in town. All Amish hymns came from the *Ausbund*, a thick book passed down through many generations. It contained only the words, no musical scores. The singing was slow, often mournful, the voices blending together into one. An Amish would say, "One with God."

The familiar hymns sharpened Daniel's emotions. Sorrow seemed strongest—or perhaps *regret* was a better word to describe the jagged feeling in his chest. And yet…he wouldn't go back if he could. He still believed he had made the right decision. He was where he belonged, protecting his people but separate from them. Daniel only wished his choice hadn't left him alone, however many friends he made, belonging neither here nor there.

Annoyed with his self-pity, he shook his head and turned his back on the large red barn, where the multitude of voices had fallen silent. He walked back to his squad car and drove away. He always tried to be present when the fellowship meal broke up. Most locals were good about keeping watch for the slow buggies and Amish on foot, but despite all warnings tourists still drove too fast. They didn't understand how quickly a car could close in on a buggy pulled by a trotting horse. Car-and-buggy accidents were too often tragic. He and his deputies dreaded being called to the site of one.

Unfortunately, he couldn't be everywhere. Three separate church districts fell completely within this county, which meant services being held at three separate homes on any given Sunday. He had assigned two deputies to patrol today while he did the same, the best he could manage given limited resources. With fewer than ten thousand people in the county, Daniel's entire department consisted of himself, a sergeant and five deputies, as well as two administrative assistants who were also dispatchers.

The two largest cities in Henness County, including Byrum, the county seat, had their own police departments.

Amish businesses might be in town, but the people rarely lived within city limits, so they were, with few exceptions, in his care. A wry smile accompanied the thought. *They* believed they were in God's care, not his. He was careful not to mention his alternate opinion on the matter in the hearing of anyone Amish.

The cars he saw as he patrolled were likely driven by tourists. Amish businesses and roadside stands were closed on Sundays, but the idea was incomprehensible to the typical American who came to sightsee.

Daniel found himself thinking about the Grabers' guests, as he had more often than he should in the three days since their arrival. They would have been in the barn, the boy still young enough to sit beside his mother on a bench on the women's side. He wondered if Rebecca had been able to surrender herself wholeheartedly to God today, or whether she held some anger or fear in reserve. However good their intentions, Amish struggled with negative emotions like everyone else. Nonetheless, her feelings toward whoever had hurt her would be far more charitable than his, he could pretty well guarantee.

Tomorrow, he decided, wasn't too soon to stop by the Graber farm and ask after their visiting family.

He refused to question why he was so eager to do so.

CHAPTER THREE

"THEY'RE AWFULLY BIG," Matthew said, standing behind the board fence and well back from the row of Percheron horses.

Rebecca stroked the cheek of the nearest gelding, which whuffled a response that startled a giggle out of her, one that made her wince as her swollen cheek protested. "They're friendly," she said. "From birth, *Onkel* Samuel and cousin Mose groom them and feed them and pick up their feet, so they like being around people. Didn't you see these four pulling a plow yesterday? That was part of their training, to work as a team. I think they will be ready for a new home soon." The horse she was petting nudged her for more attention, and she added, "They can smell better than we can, so they know we have carrots."

"They really like carrots?" her son said dubiously. He didn't mind carrot sticks, but detested cooked carrots. His pickiness where food was concerned had already brought surprise from her family here, where children weren't indulged in the same way they were in the outside world.

"A carrot is like a cookie to a horse," Rebecca said firmly. "Watch."

She broke off a chunk and held it on the palm of her hand. The horse she'd been petting promptly lipped it up and crunched with such enthusiasm that saliva and flecks of carrot flew.

Matthew laughed.

She had just persuaded him to feed a piece of carrot to another of the horses when she heard a car engine followed by the sound of tires crunching on gravel. There were innocent reasons for a car to be driving down this quiet road, even if the homes on it were all Amish owned, but she couldn't control her spike of anxiety. She turned and saw the green-and-white SUV with a rack of lights on the roof slow and turn into the lane leading to her aunt and uncle's home. It would pass right by her and Matthew. Rebecca had no doubt who the driver was.

Turning her back on the police car, she cupped Matthew's hand and helped him hold it out. He squeaked in alarm when lips brushed his palm, then laughed in delight when the carrot vanished.

"It tickled!"

The police vehicle rolled to a stop right behind them. A door slammed, and she and Mat-

thew both turned to face Daniel Byler, who
strolled around the front bumper and joined
them.

"These are beauties," he said in a voice that
was just a little gravelly. "Your uncle raises the
handsomest draft horses I've ever seen."

She smiled despite her tension. "Say that to
him, and he would then tell you about three
other Amish men he knows who raise horses
just as fine. And he would also admonish you
for admiring them for their looks, when it is
strength and willingness and heart that truly
matter."

His chuckle was a little rough, too. "You're
right, he would. Although I have no doubt he is
willing to discuss desirable conformation with
buyers."

"An entirely different thing from calling them
beautiful," she said, trying to repress another
smile.

"Why shouldn't they be beautiful?" Matt
burst out. "Aren't horses s'posed to be—"

"Sheriff Byler is teasing," she said hastily,
seeing his raised eyebrow. "And you know
Onkel Samuel is right. These will be working
horses. A horse pulling a plow could be mud
brown and have a bump in the middle of his
forehead and mismatched eyes, one blue and
one brown—"

"Like that dog we saw!" he said excitedly.

"Yep." Uh-oh. *"Ja,"* she said hastily. "Remember how funny-looking he was? But if the horse was strong and did the job, no one would mind how he looks."

"Oh." Matthew frowned, then nodded. "Can I have another carrot?"

The sheriff stayed at their side as they proffered, piece by piece, all the carrots they'd brought. Rebecca was very careful to guide their minimal conversation so that Matthew wouldn't have a chance to say anything else so un-Amish.

Sheriff Byler offered them a ride up to the house, which she would have refused except for Matthew's excitement. She held him on her lap in the front seat. The sheriff showed him how to turn on the siren and flashing lights.

Matthew reached out. "Can we…?"

"No," she said quickly. "Think how it would frighten the horses."

"Oh." He subsided. "I guess it would."

He was happy when a voice came over the radio. A deputy reported, using code that the sheriff translated, that he'd pulled over a motorist for speeding.

Byler's mouth was tight, and she knew why. Speeding was always dangerous, and particularly on narrow country roads shared by horse-and-buggy travelers.

At the house, she opened the door and let Matthew out first. Already used to the dogs, he giggled to find them waiting. "Go tell *Aenti* Emma or *Grossmammi* that Sheriff Byler is here. I'm sure he would like coffee or one of those sticky buns I saw going in the oven."

Accompanied by *Onkel* Samuel's dogs, Matthew raced for the house while the sheriff laughed. "You know your aunt's sticky buns are famous in these parts. She bakes enough so the café in Hadburg can sell them."

"Ja," Rebecca said, striving for the faint accent she heard in the speech of local Amish. "For sure, I know my cousin Sarah drove to town this morning to deliver some."

Matthew had wanted to go, but Rebecca wasn't ready to let him out of her sight. The plain clothing wasn't enough of a disguise. His hair was too short to resemble a typical Amish boy's bowl cut. His new, wide-brimmed straw hat didn't hide his face the way a bonnet did hers, and that was when he managed to keep it on his head. And if he saw his father…

Who couldn't possibly have found them yet, she kept reminding herself, for what good that did.

"You seem to move carefully," the sheriff

said, before she could leave him. "Are you healing?" Turning toward her, he laid his forearm casually on the steering wheel.

"Yes, I am mostly sore."

"Mostly?"

Being this close to him unnerved her. She was too conscious of him in a short-sleeved uniform. His forearms were strong and tan, dusted with bronze hair tipped with gold. She could see the hint of darker stubble on an angular jaw and noticed the thick, short lashes and the wave in his hair. His eyes were a penetrating dark blue. To evade them, she lowered her gaze, which meant she was looking at powerful thighs. Damn it.

"I have bruises," she admitted after a moment. "And two cracked ribs. They hurt the most."

He frowned. "You shouldn't lift your son."

"My middle—" she laid a hand over her stomach "—is wrapped for protection. Of course I must pick him up."

He made a grumbly sound she took for disagreement, but said, "What happened?"

Careful. "I stepped out in the street—" She cut herself off before she finished the sentence. The last thing she could admit was that she'd been about to get in her car. "I thought I had looked for traffic, but afterward I was confused, so I'm not sure. A car came fast and hit me. I think I was jumping out of the way, but it still lifted me in the air. I went over the hood and banged into a car coming the other way. That driver stopped to help me, but not the one who hit me."

"A hit-and-run."

"*Ja*, that's what the police called it. No one saw the license plate, so there was not much they could do."

As she had lain there waiting for an ambulance, she'd berated herself. She should have fled after the shooting. Instead, because Tim had sounded shocked about what had happened when she called him, she had given him a couple days to talk to "other people"—his vague reference. Make sure there was no repetition. Instead, he had called her back the next day to say tensely, "You've got to give those things back, Rebecca. You'll be okay if you do. I swear."

Not believing that for a second, she had packed and been ready to run as soon as she picked Matthew up at day care. That was where she'd been heading when she was hit.

This time, she hadn't been surprised when her phone rang. The message conveyed was even shorter: "Ignoring my last call, not so smart. Lucky for us, you have a weakness."

Matthew. Dear God. All she could think to do was take him and hide.

Now Sheriff Byler watched her in a way that made her suspect he knew there was more to her story, but he only said, "I'm surprised you chose to travel when you were hurt."

"I wanted to go away," she said simply—and truthfully. "Here it is quiet. Not so busy."

"Where are you from?" he asked, as if making conversation. She knew better and had been prepared.

"Pennsylvania. There, we have so many tourists." She shook her head. "I was scared every time I crossed a street or heard a car coming up behind my buggy."

A twitch of his expressive eyebrows made her realize her mistake.

"You think I am not trusting in God."

He didn't say anything.

"I do in my head," she explained, "but my heart still races and my hands shake."

"Post-traumatic stress," he said quietly.

She pretended to look puzzled.

"Your body reacts without waiting for permission from you. It takes time for that kind of response to go away."

She shivered. *"Ja."*

He laid a big hand over hers. "You're cold."

Her fingers curled into her palms and she quickly withdrew from him. "My hands and feet are always cold."

A smile crinkled the skin beside his eyes. "Even in August here in Missouri? Teach me your trick."

She wanted to laugh. Instead, she said shyly, "There is no trick. It's fine in summer, not so good in winter."

"No." His gaze rested on her face a moment longer. Then he reached for his door handle. "We should go in. I see your uncle coming from the barn."

Oh, heavens—everyone in the house was probably peeking out the window by now.

"*Ja*, you are right." She leaped out faster than she ought to have and slammed the door. "I should have been helping to cook, not sitting here like a lump."

Walking beside her, the sheriff said, "I suspect your family wants you to rest until you don't hurt anymore before you dive into chores."

"That doesn't mean I have to listen to them. It is so kind of them to take us in."

Another mistake—he must know that visiting was a favorite pastime for the Amish, who loved having family even for extended stays.

But Sheriff Byler only glanced sidelong at her before remarking, as if at random, "It occurs to me your last name isn't Graber."

Her mind stuttered in panic. She couldn't admit to being divorced. The Amish didn't divorce. Widowed. She would be widowed, except then she would have retained her husband's last name. And she'd never heard of anyone among the Amish with a last name of Gregory.

Lie? But Matthew might give her away. Oh, no—if he ever told anyone *his* last name was Gregory, they were in trouble.

"I... No," she said.

The front door opened just as *Onkel* Samuel reached them, his long strides eating up the ground. Amid the greetings, Rebecca was able to slip into the house and take Matthew to the bathroom to wash his hands. Heart still thudding, she realized how important it was that she avoid giving Sheriff Daniel Byler any more chances to corner her. She'd made too many slips already. He wasn't Amish, of course, but she suspected he knew the citizens of his county well enough to notice anomalies in her speech or behavior. And he was too interested in her.

Once back in the kitchen, she took a seat at the far end of the farmhouse table, staying silent as her uncle talked with the sheriff about local happenings, including an upcoming street fair and auction in Hadburg to raise money for the volunteer fire department. She tensed, knowing everyone would go. People would comment if she and Matthew didn't.

When Sheriff Byler finally rose to leave,

her uncle politely standing to show him out, Rebecca only joined the others in murmuring "Goodbye."

She nudged her son, who said, "I liked looking at your police car," which was only polite. That was the moment when Rebecca realized in horror that they had been speaking in English the entire time. Of course they had been. But an Amish boy Matthew's age shouldn't *be* fluent in English.

Frantically trying to think of an excuse if the sheriff ever asked, Rebecca didn't let herself meet those dark blue eyes, and she stayed seated until he was gone. Once she heard the engine, she let Matthew run outside.

Onkel Samuel came back to sit across the table from her. "Curious about you, he is."

She nodded. "I think that's why he came by this morning."

"*Ja*, that is so." Lines in his forehead deepened. "I didn't tell you, but after you got off the bus, he asked about your face."

Her *aenti* Emma and *Grossmammi* bustled in the background and didn't contribute to the conversation.

"I knew he'd seen my bruises," Rebecca said. "When we were sitting in his car, he asked how it happened. I made it sound like an accident, but told him the driver didn't stop and the police hadn't been able to find him."

His face relaxed. "That is good. There was no need to lie."

"No." *Onkel* Samuel wouldn't approve of lying, but... "He asked what my last name is. You greeted him then, so I didn't have to answer, but what if he asks again?"

He pondered that. "Outsiders join us sometimes. Someone named Holt could be one of them."

"Yes, but if he looked me up in his computers, he might find me. And Matthew's name is different from mine, besides." She hesitated. "I did lie to him. I said I had come from Pennsylvania."

He frowned. "Perhaps we should tell him what you fear. Someone must set things right. I think he can be trusted." Still, he sounded reluctant.

Inexplicably, the idea of confiding in Sheriff Byler was appealing...as was he. And that triggered a new kind of alarm. Being attracted to him was a really bad idea. Plus, a physical attraction was absolutely the wrong reason to trust him. She could easily imagine him being cocky enough to think he could solve her problems, and arrogant enough to do what he thought best without asking her first. And that was assuming he didn't have more in common with Estevez than she wanted to believe.

"The fewer people who know I'm not Amish, the better," she said slowly. "What if he tells a friend, or one of his officers, who tells someone else? So fast, everyone could know."

"If you ask him to keep silent…"

"Why don't we wait and see what happens?" she said. "He came out here and saw that I'm doing fine. He may have satisfied his curiosity."

After a moment, he nodded. "*Ja*, that is so."

Rebecca hesitated. "You don't think I'm off in the head to think someone was trying to kill me?"

"*Wu schmoke is, is aa feier,*" he said without hesitation.

That much of the language she remembered: where there is smoke, there is fire.

"God asks us to trust in Him, but He does not say to be a fool," her uncle added. "When a horse lifts a hoof and I see he will set it down on my toes, I move my foot *schnell*."

"*Denke,*" she said, torn between humor and tears.

He only smiled and said, "I must get back to work." Clapping his straw hat onto his head, he departed.

It took her a moment to collect herself enough to rise and say, "Let me wash those dishes, *Aenti* Emma."

DANIEL DROVE AWAY from the Graber farm no more satisfied than before. He knew he didn't have Rebecca's whole story. She'd failed to offer her last name, which increased his suspicion that she was running from an abusive spouse.

He didn't much like that explanation for several reasons. At the forefront was the danger to Rebecca and her kid. In his experience, domestic violence was like dynamite, volatile and deadly.

What was most puzzling was the rarity of an Amish woman fleeing from her husband. They were a peaceful people, committed to nonviolence. Domestic abuse existed among them, but forgiveness was so ingrained that women rarely gave up on a husband. Or perhaps it was more that the women knew how few alternatives they had. If the abuse was bad enough, she might go to her bishop, who would chide the husband, maybe going so far as counseling him and demanding he confess and beg forgiveness from the entire congregation. But for the wife to take her child and run... Daniel had never heard of such a thing.

Even as he brooded, Daniel noted how well the corn seemed to be coming on, thriving in the heat. Many local farmers would plant a second crop once the corn was harvested—soybeans had become a success in the difficult northern Missouri climate, but many of the Amish chose a cover crop like forage turnips, which provided good grazing for livestock and kept down weeds. Even the Amish moved with the times, just with more deliberation than their neighbors.

He wasn't sure what more he could do to help Rebecca when she so clearly didn't *want* his help. Daniel fully understood the stubborn refusal of the Amish to turn to outsiders. Samuel Graber was a capable man, and he had extended family in the county. Yet he was ill equipped to counter violence. The best he could do was slow down an intruder to give Rebecca and Matthew time to hide in the barn or the woods at the back of the property. Samuel would let himself be shot rather than strike a blow.

And that was where Daniel had collided with the *Ordnung*, the rules directing the people that had once been his.

No, his decision to go out in the world had been more complicated than that, as nearly every life-altering decision was, but he knew his father or mother would say sadly, "Daniel could not forgive."

To them it was that simple.

He wished he thought any of the Grabers would call him if a dangerous man came seeking Rebecca.

"SLEEP TIGHT." REBECCA kissed her son's forehead and stood. She lifted the kerosene lamp to light her way back downstairs. Thank goodness Matthew had never been afraid of the dark.

"Mommy?" he whispered.

She paused and turned back.

"Can Daddy come see us here?" Matthew asked. "I bet he'd like the horses, too."

He'd asked about his father when they first set out, but not since. After a moment, she returned to sit on the edge of his bed again. Smoothing his hair, she said, "You know how hard he works. He wouldn't be able to get away for days and days. This is our adventure."

"But…what about when it's *his* weekend?"

His weekend had just come and gone. She didn't like to think about how he'd reacted.

"We'll make up for it later," she said. "Just like we do if he has to travel for work and can't be home for his weekend."

Matthew was quiet. She knew he understood that much.

"I don't know when we'll go back," she said softly. Or *if.* "Aren't you having a good time?"

"*Aenti* Emma makes good cookies. And I liked fishing with Abram and his dad."

Mose, the son who farmed alongside Samuel, had his own house and a growing family on the far side of the cornfield. In his thirties, he already had four children, the oldest almost eleven. Like Matthew, Abram was six.

"Only, Abram doesn't talk that good."

"That *well.* And Abram talks just fine, but he's only starting to learn English. I actually thought he was doing pretty well with it for his age."

"But how come he doesn't speak English? *Everyone* does."

So she explained again how the Amish people spoke their own language, and that children weren't usually exposed to English until they began school at six years old. By the time they finished eighth grade, they would be able to speak two languages, which was more than you could say for the typical American student.

Matthew was quiet long enough that she hoped she could slip out, but then he said, "Abram wants me to go to school with him. He says *Sarah* will be his teacher." He sounded astonished.

Rebecca smiled despite feeling a pang. When

would she be able to have her own classroom again? She could hardly apply for jobs now. "It's true. Cousin Sarah is a teacher. Just like teachers and kids at home, she has the summer off. She told me that tomorrow she is going to the schoolhouse to start preparing for the new school year. I offered to help her clean. You can come with us, if you'd like."

"Can Abram come, too?" he asked, with eagerness that encouraged her.

"If his *mamm* and *daad* say he can. Now." She made her voice firm. "Sleep, and no argument."

"'Kay," he murmured. "But you'll come to bed real soon, too, won't you?"

"I will." Without electricity or television or smartphones, there was little temptation to stay up late. And on a farm, the work began early.

She kissed him once again and this time made her escape, taking old worries and new ones with her. What would she say if Matthew kept asking about his father? If he begged her to let him call Daddy? And how would she react when he found out he likely wouldn't be in Mrs. Chisholm's first-grade classroom this fall, but would instead be joining his cousin Abram and the other children in their church district in a one-room school?

He was young. He'd adapt.

But Rebecca knew she'd keep asking herself

if this huge adjustment she expected of him was
fair or even possible. And yet Tim had let her
know he couldn't protect her or Matthew. Her
priority had to be keeping herself and Matthew
safe. If Tim truly loved their son, if he felt even
a shadow of affection for her, he would understand what she'd done.

How long would they have to stay in hiding?
Right now, all she could do was check the internet for any news about Steven, Josh, Tim or the
construction company when she could make it
to the library in Hadburg. If she found no news
about an arrest or closing of the investigation, at
some point, she had to talk to Tim again.

But not yet.

CHAPTER FOUR

A WEEK AFTER his visit to the Grabers', Daniel strolled down the middle of Grove Street, the main drag in Hadburg, closed today to motorized vehicles and horses and buggies for the three-block length of the business district. Instead of the usual traffic, stores had flung open their doors and spread out onto the sidewalks. Booths and tables offering crafts, fresh-picked produce, desserts and a bounty of home-canned goods lined both sides of the street. The quilt shop had attracted a crowd of locals and tourists with half a dozen tables covered with packets of coordinated fabrics and small quilts, mostly Amish made. Even the Amish Heritage Furniture store displayed small side tables and quilt racks on the sidewalk.

So far, so good. The cop in him leaned toward pessimism, but there was no reason to think there'd be any trouble. Support for the volunteer fire department was genuine hereabouts. People recognized its importance in their lives. Today's fair was part of an effort to buy a new tanker for the department. Naturally, the Amish were the big draw for outsiders. The tourists were thrilled because the street was thronged with Amish, buying and selling.

The impetus for the event had been the fire out at the Bontrager place in early July. The barn had not only burned to the ground, but sparks had caught on the roof of the house and they'd lost it, too. A tanker truck full of water might have made a difference. The drought had left the creek at the back of the property running too low to be any use.

Although Amish and *Englisch* neighbors alike had joined to rebuild, Eli Bontrager ran his harness business out of that barn. His tools, supplies and finished products had all been casualties, as had a young horse that pulled his daughter's open buggy.

Shaking off the memory of the horse's screams and the devastation on the faces of the entire family, Daniel ambled for another half block, exchanging greetings. He was glad to see so many people supporting the fire department. Their town didn't usually draw tourists the way the larger and better-known Jamestown did.

Today was hot as sin—a saying his father had particularly disliked. Had to be over a hundred in the shade. The stifling humidity didn't help. His summer-weight uniform already had wet circles beneath his arms. He could feel sweat running down his spine. Water stations up and down the street offered relief, and merchants and police alike knew to watch for the effects of heat on shoppers.

He'd have been happier if the plan hadn't included a beer garden, set up in the small park, which also boasted a bandstand and a bronze statue of a local Civil War hero, a major in the northern army. Some still muttered that there ought to be a statue representing the Confederate side, as well—or instead. Missouri had been torn in two by conflicting loyalties and an ugly guerrilla war between the Union army and the raiders with Confederate ties.

Food booths in the park were doing good business. His stomach rumbled at the smells emanating from grills. Seeing that Anna Ropp was selling her pierogi, Daniel veered in that direction.

But he detoured at a raised voice in the roped-off beer garden. He shook his head at the sight of an all-too-familiar face, flushed with anger and a beer or two too many. Billy Shaver. No surprise, his brother Damon was with him. Daniel had intended to make one of his every-couple-week stops at their run-down rural property in the next day or two, anyway. The two younger Shaver brothers had walked out of the penitentiary only four months ago after serving time for operating a meth lab in their barn. The oldest Shaver, Jethro, had another six months to go.

Stopping just outside the rope, Daniel caught their attention. "How you boys doing? Good you're out here supporting the fire department."

Billy, the hothead, opened his mouth but swallowed whatever he'd been about to say when Damon elbowed him.

"Just having a beer," Damon said. "Thinking about some lunch. Nothin' wrong with that."

"Not a thing," Daniel agreed, aware of their audience. "I was heading that way myself." He looked over the park. "Hadburg is doing itself proud today. Haven't been called for so much as a shoplifter."

Billy snickered. "Guess them weirdos think God would strike 'em dead if they stole a stick of gum."

Quelling his instinctive dislike for this weasel, Daniel only said easily, "Don't know that it's that extreme. They're raised to believe taking something they haven't earned is wrong. They don't lie, either."

"So that guy over there—" the little creep jerked his head toward a middle-aged Amish couple walking side by side "—tells his wife she's a fat cow before he climbs on top of her?"

"That's a good woman," Daniel said quietly.

"She deserves respect." Figuring he'd about reached the end of his store of tact, he nodded and said, "Enjoy yourselves," and walked away.

As much as he disliked the Shaver brothers, he had to wonder how much of a chance any of them had ever had, being raised in that house. Their father had been even more notorious than they were. Once Daniel became sheriff, he had reviewed the domestic violence calls to that address, ending with Clara Shaver dying from a supposed fall down the stairs. Her husband had ultimately drunk himself to death, but not before he'd ruined his sons.

Behind him, a woman's voice rose above the hubbub. "Matthew! Matthew!"

He swung around to see a frantic Rebecca spinning in circles as she screamed her son's name. People hurried to her, trying to help, but she didn't even seem to see them.

Daniel reached her in a few strides. "Rebecca." More sharply, he repeated her name, and she finally focused on his face.

"When and where did you last see your boy?"

"I was buying carved wooden horses from Ike Schwartz, and when I turned around Matthew was gone." Wringing her hands, she cried, "He knows better! What if somebody—"

"I think I see him," he interrupted. Without conscious thought, he slid into Deitsch. "*Ja*,

there is Mary Yutzy, holding his hand. See?"
He risked touching her, nudging her to face the
woman who hurried toward them, holding the
little boy's hand.

Her body quaked until she spotted her son,
and then she sagged. Afraid she'd go down onto
the concrete sidewalk, he supported her with
his arm. But she sprang to life, leaping first to
hug Matthew, then to scold him. She appeared
to be unaware of the many people listening and
probably wondering, as he did, that she spoke
English. Did her boy not know Deitsch at all?
Daniel speculated. How could that be?

Finally she wound down enough to thank
Mary and him. Mary patted Rebecca a few
times before hustling back to her table, where
she sold honey from her hives.

"Have you two had lunch yet?" Daniel heard
himself ask.

Her sky blue eyes widened. "I—"

Matthew shook his head. "Uh-uh. I'm hungry, Mom. Did you see those giant pretzels? I
bet they're good. That's where I went. I woulda
come right back, 'cept you weren't there." The
accusatory tone suggested that if Mom hadn't
panicked and started running around like a
chicken with her head cut off, she'd have seen
him right away. That she'd been afraid he was
lost wasn't *his* fault.

Daniel didn't show it, but he thought if Matthew wasn't an all-American kid, he'd eat his hat. The one he rarely wore, of course. Speaking of which...

He ruffled the boy's blond hair. "Did you lose your hat?"

Matthew ducked his head guiltily. "I don't know where it is."

His mother rolled her eyes.

"Come on." Daniel smiled at her. "I'll buy you lunch."

That earned him another wide-eyed look of alarm. "Oh, you don't need—"

"I'd enjoy the company." He glanced at the boy. "Best get Matthew out of the sun."

"Oh!" she exclaimed. "I left my bag—"

While he waited with Matthew, Rebecca hurried back to Ike Schwartz's booth, returning with a woven-grass shopping basket that bulged with her purchases.

He set them moving across the lawn toward the food booths and tents that lined the north end of the park. The location had been chosen to take advantage of the big shady sycamore trees. A couple dozen plastic tables and chairs provided a place for folks to eat.

While mother and son looked at the vendors, Daniel radioed to let his officers know he was taking a break and where to find him. Matthew didn't seem to have ever seen a pierogi and went for a hot dog, while Rebecca chose chili and corn on the cob. Daniel bought giant snicker-doodles for all of them. Matthew decided they were *almost* as good as his *grossmammi's*.

Daniel grinned at him. "Even if they were better, a smart boy wouldn't say so, would he?"

"Uh-*uh*." He had a cute grin that gave him dimples and displayed missing teeth.

Rebecca's bruises had faded and the swelling had gone down, letting him see that she had a classic heart-shaped face, a high fore-head framed by rich chestnut hair parted simply down the middle, in the Amish way, and a gauzy white prayer *kapp* with the ties loose. The lilac color of her dress and apron enhanced the blue of her eyes. He guessed her to be five foot six or seven, and curvy. Despite the mod-est dress with a hem at midcalf, he could tell that much.

Watching her smile at her son, he knew the tug he felt every time he saw her wasn't ex-plained only by her looks. He liked that she wasn't good at hiding what she felt. It all showed on her face. This wasn't a woman used to lying or with any aptitude for it. Her fierce need to protect her son pleased him, too, as did her soft-ness toward him.

Seemed his determination not to think about

her this way hadn't lasted past setting eyes on her again.

Predictably, Matthew finished eating first and wanted to go watch the older boys playing a casual game of baseball in the nearby diamond. After making him promise to stay where she could see him, Rebecca let him go. The way her gaze followed him, Daniel could tell she wanted to keep the kid on a leash.

He'd have preferred not to add to her stress, but knew he might not get another chance to talk to her alone. So he asked right out, "Matthew was not raised plain?"

Those beautiful eyes met his, the color deepened by worry and inner conflict she wouldn't like to know she was betraying.

Her shoulders slumped. "I... No."

He raised his eyebrows.

"His father..."

She sneaked a desperate look at him. "We're running away."

No kidding.

Her gaze went to her son, then back to his face. "*Onkel* Samuel thought we should tell you. In case, well..." She hesitated.

"Your husband comes after you?"

Rebecca pressed her lips together. "Matthew's father, but not my husband." She swallowed. "Ex-husband."

Daniel didn't even blink as he stared at her, absorbing the words that changed everything.

SHE SAW HIS SHOCK, followed by understanding.

"He's not Amish. You jumped the fence," Daniel said.

Beyond the instinct that insisted he wasn't anything like the San Francisco detective, Rebecca didn't know why she was telling him anything. But she'd seen his expression as he'd gently teased Matthew and listened to him chattering away over lunch. He already knew. Not everything, but too much. They shouldn't have come today. She'd been foolish to let herself be persuaded by her aunt.

Now she had to make a quick decision. Still, there was no reason to lie about her background, given how much he had guessed.

"No," she said, staring across the grass to Matthew, whose fingers were wrapped in the chain link as he watched avidly. At home, he had been begging to play T-ball. "Not me. My mother. She fell in love with my father, who was a grad student here studying the language. He wanted to know how quickly it changed as the Amish migrated."

The sheriff nodded, although it was safe to say he didn't care how her parents had met.

"They were happy. He became a professor.

They were, um, killed a few years ago. Matthew doesn't remember them."

Still not getting to the point.

"The thing is, Mom wasn't rejecting her faith or her roots when she left. She hadn't been baptized yet, so she was able to stay in contact with her family." The Amish were not baptized until they fully committed to the church in their late teens or early twenties. "As a child, I spent summers here with my grandparents."

"The Grabers."

"Yes. I hadn't seen them in ages, but when I wrote asking for help, they didn't hesitate."

"They wouldn't," he said mildly.

"So…here I am." Was that enough to satisfy him?

"Did he hurt you?"

He was a cop. Of course he'd have questions. Probably lots of them.

Her gaze shied away. "No, it's not like that." Wait, she *wanted* him to believe her ex-husband was a stalker. Fumbling, she said, "At least, I… don't know for sure. He's been…threatening. And then, well, a couple things happened that really scared me." She nibbled on her bottom lip as she debated whether she needed to edit the next part. No. There was much she had to keep secret, but not this. "First, I was almost shot," Rebecca told him. "The police thought it was gang related and I just happened to be in the way." The phone threat… No, she couldn't tell him about that, not unless or until she had to admit to the entire story.

"What city?"

"Do you have to know?"

His eyebrows twitched. "We'll talk about that after you tell me the rest of what happened."

Wonderful. This was why it would have been better if she had been able to stay off his radar. But…*Onkel* Samuel was right. Sheriff Byler could be a first line of defense. She just had to convince him not to research any of what she'd told him.

She glanced at her son again before her eyes met his. She had a bad feeling she was baring too much of the pain and fear that filled her every time she thought about Tim. He had turned into a man she didn't like or respect, but she *knew* he'd never have said, *Sure, shoot my ex if you have to. And a threat against my son? Great idea.* He was being terrorized, too—she had to believe that.

Needing to answer the sheriff's question, she touched her cheek gingerly. "This. It happened only two days later. Like I told you, I was crossing the street to get to my own car, parked on the other side. I looked both ways, I swear I did. I'd almost made it when this dark SUV just came out of nowhere. I was flung into the air and came down on the hood of a car coming the other way. I was lucky. So lucky."

"You were," he agreed, his gaze lowering to her hands, clasped tightly together on the plastic tabletop. "Nobody saw the license plate?"

Rebecca shook her head, fluttering the white ribbons. The *kapp* still felt alien. She never wore hats. "Someone just coming out of an apartment building said the driver swerved and accelerated. The woman heard the tires squeal as he went around the next corner. She's the one who called 911."

"You didn't get a good look at the driver."

"Nooo." Uncertainty stretched the word. "I know it was a man, not my husband, but…" She half shrugged. "He could have hired someone." *Please forgive me for the lie*, she thought. But she couldn't tell this man that she didn't believe the real enemy was her ex-husband.

"He could have," Daniel said quietly, although she could tell he had his own thoughts about that. "Had he been stalking you?"

"Not…exactly." She'd intended to stick with the stalking ex-husband scenario, but Daniel— no, no, she had to keep thinking of him as the sheriff—had seen how extreme her panic had been when she lost sight of Matthew. He must have guessed Tim was focused on their son, too. "He wasn't happy about the divorce," she offered. When he didn't leap to fill the silence, she squirmed. "Our big conflict was over Matthew. My ex-husband works ten, twelve hour days at a minimum, but he demanded joint custody." She made a face. "Actually, I'm pretty sure the demands came from his father, who I suspect just wanted me out of the picture. Matthew is *his* grandson, and that's all he cared about." Letting this man hear her bitterness, she added, "I doubt he'd have been the slightest bit interested if Tim and I had had a daughter instead." Oops. She hadn't meant to use his name. But really, a first name didn't tell the sheriff much.

"Are you afraid of your ex-husband or your father-in-law?" he asked.

"I'd say my father-in-law, except… Tim has this *huge* need to impress his father. I wish I thought he was capable of saying no to him, but…" She trailed off.

Matthew turned away from the baseball game and started toward them. Following her gaze, Sheriff Byler said, "Rebecca, if I'm to be of any help, I need to know where you came from. And your ex-husband's full name." His mouth quirked. "Yours, too."

WELL, SHE'D TOLD him that much, if she hadn't lied. Which he was reasonably sure she had, even if not about her name.

Daniel had escorted her to her aunt, whose head had been turning until she spotted Rebecca.

"Do you want to stay longer?" Emma asked. "Samuel and I need to take Ephraim and Ruth home. Ephraim keeps saying he is fine, but he doesn't look so fine. We can come back later for you. Or Sarah says Katie and Paul Kurtz will bring her home. You and Matthew could ride along with them."

Ephraim and Ruth were Rebecca's grandparents. Ephraim's heart was failing, Daniel knew. He was surprised the old folks had decided to come out on such a hot day.

Naturally, Rebecca insisted she and Matthew were ready to go, too, which maybe they were. Was Matthew of an age to still take naps?

Daniel returned to his foot patrol after checking with his two deputies that there'd been no disturbances while he ate lunch. He caught a glimpse of a buggy briskly receding down the street in the direction of the Grabers' farm, the reflective orange triangle obvious on the back. Daniel was grateful that the church districts in his county embraced some modern safety standards. In Old Order settlements, every decision was made with a rigid belief that they must trust in God, not modern technology, to protect them. In some, the *Ordnung* did not allow for reflectors on the buggies, far less the battery-operated lights the more pragmatic local bishops permitted. Bishop Jonas had told Daniel their concern was not so much for themselves but for the *Englischers* who might be injured in an easily preventable accident.

Rebecca Holt. Daniel had committed the other names to memory, too. Timothy Gregory. Robert Gregory. Presumably, her kid was a Gregory, too.

He could find more information in a heartbeat now that he knew she'd come from San Francisco, not Pennsylvania. Except he'd made a promise.

"Please," she'd begged, keeping her voice low. "*Please*. Promise you won't contact San Francisco PD in *any* way. Tim's family is prominent enough, I'll bet they have an in at the police department. And that Tim has hired a PI by now. If you do anything, it will draw attention."

Matthew reached them at that inconvenient moment, leaning against his mother, his eyes fastened on Daniel.

"Not without talking to you again," he agreed. He hadn't had a chance to ask why she believed the man she'd been married to wouldn't know her grandparents' names or where they lived. Had her ex never met them?

Daniel had learned to swear casually when he went out in the world, part of the camouflage that had helped him blend into police culture even before his slight accent faded. Now he was trying to unlearn the words. His Amish constituents in particular would be shocked, and he found he didn't like that kind of language. But listening to her talk about the drive-by shooting, as well as being flung into the air by a speeding car, had strained his ability to maintain a professional demeanor. He'd had to bite back a few pungent words.

Even as he exchanged greetings with people, asked how sales were going, helped a frail older lady without the sense to get out of the sun before she collapsed, he kept mulling over what Rebecca had told him—and what she hadn't.

Taking her fears at face value left too many questions in his mind. If the Gregorys were so all-fired powerful—which usually meant wealthy—why hadn't they challenged the custody agreement in court? Or fought harder for joint custody *before* the divorce was final? Murder was a pretty extreme solution for anyone but a mob figure.

And, while it was possible someone was trying to kill her, he had a lot of trouble believing it was a stalker ex-husband. Usually, domestic violence was up close and personal. Sure, there were instances when a person paid someone to knock off an inconvenient spouse. But those *were* the exception.

In Rebecca's case, she'd had two frightening experiences and, probably because they occurred so close together, leaped to the conclusion that somebody was trying to kill her. He could tell she didn't want to believe that somebody was her ex-husband. Better to blame the former father-in-law she so obviously disliked.

Coincidences bothered him, as they did most cops. But in this instance, he couldn't help thinking that the two near misses actually could have been coincidental. Cities did have more crime and crazier drivers than rural Missouri did. Had she checked to find out whether the drive-by shooting suspect had been arrested? By now, even the hit-and-run driver could have been charged. The police took things like that seriously, and they likely had a scrape of paint from the vehicle, which was a good start.

Had she ever sought a restraining order? He guessed not. That especially bothered him now that he knew she wasn't Amish. What if the cops were after *her* for some reason?

Knowing how easily he could get some of his

questions answered left him frustrated. Still, his promise didn't mean he couldn't do a general search for her ex and his father. He'd have to use his tablet—the police-department computers trawled the internet closer to the speed of a rowboat than a powerboat.

What kind of man had Rebecca Holt married? This need to know was more than curiosity. If it was an itch, it was the kind you got from poison ivy.

"DAD WOULDA HAD fun today, too," Matthew said wistfully, shortly after they left town.

Rebecca's grandmother was preoccupied by Ephraim, who kept irritably shaking off her concern even though they could all tell his breathing had worsened. If she heard Matthew at all, *Grossmammi* didn't react.

"Actually—" Rebecca injected amusement into her voice "—I think your dad would have hated it. He wouldn't have been interested in anything that was for sale." She smiled. "Maybe a straw hat. It is *hot*."

Her son's nose wrinkled. "Really hot. I wish it would get foggy."

She smoothed a hand over his hair. "I doubt we'll get that lucky."

He lapsed into silence again, and she couldn't tell if he was satisfied with their exchange or still thinking about his father. Her eyes caught her grandmother's, and Rebecca realized she'd been listening, after all.

"A nap will be good, *ja*?" she said. "This evening will be cooler. I'm thinking Mose might take you and Abram fishing tonight or tomorrow. Fresh, fried catfish, yum."

"Or sunfish," Rebecca said suddenly. "I remember pulling in a few of those from the pond."

Matthew's eyes widened. "Would I have to kill 'em?"

"I think Mose would do that part," Rebecca said. "He knows the fish you've eaten before came from the grocery store."

"'Cept at Dad's," he argued. "Justina says she buys fish at one of the piers, right off the boats. So it's fresh."

Tim had changed housekeepers right after the divorce. Justina was full-time and, according to Matthew, prepared dinner for Tim as part of her duties. Matthew liked her, and Rebecca had felt confident he was safe with her. The meals she'd prepared were considerably more gourmet than what Rebecca whipped together after a day's work. The comparison might have annoyed her, except six-year-olds didn't generally appreciate gourmet. Matthew was happiest with fast food or macaroni and cheese out of a box.

"Did you like the fish she prepared?" Rebecca asked.

He wrinkled his nose. "It was okay, 'cept she always put gunk on it. Sometimes Dad got mad when I scraped it off."

"Gunk?" *Grossmammi* queried.

"Sauce."

Matthew didn't like *any* sauce. He preferred his foods carefully separated and undisguised.

"Ah," *Grossmammi* said, her face crinkling with humor. "*Aenti* Emma, she won't put this *gunk* on any fish you catch."

"Fishing might be fun," he decided. "I like Abram's *daad*. He helps us talk together."

"*Gut,*" Rebecca said, teasing a bit, then intrigued to see that he didn't seem to notice she'd used Deitsch. She'd picked it up quickly her first summer here, when she was… She had to think. Six or seven. A new language was so much easier to learn at that age.

Matthew was silent for a couple of minutes. Then he mumbled, "I bet my *daad* would like fishing, too."

Rebecca smiled, but worry ratcheted up a notch. Back in San Francisco, Matthew had hardly mentioned his father between visits. So what was this really about?

CHAPTER FIVE

IT DIDN'T TAKE Daniel long to discover that Rebecca Holt was right about her former husband and father-in-law's status in San Francisco. The father lived on Nob Hill, while Tim Gregory had built a monstrosity of a house—featured in a local magazine as an architectural gem—in a neighborhood described as SoMa. Robert Allen Gregory was a venture capitalist, which meant he owned pieces of a lot of other businesses. Mostly high-tech, it appeared. Tim had grown up privileged, but one article mentioned in passing his degree from a state university. Given the younger Gregory's background, Daniel would have expected him to go to Stanford or someplace like that. Had he rebelled? Or had even Dad's influence failed to get him into a school with a fancy name?

Whatever his educational background, Tim had done well for himself, launching a construction business not long out of college with two partners. The senior Gregory's influence might have come to bear there, because they almost immediately made a name erecting ugly but enormous houses and condominiums for people made newly rich with tech start-ups.

Daniel studied a few G, G & S buildings and tried to imagine living in one. Why would anyone want a house big enough for five families when you didn't plan to fill it? As a boy, he had liked being able to hear the murmur of adult voices after he'd gone to bed. He would have been scared to be alone in a bedroom two floors away from the main living space. Apparently, these houses were "wired" to compensate for the great distances between rooms. A little boy could call for Mommy using his intercom.

He shook his head and went back to an article profiling the successful partners of G, G & S Construction. Tim Gregory and a second partner, Steven Stowe, were lean, handsome, tanned men with expensively cut blond hair and flashing smiles. In contrast, the third partner, Josh Griffen, had darker coloring and a bullish build. He came across as more blue-collar, which made sense since, in managing the job sites, he was the one who seemed to do the actual building. He hadn't bothered to summon a smile for the camera. Daniel found a photo of Tim and Rebecca. Its caption mentioned but didn't show Matthew. The other two men were described as "eligible bachelors," often seen on the city social scene.

Most interesting was the succession of articles in the *San Francisco Chronicle* and other newspapers about the shocking embezzlement of funds some ten months before from G, G & S by Steven Stowe, who had handled the money for the firm. The implication was that Griffen and Gregory had begun to suspect some malfeasance and perhaps confronted Stowe, who then disappeared with the money. The amount hadn't been disclosed, but the writer suggested it was "certainly" millions of dollars. Investigators were initially reported to be confident that they would find Stowe and be able to recover some, at least, of the stolen money. Later articles became shorter and moved from the front page to inside sections. Stowe appeared to be staying on the move. Customs was on alert to prevent him from fleeing the country with his stolen wealth.

Days and weeks between articles followed. Daniel read an interview in a business magazine with Tim Gregory, who expressed heartfelt dismay that a friend could betray him and Griffen. At the same time, he was confident G, G & S would survive and continue to grow. He deftly directed attention to ongoing projects, including the new headquarters for a bank in the financial district.

Months later, that was where the situation remained, without Stowe having been dragged back to the city to stand trial, and with the construction firm seemingly bouncing back from the significant loss of operating capital. *A little help from Daddy?* Daniel wondered.

He was unable to determine when the divorce had happened without the kind of digging he'd promised not to do. The article that included the picture of Rebecca was dated eighteen months ago. She hadn't mentioned the embezzlement. Because she had already separated from her husband?

What were the odds this had nothing to do with her problems? The marriage might already have been history, or the separation and divorce happened later but had nothing to do with the uproar at her husband's company. Or it did, but only because stress exacerbated other problems.

He wasn't buying any of that.

He typed in a query about Robert Allen Gregory's wife and came up with an obituary dated sixteen years before. Quick calculations told Daniel that Tim would have been seventeen. Tim's looks must have come from her: Robert was undistinguished in appearance, except for a certain intensity the camera had captured.

Like Josh Griffen, he never seemed to be smiling when the shutter clicked.

Daniel checked email and then turned off his tablet, disturbed. Instinct told him that Robert Gregory could be a dangerous enemy. With Tim, it was harder to determine—but Daniel had seen Rebecca's ambivalence where her husband was concerned. She didn't want to believe Tim was behind the assaults, which was dangerous in and of itself. If he found her, would she give him the benefit of the doubt for what could be a fatal instant?

After a minute, Daniel reached for his remote to turn on the TV.

Staring unseeing at the television screen, he tried to decide what, if anything, he could or should do about Rebecca Holt. Did she really need him?

The answer was very likely no. Given his uneasy feeling she still wasn't offering the entire truth, it might be best if he stayed away from her.

HER METAL BUCKET overflowing with weeds, Rebecca straightened with a groan, then was hit with a wave of light-headedness. Even midmorning, it was roasting hot out here.

The summers of her memory had always

been hot, but not like this. *Onkel* Samuel and her cousin Mose weren't saying much—the weather was in God's hands and they wouldn't chafe against His decisions—but she'd seen worry on their faces nonetheless. There hadn't been so much as a thunderstorm since she'd arrived. The corn looked dry. If the cobs didn't mature in time, the entire crop would be a failure. Even the weeds she'd been pulling from the vegetable garden looked anemic, and at least this patch *was* being watered.

Laughter and shouts came from the back of the property. The creek there, while lower than she remembered it, still had enough water to entertain the children. Earlier, Sarah had taken Matthew, Abram and two of Abram's younger siblings to play in the water. Rebecca wanted to join them. Oh, to take off the stockings, hoist her skirt and dip her feet in chilly water! But she had resolutely shaken her head when they'd invited her. *Aenti* Emma had to spell *Grossmammi* in caring for *Grossdaadi*, who wasn't feeling well. He was irritable at the women hovering, but they were afraid to leave him alone. The least she could do was maintain the garden that supplied a good part of the family's food throughout the year.

She should count her blessings they weren't

canning today. The hot stove would raise the temperature in the closed air of the kitchen unbearably.

The sound of a car engine came to her. Tensing, she made herself keep trudging to the compost bin. Even here, occasionally cars came and went. The near neighbors were Amish, but they had *Englisch* friends, or their teenage children did, or a sheriff's deputy patrolled, or…

Even if Tim drove up the lane right this minute, Matthew was out of sight and she could disappear by stepping into the cornfield. He would be greeted by puzzlement. Rebecca? *Ja*, they remembered her, she had visited when she was a *kind*, but here now? Why would he think such a thing? Was something wrong? They would pray for her well-being. They could imply much without actually lying.

But this car continued by and her shoulders relaxed.

Rebecca had learned something about herself in the past few weeks. She was very bad at waiting. And that was what this felt like: knowing the other shoe would inevitably drop, but when?

Almost more bothersome was the alternative. What if no one ever came looking for her and Matthew, or they simply never found them? What would she do? Become plain in truth? Raise her son Amish?

In her haste to find safety for herself and Matthew, she hadn't given any thought to a future beyond the coming days and weeks. Now the necessity was becoming unavoidable.

As increasingly comfortable as she was becoming in the Graber household, she knew that staying wasn't really an option. She might be able to give up her telephone and computer—although right now she'd have given a lot to go online to see if her disappearance had become public. But if she stayed and was baptized, Matthew would be limited to an eighth-grade education, and even though she understood and sympathized with the Amish reasons for limiting further education, she wanted something different for him.

Obedience would be a big problem for her, too. In the Grabers' hearing, she *said* the right things but knew that in her heart she was incapable—okay, *unwilling*—to yield herself to a higher authority completely. Rebecca remembered becoming impatient when she was a kid, annoyed at being forbidden to do something because the *Ordnung* said it wasn't allowed, and *Grossmammi* lecturing her on accepting the will of God and others better able to judge His will, such as the bishop. *Gelassenheit*, the Amish called this yielding. *Grossmammi* claimed that it led to a calm spirit, in contrast to the seemingly eternal discontent of moderns.

Rebecca understood the Amish puzzlement with the frenetic way outsiders lived—always wanting more than they had, to get places faster whether there was any urgency or not, suffering boredom when life slowed down. But she didn't believe herself capable of giving up her independence or her right to make decisions for herself—and for her child.

No, like a turtle, eventually she would have to stick her head out of her shell to see whether danger had passed.

There had to be a way to find out who had made those threatening phone calls.

She smoothed damp strands of hair off her sweaty face, tucking them beneath the *kapp*, and carried her empty bucket back to the garden.

A bright flash of blue caught her eye. The bird settled for just an instant on a post at one end of a row of raspberries before taking flight again. Not big enough to be a blue jay. A long-ago memory surfaced. An indigo bunting. *Grossmammi* liked to identify birds and had had a book about them. Rebecca wondered if she still had that book. She'd seen half a dozen different birds today and had no idea what they were. Matthew might be interested, too.

She dropped to her knees and started on a row of green beans.

Another worry crept out of hiding. Had Sheriff Byler kept his word? She'd seen his skepticism and had expected him to appear with more questions, but four days had passed without him dropping by. She ought to be relieved, but for reasons she didn't understand, his absence left her...anxious.

DANIEL STEPPED OUT of the courtroom. He'd just testified in juvenile proceedings having to do with a teenager who had spray-painted obscenities all over two Amish barns. Daniel saw the Byrum police chief walking down the hall toward him.

"Ben."

Around Daniel's age, Benedict Slater had become the chief here in Byrum, the county's largest city and center of government, only a year ago, after the previous police chief suffered a heart attack. The ultimate outsider, Slater had come from Camden, New Jersey, right across the Delaware River from Philadelphia. Nobody seemed to quite know why he'd left a job in a major metropolitan area to take a job in Missouri. Daniel hadn't asked and didn't intend to. The two men were cautiously becoming friends and developing a level of trust, but they hadn't exchanged much that was personal.

Ben was tall and lean, with dark hair and eyes. He smiled and said, "Don't suppose it's anything good that brought you here."

Testifying wasn't Daniel's favorite way to kill half a day. Cops rarely enjoyed the experience of having defense attorneys trying to discredit them.

"Vandalism, believe it or not. And just a kid." He grimaced. "I let him slide the first couple times we caught him, but he won't let up, and he's targeting our Amish families."

"Doing?" When Daniel told him, Ben grunted. "I'd have lost patience, too." He raised his brows. "Do you have time for lunch?"

Ten minutes later, they had taken a booth in the back corner of a Mexican restaurant. After ordering, they exchanged news about ongoing investigations and problems.

Ben had just fired an officer for stealing money and drugs that should have been safely locked in Evidence.

"I'm having trouble holding on to the best officers," he grumbled. "Once they get some experience under their belt, they want to head for the big city."

"Same crimes wherever they go."

He dipped a chip in salsa. "Can't convince 'em."

"I've been lucky," Daniel said. "My deputies all grew up around here, want to stay near family. It helps that they know everyone, and I like that they understand when we need to be flexible and when we can't be."

Having heard only the basics, he asked more about the armed holdup of a popular restaurant here in the county seat. The thieves had struck after closing and gotten away with a surprising amount of cash.

"Including the tip money out of two waitresses' pockets and what the staff had in their wallets." Ben shook his head in disgust. "The employees were all forced to lie facedown on the floor in the kitchen. I think they half expected to be executed."

"Nobody recognized a voice?"

"Nope. The consensus was they sounded like Northerners."

Daniel grinned. "Kind of like you?"

Ben laughed. "Afraid so." Once their entrées had arrived, he said, "Got any suggestions for persuading an Amish man to testify even if he has 'forgiven' his assailant?"

"Not happening." Daniel took a bite of his burrito, enjoying the spicy flavor, before shrugging. "I shouldn't say that. Mostly, if the assault was personal, you won't get anywhere pursuing it. It's different if the Amish can see that

the person you've arrested will continue to be
a danger to other people. Cooperation might
be possible. They can forgive him for whatever
wrong they personally suffered, but testify as
to the facts to ensure there are consequences.
They hope a stretch in jail will give a wrongdoer time to repent."

Ben gave a sharp, hard laugh.

"Your best bet," Daniel continued, "is to
speak to the bishop. Without his permission,
no one in the church district will go along with
you, whatever their feelings. It pays to try to
build relationships with the bishops and ministers in every church district."

Lines in his forehead, Ben said, "My only
dealings with them have to do with the businesses that are within the city limits. Not many
actually live in Byrum."

Daniel hesitated. "I have more of a history
with the Amish. If it's someone I know..."

They talked about the situation, and Daniel
shook his head. He knew the bishop in question.
"I think you have to let this one go."

"I was afraid of that." Ben gave him a specu-
lative look. "I thought you'd been in office only
three years."

"I have." He could, and usually would, leave
it at that. But he didn't want to shut the door on
potential friendship, not when he had been so

aware lately of the distance between himself and others. "I grew up Amish," he said abruptly. "My family lives here in Henness County."

He explained why he wasn't under the *bann*, but that his relationship with his parents and brothers and sisters wasn't an easy one, either. "Jumping the fence is one thing," he said, "but being a cop is something else. We're taught to turn the other cheek, not fight back."

Ben winced, then pushed his almost empty plate away. "Do you mind me asking how it happened?"

Daniel couldn't remember ever telling his story. The reason his family had moved to Missouri from their previous home in Illinois and that he'd jumped the fence was known only among local Amish.

"You know Amish businesses rarely accept credit cards."

"Which means they tend to have a lot of cash on hand."

"Yes. This happened when I was a teenager. The father of a friend of mine owned a furniture and cabinet shop. He had just been paid for a big order, so he had an unusually large amount of money on the premises. He got a call that his mother had taken a bad turn and been transported to the hospital here in Byrum. As it turned out, she'd had a stroke." That part still made Daniel cringe. His friend Josiah had shrugged, insisting that his grandmother was always complaining and this wouldn't be any different than usual.

Ben's gaze never left Daniel's face.

"My friend was working for his dad by then. He promised to close up and take the day's receipts straight to the bank. But he figured, what was the hurry? He could take the money home and drop it at the bank in the morning. His *daad* would never notice. He had a cell phone, as plenty of teenagers do during *Rumspringa*. He called around, said, 'Let's party.' One of the other boys brought beer. There ended up being seven of us there, including two girls."

Daniel didn't like how vivid this memory was, but it wasn't surprising. In something like forty-five minutes, so many lives were damaged, his changed forever.

"It came out later that my friend's father had talked to a fellow merchant about when he was getting paid, and was overheard. Three young guys decided to rob him. When they stormed in, armed, my friend agreed to let them take the money. No matter our belief system, we couldn't have stood up to them bare-handed."

"But the money wasn't all they wanted," Ben said softly.

"No, it wasn't. We stood between those men

and the girls, kept blocking them, but doing more than that is in violation of Amish beliefs. They slugged us, knocked us down. I…broke, I suppose you could say. I ripped one of the men off a girl, hit another. I was pistol-whipped and barely conscious from then on. Both girls were raped while the other boys watched. Every minute of it." Anguished, but abiding by their beliefs. "Ultimately, the girls and I were taken to the hospital, so the police were involved, but our bishop was rigid. I had recognized two of the assailants. All three were arrested and most of the money recovered. I was the only person who had been present when those girls were assaulted who was willing to testify against the assailants in court. The bishop reluctantly conceded that I should, but wanted me punished for transgressing our beliefs in fighting back. My father had more mixed feelings, but we still had raging arguments. I felt so guilty, so angry." Meeting Ben Slater's dark eyes, he smiled wryly. "I suppose, in a way, I wanted vengeance."

He still believed he had made the right choice for himself, but he had never entirely quieted doubt, either. "Vengeance is mine," the Lord had said. When would that vengeance be taken? he had asked himself. In the afterlife? How many women had those men already raped?

How many would they have gone on to rape, had they been allowed to go free? And yet, his childhood beliefs ran deep. He still had moments when he feared God had tested him, and he had failed.

"My parents understood my decision enough to choose to leave our church district. They pulled up roots and moved here, to Henness County. I stayed at home for a while, but I no longer belonged."

Daniel had no idea what Ben saw on his face, but, after a minute, Ben said, "Becoming a cop hadn't even crossed my mind when I went to college. I was thinking law school. Big, prestigious firm, lots of money."

Both men smiled at the irony. There weren't a lot of zeroes on either of their paychecks.

"My older sister was raped," Ben said abruptly. "No arrest was ever made." His jaw muscles spasmed. "She was never the same. I changed my major to criminology."

Stunned to learn that such similar events had driven them both, Daniel could only nod his understanding.

Ben sighed. "And I have an appointment with the mayor in fifteen minutes, so I need to get moving."

Both dropped twenties on the table and they

walked out together. Ben held out a hand. They shook, nodded again and parted ways.

Daniel wondered how Ben Slater felt about baseball. Maybe he'd enjoy a drive to St. Louis to watch the Cardinals lose to whatever team came to town to whip their asses.

MATTHEW SQUIRMED ON the bench beside her. He had been restless almost from the beginning of the service. Rebecca could follow along in the *Ausbund*, the fat hymnal that held all the words but no scores. The hymns were sung from memory, passed down from one generation to the next. The *Ausbund* was in High German, not the dialect spoken day to day, but enough had come back to Rebecca that she was better able to follow along. She had sung these hymns before. Traditionally coming second in the service, *"O Gott Vater, wir Loben dich"*—"O God the Father, We Praise You"—came to her as if it had been last summer she'd attended the every-other-week services, not eighteen years ago.

Amish children were included in prayer from the time they were toddlers, held on a parent's lap with their hands clasped together for the prayer before meals. Only now that she was a parent did Rebecca realize that she had been coached in much the same way by her mother. Rebecca had never required Matthew to sit still without entertainment for more than half an hour at a time. TV was always available. Games, toys, books.

To him, the sermons in German had to be white noise. Even Rebecca had forgotten how hard it was to sit for hour upon hour on a backless bench. Very young children were sometimes taken out, nursing mothers were excused if they slipped out midway and the elderly were known to fall asleep, but everyone else remained attentive.

Rebecca gently rubbed Matthew's back and hushed him quietly a couple of times. But he kept squirming. Right in the middle of the sermon, he slid off the bench to his feet, his voice ringing out.

"Mommy, I'm bored!"

The minister fell silent. Heads turned.

She closed her eyes in mortification but recognized defeat. Grimacing an apology at the women she had to pass, she hustled him outside and a short distance across the packed gravel to the scanty shade of an apple tree.

"Being bored is not an excuse for rudeness," she said quietly. "You knew from last time what church would be like. I would have held you on my lap, or you could have leaned against me and napped. You're a big enough boy to know better than to interrupt like you did."

His face crumpled, but instead of crying, he spit out, "I want to go *home*! *Dad* wouldn't make me come here." Then he wrenched himself free of her hands and raced toward the house.

Feeling helpless, Rebecca stayed where she was, watching until another woman bent to catch him, spoke to him and led him to the long tables being set with food for the fellowship meal that followed the service. Confident he was safe and desperate to steal a moment to collect herself, she walked behind the parked buggies, then slipped between two of them and rested her arms on the fence. The fawn-brown dairy cows grazing in the pasture beyond the fence continued grazing, uninterested in her.

Had Matthew been using her to twist Tim with guilt into doing what he wanted? She would have liked to ask Tim, except...well, for the fact that he might be going along with a decision to kill her. She laughed without any humor. Yep, just a little complication in their ability to co-parent.

It stunned her that Matthew seemed so angry at her. She hadn't seen any displays of stubbornness or defiance with his aunt and uncle or grandparents. Perhaps she should ask Mose. Especially now, with *Grossdaadi* failing, Mose frequently kept Matthew with him along with Abram. Matthew was proud because he was learning some farm chores. He had helped throw hay into mangers and even, in a small way, to harness a horse. Yesterday, Mose had put the two boys to work scrubbing a buggy. Matthew hadn't seemed to mind.

So, why the anger at her? Had he guessed that she might really be taking him away from his father forever?

At the sound of an engine in the somnolent heat of the day, she turned her head. A marked police SUV approached slowly along the road. Feeling a flutter in her chest, she thought of stepping back between buggies. Would the driver see her?

When the vehicle eased to a stop on the shoulder of the paved country road, she knew he had.

CHAPTER SIX

THIS WAS STUPID. Daniel knew he should drive on. But he'd already set the emergency brake and turned on the warning lights. Ignoring his better judgment, he hopped out and strode up the lane to where Rebecca Holt stood, alone, hidden from the rest of the fellowship by the row of black buggies. The service couldn't possibly be over. Why wasn't she still in the barn?

"Rebecca."

She eyed him skittishly. "Sheriff. What brings you out here today?"

"My deputies and I make a point of patrolling before and after church services. I worry with so many buggies on the roads."

Fortunately, she didn't point out that he was more than a little premature.

"Where's Matthew?" he asked.

She turned back to face the dairy herd, her shoulders slumping. He hungrily studied the graceful line of her neck, bared between the simple, collarless dress and the *kapp*.

"He threw a temper tantrum in the middle

of a sermon," she said. "I had to take him out of the barn. When I let him know I was disappointed because he couldn't be any more patient, he yelled at me and ran off."

Daniel went on alert despite the stultifying heat. "You're looking for him?"

"No, one of the women setting out food has him. I should be helping her since I didn't go back into the service."

"Do you understand the sermons?"

She smiled a little. "I'm afraid not. The Deitsch is coming back to me. Just everyday conversation, you know. But I can't claim to be grasping the subtleties."

Daniel leaned on the fence, too, but facing her. "It's hard for a little boy when he doesn't understand a word."

Rebecca wrinkled her nose. "Are you chiding me? You don't have to. *I'm* the one who was impatient. And everyone there knows—" She came to a sudden stop, the whites of her eyes showing.

"That neither of you are Amish?" he said sardonically. "That he doesn't speak Deitsch, far less understand the High German used by the ministers?"

"I don't suppose he'd appreciate what they were saying even if he did."

He laughed. "No, I remember being hideously

bored during church services. I was glad when I was old enough to sit with friends and not be under my father's eagle eye. We managed to pass a few notes and poke each other with our elbows, unseen by our elders."

Rebecca smiled at him, her eyes sparkling, the curve of her lips tempting. "I'll bet *you* didn't announce how bored you were out loud."

"Is that what he did?" Chuckling, Daniel shook his head. "I wouldn't have dared. Was it Bishop Jonas speaking? My impression is that he, at least, has a sense of humor."

She rolled her eyes. "Of course not. It was Amos King."

The stern owner of the custom butcher shop. Daniel hid a grin. He had sometimes wondered why Amos hadn't moved to southern Missouri, where the Amish settlements were considerably more conservative.

"I should go back."

He leaned against the fence. "I've been meaning to catch up with you, anyway. Unless someone will worry?"

He could tell she wanted to make an excuse to escape, but after a moment she shook her head. "No, I doubt anyone will miss me for a few minutes."

She returned her gaze to the cows. He looked at her.

"I searched for your ex-husband and father-in-law online." When he saw the alarm flaring on her face, he shook his head. "I read newspaper articles on my personal tablet, that's all. There were plenty of them. Even your house was featured in a Sunday supplement."

She must have heard the question in his voice, because she said, "Tim built it for me. Only, he never asked what I liked." Her sigh was almost soundless and somehow...sad. "It's hideous. The house, I mean."

"Wouldn't appeal to me," he admitted, thinking that was more tactful than an outright agreement.

For a minute, the familiar drone of cicadas was the only sound. Then Rebecca glanced at him. "I suppose you read about the embezzlement."

"Kind of jumps out at you. I couldn't help wondering if you were still married during that mess."

She nodded. "The worst was the several months before it all came out."

"All came out? You mean, when Stowe took off."

Her eyes skipped away from his, then came back. "Yes. I knew something was wrong. Tim was...tense, all the time, but he would never say why. He just...withdrew. I found myself living with a stranger. If I pushed him to talk, he'd get angry. Once he—" she sneaked a look at Daniel "—he shoved me so hard, I slammed into the corner of a kitchen cabinet. That was the only incident I'd call violent, and he horrified himself." She hunched her shoulders. "Weirdly, once everything came to a head, I could tell he was relieved. He became, I don't know, more himself again."

"Relieved?" Not the usual reaction to finding out a trusted partner had just ripped off a significant portion of the assets of the company you'd built.

Rebecca nibbled on her lip. "It…seemed odd to me, too, but I decided that the hardest part had been knowing something was wrong, but not what. I'm guessing he and Steven and Josh were arguing. Blaming each other for financial problems. Once Tim knew what he had to deal with and could make a plan, he seemed certain they could ride it out."

Daniel supposed that made sense. The unknown was the most frightening. He couldn't feel a drop of sympathy, however.

"So he gave a sigh of relief and took you out for a romantic dinner?"

"Something like that." Now she met his eyes squarely. "He thought we could go happily on, as if the past few months hadn't happened. That's when I left him. I supported him through the worst, but I no longer liked or respected him."

A sudden burst of voices from the direction of the barn signaled that his time was up.

"Do you have a cell phone?" he asked.

"No, I left it behind so it couldn't be used to trace us. And I promised my aunt and uncle that, while we're with them, we will live plain."

"You might talk to them. If you agree not to use it except for emergencies, they might agree. We could get you a cheap, pay-as-you-go phone."

"But I'd have no way to charge it," she pointed out. "And the phone shanty isn't far."

No, it wasn't; it sat right between the Grabers and the neighboring farm, owned by Noah Yoder. But getting to it meant cutting through a cornfield and squeezing through strands of a barbed-wire fence or walking down the road. The small wooden enclosure was open to the road, too—no place to hide if someone was hunting you.

"All right," he said reluctantly. "You've been here, what, two and a half weeks? And there hasn't been even a hint that your ex-husband has located you? He may just be waiting, assuming that because of Matthew you'll eventually get in touch."

"Maybe," she agreed, but doubt leaked through.

She didn't believe Tim Gregory would wait, maybe because she knew the man to be impatient by nature. Daniel could understand a father frantic to find his missing child.

He would really like to see the custody agreement. Something about Rebecca Holt got to him, which made him vulnerable to being manipulated. Her family here would have accepted whatever she said at face value. But what if *Tim* had primary custody, not her at all, and she was the one breaking the law by fleeing with her son? The rest of her story could be a smoke screen.

Except he'd seen her bruised face. And seen how afraid she was, how haunted. He half lifted his hand, wanting to comfort her, to touch her cheek, rosy now like the sun-kissed skin of a ripe peach.

"When you looked online," she said suddenly, "did you see anything about me taking off? It might have made the news if he'd reported Matthew and me missing."

"Nothing," he said. "Custodial interference would be taken seriously, of course." She didn't noticeably react, so he continued, "I doubt the police would have taken a missing-persons report if it was obvious you had packed up and left voluntarily."

"We…didn't take all that much with us. Because I knew we wouldn't need electronics or our *Englisch* clothes, and handling heavy suitcases when we kept changing buses didn't seem like a good idea."

"In other words, someone glancing around your apartment—house?—might not have been able to tell you had packed at all."

"Except I had my purse, of course. And I paid the rent a few months in advance. Oh, and I got rid of all the disposable food." Her nose wrinkled. "I couldn't leave stuff rotting in the refrigerator or molding in drawers."

"Who else had a key to your place?"

"Only the building management. They have to let themselves in for maintenance sometimes."

They both heard a woman calling her name.

"I have to go." Without so much as a goodbye, Rebecca whirled and hurried away. He lost sight of her as soon as a buggy blocked his view.

Daniel didn't linger. He wouldn't be welcome here on a church Sunday. If he was spotted, it would be an embarrassment to his parents. Getting into his patrol vehicle, he wondered if Rebecca had gotten to know his mother or sisters at all. It was a strange thought. As members of the same church district as Samuel Graber's family, they had known she and her son were hiding from a bad man and weren't really Amish long before he did.

As always, thoughts of his family made him aware of the hollow, chronic ache in his chest.

THE FOLLOWING SATURDAY, Daniel sat by the window in the Hadburg Café, idly watching the very occasional passerby as he sipped iced tea and waited for his burger and fries. Hot as it was, no one much wanted to be outside. Sometimes a heat wave led to an increase in crime, but this one seemed to have made people too enervated to cause trouble. His radio had been mostly silent today.

A few cars had passed, as well as some horses and buggies. While he watched, a few Amish men in their dark trousers, blue shirts, suspenders and straw hats had gone into the harness shop, some carrying straps of leather and buckles that probably needed to be repaired or replaced. From this angle, the only one Daniel had recognized was Isaac Bontrager, a man with a distinctively stork-like build and jerky gait.

Daniel's food still hadn't arrived when a silver sedan pulled to the curb across the street in front of Olde Country Antiques. The man who got out wore chinos, a powder blue polo shirt and sunglasses with a gold sheen. Everything he wore looked expensive. He closed his door, then took his time studying the businesses lining Grove Street. Odd to park before he'd spotted his destination, Daniel thought.

Deborah Chupp set his food down in front of him, but he kept an eye on the stranger even as he thanked her. If the man had been accompanying a wife eager to browse gift and quilt shops, Daniel wouldn't have paid the same attention. As it was, the guy looked out of place.

Apparently making up his mind, the stranger walked halfway up the block to Miller's General Store. Heck, he might have just stopped on his way through town for something cold to drink or a snack. Still—why hadn't he parked right in front, or in the lot to the side?

He strolled out a few minutes later, hands empty. Daniel popped a French fry in his mouth and watched as the man went into the fabric-and-quilt store, the harness shop, the creamery and an Amish furniture store. In fact, every business he had entered was clearly posted as Amish. He skipped the liquor store, the gas station and the town's one-and-only real estate agency.

Then he crossed the street so that Daniel lost sight of him.

Done with his meal, Daniel dropped bills onto the table and called his thanks to Anna Mae Kemp, a distant cousin and widow who ran the café. When he stepped out on the sidewalk, he couldn't see the stranger, so he crossed the street and went into the general store.

Slow day like this, Yonnie Miller seemed to be alone, desultorily stocking shelves that held single-serving snack foods.

"Yonnie." Daniel nodded. "A fellow came in here a minute ago."

"Ja, Englisch."

"Looking for something you don't sell."

"Seemed so."

"Mind telling me what?"

Yonnie considered for a minute. "Said he heard some Amish hereabouts breed Percheron horses." He shrugged. "I told him about Willard Hostetler and Big Ike and Little Ike Mast."

"Not Samuel Graber?"

"No. Thinking two was enough."

"Did he ask for directions?"

"I offered and wrote them down. He shoved the piece of paper in his pocket, not so careful."

Daniel had no trouble with the subtext of this conversation. Yonnie wasn't a member of the Grabers' church district, but he had heard something, enough to know not to send a stranger to Samuel Graber's farm.

"Denke." Daniel then said in Pennsylvania Dutch, "Just curious, I am. He seems to be walking around town asking questions."

"Ja, lots of questions, that one."

Back out on the sidewalk, he took the time to jot down the license-plate number and make and model of car, although he felt sure it would turn out to be a rental. Then he went into the fabric store, where his appearance created a flutter of interest in the group of ladies seated around a quilt frame in the back room. A log-cabin quilt in sunny colors was stretched in the frame.

"Don't get up," he said when Gloria Wagler started to stand. "Just wondered what the *Englisch* man wanted. He seems to be checking out all the businesses."

The women exchanged glances. Rose Chupp, sister-in-law of Paul Chupp and aunt of Deborah, who had just served Daniel at the café, spoke up.

"He said he thought to buy a quilt to surprise his wife. He looked at the ones displayed—" she nodded toward the front room, where quilts hung from wooden dowels on the walls "—but not as if he saw what he wanted. He said he was told Ruth Graber was an especially fine quilter."

"Which she is," one of the other women chimed in.

Rebecca's grandmother.

Gloria, whose shop this was, said, "I showed him two quilts she made, one for a bed, one smaller. He barely looked at them. He wanted to speak to her, ask her to make a custom quilt."

Rose Chupp, who it so happened was a good friend of Daniel's mother, said, "I told him Ruth's husband is in poor health and she has no time to make new quilts."

"We suggested other quilters. So many fine ones whose quilts I sell." Gloria's gaze was opaque when it met his. It appeared that she was aware of Rebecca Holt's situation, but didn't know *he* knew. "I said if he didn't like these, there are places in Byrum and River Grove for him to look. Or he could go to Jamestown. He said he just wanted to talk to Ruth."

"Hope you didn't tell him how to find her. She doesn't need to be bothered right now."

"I didn't, but someone else might."

"Thank you."

He stepped out to see the man crossing the street toward him. And not pleased to see a uniformed police officer, Daniel decided.

He waited on the sidewalk, smiling pleasantly. "Don't know how you can resist buying something," he observed.

"I always like to look first, think about what I saw," the man said. His salt-and-pepper hair was cropped short, the crease in his chinos sharp. Thin but athletic, he was likely in his forties. He pulled his keys from his pocket. "Not a lot here, in a town this size."

Daniel really would have liked to see his

eyes. Hard to judge a man hidden behind dark glasses.

"If you're looking for Amish crafts," he suggested, "you might prefer Jamestown."

"You're the third person to say that." He sounded irked. "Thought I might get better prices off the beaten track."

"Are you staying locally?" Daniel asked pleasantly.

His face tightened. "Haven't decided. Now, if you'll excuse me…"

"If there's anything I can do to help, you let me know."

The man took a couple of steps, then stopped and turned. "Maybe there is. I'm looking for a young woman who might be staying with her grandparents. Ephraim and Ruth Graber. You wouldn't know them, would you?"

"Amish, are they?" Daniel scratched his head. "We have a lot of Grabers in these parts. You know how many kids they tend to have. I imagine you could find some Grabers down in Daviess County, too, and probably Livingston. Of course, they aren't listed in any phone book. Don't believe in having phones."

"Ruth is a quilter, I'm told."

"Did you check at the quilt shop? They'd probably have heard of her."

"The woman there said her husband is ill and

she's not taking commissions right now. Really, I'm more interested in her granddaughter and great-grandson who might be visiting."

"Did you tell the ladies that?"

He hesitated. "No. This is…a delicate situation."

"If that's so, why don't you come on over to the station and we can talk. I'm the Henness County sheriff, Daniel Byler."

"I appreciate the offer, but I'd rather keep this casual for now. I'd just like to talk to the woman, that's all."

"May I ask why?"

"Nothing you need to be concerned with," he said, sounding a lot less friendly. "Excuse me."

Daniel watched as he got in his car and drove past without his head so much as turning. Pondering, Daniel started down the sidewalk toward the sheriff's department headquarters, two blocks east and one block down a cross street.

The stranger wasn't Tim Gregory, Robert Gregory or Josh Griffen. Daniel would have recognized them. He wasn't Steven Stowe, either, assuming the missing man would have any interest at all in Rebecca or her son. A PI, Daniel suspected. He surely had stood out in this small, dusty town. Daniel wanted to think the guy would widen his search to Byrum and beyond, but something told him they wouldn't be that lucky. The fact that he had Ephraim's and Ruth's names, knew she was a quilter and that Ephraim had bred Percheron horses meant he was too close to his target.

Daniel wished Yonnie had pretended not to know anyone who bred Percherons. Either Willard Hostetler or one of the Masts, father or son, might generously share the name of a competitor.

Speaking of names... First thing he'd do was run the plates. Call the rental company, if the car was indeed a rental.

And then he'd better take a drive out to talk to Rebecca and Samuel.

REBECCA WAS RETURNING from the *grossdawdi haus* with a tray of dirty dishes when she saw the familiar sheriff's department SUV turn into their lane. Feeling a squeeze of fear, she prayed Daniel Byler was here only to ask more questions. Nosy as he was, that was likely, she told herself.

She slipped into the house and set the tray beside the kitchen sink. Her aunt smiled at her. "*Denke* for fetching those. It's *gut* to see Ephraim must have finished his soup, at least."

"He looks a little better." She smiled. "He scolded me for not wearing my *kapp*, so I asked why he wasn't wearing his hat."

Aenti Emma chuckled. "A stickler he always is." She sobered. "It's this hot weather. When it turns cool, you'll see, he will feel better."

Rebecca knew that nobody except possibly her grandmother really believed that. They all knew the end was coming. The inevitability made Rebecca glad she had had a chance to see him again, and that Matthew was old enough to remember meeting his great-grandfather.

A rap on the door had her aunt starting. "Who—"

"The sheriff is here again."

"Ah." Her face relaxed. "Then it is you he wants to see."

"Is Matthew actually asleep?" He only occasionally napped, but had been droopy today in the afternoon heat.

"I haven't heard a peep."

Nodding, Rebecca went to let the sheriff in. She hoped each time she saw him that the impact of his presence would lessen, but once again she felt breathless the minute he stepped into the kitchen. Aside from his strong build and too-perceptive eyes, he had an air. He wouldn't be a very good subordinate, she thought—people would always assume he was in charge. She bet that even as a boy, he had been the leader of his crowd.

"Let me cut you a slice of raspberry pie,"

Aenti Emma said briskly. "The coffee is always on, but we have lemonade, too."

"Thank you," he said, "but nothing this time. I ate at the café in town." He patted his stomach.

"*Ach*, if it's Rebecca you need to see, why don't you two sit out on the porch? There might be a breeze, *ja*?"

Of course there wasn't a breeze. *Aenti* Emma was offering a degree of privacy.

"I'd hoped to speak to Samuel, too," the sheriff said, his tone grave.

Rebecca's heart constricted. "I'll run and get him."

The farrier had come to shoe several horses, so she found her uncle where she'd expected, in the barn holding one of the massive beasts. Mose was there, too, as was Samuel's youngest son, apprenticed to the farrier. When she told them her errand, Mose gripped the horse's halter and Samuel accompanied her out of the barn.

"Did the sheriff say why he needs to speak to me?" he asked.

"No. But he looked worried, I think."

With his big, callused hand, he patted her shoulder. "Trust in God, Rebecca. You take too much on yourself."

She managed a smile at him and kept her rebellious thoughts unspoken.

Daniel was waiting for them on the porch, his

shoulder resting against an upright. He watched as they approached, lines scoring his forehead. He exchanged nods with her uncle. Samuel urged her to sit on the porch swing, and even joined her when Daniel said, "I sit too much of the day already."

Then *Onkel* Samuel asked, "What is this about?"

"A man came to town today looking for Rebecca and Matthew."

Rebecca pressed her hand to her mouth.

Regret darkened Daniel's eyes when he saw how stricken she was, but he continued, telling them about the stranger who went to most of the Amish businesses in town, framing his questions differently in each. "At the quilt shop, he had heard what a fine quilter Ruth is and wanted to talk to her about taking a commission. At Miller's and in the harness shop, he was asking about breeders of Percherons. He wasn't satisfied by the names he was given, the Masts and Willard Hostetler. In each store, he tried a different story. Only with me did he admit he hoped to locate Ephraim and Ruth's granddaughter, maybe here for a visit."

A sound escaped from behind her fingers, one she didn't recognize. Daniel straightened. Her uncle took her free hand in his.

"We have to leave. Right now." She started to stand.

Onkel Samuel pulled her back down. "Let Sheriff Byler tell us the rest. Was this man Matthew's father?"

"No." His eyes locked on to hers. "He was a private investigator. I looked up the license-plate number on his car, determined it was a rental and called the company. The woman there gave me the man's name and I found him online. He owns a private investigation firm based in San Francisco. If he doesn't get any cooperation, he may not want to stay here long. Nobody in town I spoke to told him how to find this place. They went out of their way *not* to, Rebecca. Some aren't in your church district and probably don't know, but they didn't trust the man today, and they didn't want to give him what he asked. Everyone sensed there was something wrong with his interest."

"Somebody will tell him," she burst out. "*Onkel* Samuel's Percherons are well-known. Even in Byrum, people will say, go talk to Samuel Graber."

Her uncle didn't express his usual humility, because she was right. He had buyers from up in Iowa and down to southern Missouri, maybe farther away.

"Your ex-husband was only making a guess when he sent the PI to check here." The father-in-law was another possibility, Daniel had realized. Tim Gregory might have shared what he knew about Rebecca's grandmother being a quilter, her grandfather breeding the magnificent draft horses. The guy had paid more attention when she talked about those summers spent here than she'd believed. "It might be best if this man does get this far. If there is no sign that you and Matthew have ever been here, they'll move on to searching elsewhere."

She stared at him, aghast. "You're suggesting… what?"

"That you stay close to the house and keep Matthew out of sight, too. If Samuel and Emma are willing to mislead him…"

He was careful not to say "lie to him," Rebecca noticed.

"Ja," Samuel said. "No one needs to know we have family visiting."

"He'll try to insist on talking to Ruth or Ephraim," Daniel warned.

Her uncle's expression became forbidding. "Bothering them, I will not permit."

"How is Ephraim?" Daniel asked, his voice becoming gentler, as if he really cared.

Samuel shook his head. "Not good, no. His heart is giving out."

"So my mother said. I'm sorry. He will be missed."

"Ja." Her uncle cleared his throat. "I still

need his advice. No one knows horses like my *daad*."

His grief touched Rebecca even through her fear. Did she dare stay? What if the PI didn't drive openly up to the house, but sneaked across the field, instead, and saw her or Matthew outside?

"Did that man look like someone who would sneak around in the woods or fields?" she asked, surprising both men.

Daniel's mouth curved. "He looked like he'd never been out of the city. He wouldn't want to snag his fancy trousers on a fence or step into a pat of manure. I don't think you need to worry about that."

Onkel Samuel was chuckling. "The horses would be curious about a stranger in their pasture. They would follow him, lip his hair thinking it might be a new kind of hay, even step on his heels."

Daniel laughed out loud. "I'd like to see that. This man didn't seem the type to have ever been in touching distance of a horse. And such a big one?"

Rebecca still felt reassured despite her exasperation at the two men's open merriment. Daniel was right—if they could fool the PI, he'd go back to San Francisco and tell Tim she wasn't here. The challenge would be keeping Matthew close.

"Thank you," she said, letting herself meet Daniel Byler's dark blue eyes. "It was good of you to let us know someone was asking about me."

He stayed still for a moment that felt a little too long. "Did you think I wouldn't?"

"No, I—"

He gave her no chance to explain or apologize, only dipped his head, said, "Samuel, Rebecca," and walked away.

CHAPTER SEVEN

"REBECCA GREGORY?" *ONKEL* SAMUEL repeated the name the stranger had given him, then seemed to ponder. He took off his straw hat and slapped it against his thigh. "I have a cousin Rebecca," he said helpfully. "She married Marvin Bontrager, over Hickory Creek Way. But she was a Troyer before she married. This Gregory…" He shook his head.

Rebecca could see only the strange man's back from where she stood tensely to one side of the window in Sarah's bedroom, looking out to the driveway. Would he turn so she could catch sight of his face? She didn't recognize the mix of dark and gray hair, salon-cut in contrast to her uncle's thick bowl-cut. He had to be the private investigator Daniel Byler had told them about Saturday. Truthfully, she was surprised it had taken him two days to find them.

Rebecca, who had been in the kitchen when the car drove up the lane, had seen how quickly her uncle strode from the barn, intercepting the man as soon as he got out of the silver-gray sedan. *Onkel* Samuel hadn't so much as glanced toward the house.

Aenti Emma had flapped her dish towel at Rebecca. "Shoo! Upstairs with you, but not to worry."

How could she not? Matthew was playing with Abram, and though Mose's wife, Esther, knew to keep the boys close, would Matthew come over if he heard the car?

Sarah's window was open but screened, so Rebecca could just hear the voices drifting up. Even as she strained not to miss a word, she kept glancing toward the cornfield or creek where Matthew would appear if he returned unexpectedly.

"I should have said Rebecca Holt," the stranger said. "She went back to her maiden name after the divorce."

"Rebecca Holt," Samuel repeated, sounding enlightened. "*Ja*, her I remember. Little girl, used to visit summers. My niece, she is. Loved to fish and run wild with the boys. Her *grossmammi* tried to teach her to quilt, but that girl had no patience for sitting down." Smiling, he shook his head.

"I'm told she's visiting you now, her and her son, Matthew." The quick, sharp voice suggested the private investigator was struggling for the same patience Rebecca had lacked as a girl. *Onkel* Samuel's deliberate way of speaking would be driving the outsider crazy.

"Visiting?" *Onkel* Samuel sounded surprised. "Who told you that? She came… Let me think." He stroked his beard. "My Mose was having his *Rumspringa*. He might have been sixteen? Seventeen? He has four *kinder* of his own now, a blessing they are. So I think my niece Rebecca was eleven or twelve. Such a nice little girl. My *mamm* and *daad* were real sorry when she didn't come again. Her *mamm*—who was my sister, you know—wrote to say that Rebecca wanted to stay close to her friends. She writes sometimes, Rebecca does."

"Recently?" The question shot out with the explosive force of a gun firing.

"She did write of her divorce. It might have been in January or February the letter came. Sorry we were to hear about it, but he wasn't such a good man." He shook his head in obvious dismay. "Is it him who sent you looking for her?"

"Yes. She took off with his little boy. He is desperate to find his son."

"She might be afraid he would hurt the boy, seems to me."

"He loves his kid," the PI snapped.

"Men who say they love their wives and children sometimes hurt them, anyway," *Onkel*

Samuel observed, an edge in his voice for the first time. "A man like that might hire someone like you to find a wife and son who ran away because they were afraid."

"You're saying that's why she took off?"

"No, no. How would I know?" Samuel did *perplexed* well. "No, I was asking *you*."

"I'm told they were having a custody dispute. She didn't want Matthew spending time with his father, which is wrong. A boy should grow up knowing his dad, don't you think?"

"Usually that is so, *ja*. But I can't help you find her so you can ask." He shrugged and clapped his hat back on his head. "Is that all?"

"No. If you'd point me their way, I'd like to talk to Ephraim and Ruth. They may have heard from her and not told you."

"Not so. They would have shared such news. And I will not let you bother them. My *daad's* heart is failing, and it's all my *mamm* can do to care for him. She does not need to worry more, this time about her granddaughter." There was no give in his voice. The PI was fortunate he hadn't been foolish enough to come here yesterday. Sundays were not to be defiled by such errands. *Onkel* Samuel took a step back. "I have told you what you need to know. I think you should leave now."

The PI, at least temporarily accepting that

he'd worn out his welcome, handed *Onkel* Samuel a business card and asked for a call if he heard from Rebecca, thanked him for his time and got back in his car. Still hovering out of sight in case he looked up at the house, she watched as he backed up a couple of times to turn around, then drove down the lane, dust rising behind him.

Still without a glance toward the house, *Onkel* Samuel returned to the barn. Knees suddenly weak, Rebecca let herself sink onto the edge of the bed. Her breath came fast. Had the man been convinced? She wished she could have seen his face.

When she thought back, she realized that *Onkel* Samuel hadn't once lied. He'd never said *I haven't seen her in years* or *I've never even met her son*. Would the private investigator run through the conversation in his mind as he drove, and realize there had never been a denial, only reminiscences about those long-ago visits? If so, would he dare come back?

The panicked part of her wanted to grab Matthew and run. The more rational part asked where she would go, and how she would get there. With this investigator prowling around town, she couldn't catch the bus here. And what if he decided to watch the farm? He might follow if Mose or *Onkel* Samuel set off with a woman and child in a buggy.

And even if she succeeded in getting away, what then? She was back to the same worries about the future that had been keeping her awake nights. She had money, but it wouldn't last forever. And going on the run would mean not enrolling Matthew in school.

Stay, she decided, even though when she looked down, she saw that her hands shook. All she could do was hope Daniel was right, that the PI would go back to San Francisco now and tell whoever had hired him that she and Matthew weren't here.

Staring at the bright rectangle made by the window but not focusing on the blue sky outside, she wondered whether they would be satisfied if she mailed the ring and wallet to Tim. If she no longer had the proof that Tim had been involved in Steven's likely fatal disappearance, would he still consider her a danger?

Maybe not...but what about Josh? She was still a witness—and she believed Tim when he said it was Josh, always an enigma to her, who was the real threat. If Tim had been sincere when he claimed he hadn't had anything to do with Steven's death or the threats against her, that left Josh. Even if she relinquished the physical proof, she *knew* Steven wasn't out there dodging cops and somehow enjoying his embezzled millions. And she trusted Josh considerably less than she trusted Tim.

Besides, there was still Matthew. Tim *couldn't* let his son go, not without standing up to his father in a way he'd never been able to do. Squeezing her fingers together until they were bone white, she realized how foolish she'd been to take the ring and wallet in the first place—and to succumb to the temptation to use them in a kind of blackmail.

But I might have lost Matthew.

And she couldn't go back and do anything differently.

She ached to tell someone the whole story, ask for advice. She knew who she wanted to tell, but she was too afraid to take such a risk. All the same qualms nipped at her like hovering mosquitoes. He would want her to go to the police in San Francisco, which meant Detective Estevez. If she did that, she would again be within Josh Griffen's reach. Tim would likely be tried and convicted for, at the very least, aiding and abetting in a murder—assuming she lived long enough to testify. With Matthew's father behind bars, Robert would gain custody if anything happened to her. No court in California would award custody to an Amish aunt and uncle over a respected, wealthy local businessman, and that was assuming her family asked for custody. Going to court wasn't something the Amish did.

The dilemma hadn't changed. The wallet and the possibility of her testifying were all she had to hold off the man who had made those calls, as well as Robert's hunger to control his grandson.

Gradually, she succeeded in calming herself. She needed to help start dinner. She could let herself believe that she and Matthew were safe here now. It made sense to stay cautious, yes. But living in fear wouldn't keep them any safer.

And it would be best if Sheriff Byler didn't drive out here again. If anyone was watching, that would only draw attention. If she was going to keep quiet about what she had done and the secret she had cached beneath a floorboard in the barn, she needed to avoid drawing *his* attention.

So far as Daniel could tell, Clint Myers, the private investigator, had left town. Later in the day, after Daniel had spoken to him, Myers had checked into a bed-and-breakfast in Byrum. Waiting, unable to do anything beyond give Rebecca the warning, Daniel had spent a restless, edgy day and night until the owner of the B and B called on Monday to inform him that Myers had left after a two-night stay.

That same morning, Anna Mae Kemp rushed out of the café as Daniel walked past, calling his name.

"A message," she said, sounding breathless, "from Sarah Graber. She brought her *mamm's* sticky buns for me to sell, and asked me to tell you that the man came out to the farm and her *daad* talked to him. She said Samuel sent that man away, no problem, and you would know what she was talking about."

"I do," he agreed, wishing he could feel more relief. He'd give a lot to drive out to the Grabers' and find out exactly what was said. How had the PI justified his search for Rebecca? Disturbed, Daniel knew she might take off again with him being none the wiser. No way to stop her. Why hadn't he told her to stay in touch with him, no matter what happened?

Not that he'd have believed a promise. Rebecca didn't trust him, not yet. Maybe because her troubles were more complicated than she had admitted. Maybe because she hadn't told the truth at all—or, at least, not the entire truth.

Frowning, he got into his patrol car and sat for a minute. How could he be so attracted to a woman he knew might be lying to him? Going as far as thinking he might scrap his integrity and help her escape even if she was the one in the wrong?

Yes, she might be stealing her son when she didn't have full custody. It happened. If that was so, he felt strangely certain she had a good reason. After seeing her battered face, yes, he believed she could very well be afraid that her ex-husband would abuse her little boy, too.

During the night, he'd had the uncomfortable thought that she might have something to do with the embezzlement. Her flight could be out of fear her role would be discovered. Or she could have had an affair with Steven Stowe. What if they had arranged to meet up later, when they thought it would be safe? Would another stranger, a handsome blond one, show up in Hadburg? But Daniel trusted his own judgment of people enough to instinctively reject any scenario where Rebecca had stolen millions of dollars. It was stupidly credulous, maybe, to be so certain, but he was.

He would help her if he could, but he needed to quit thinking there could be anything between them. If she'd been Amish, that would have been a nearly impossible obstacle. She wasn't, but that only meant she had no reason to stay in this remote corner of Missouri once she could safely leave. And that was assuming her life didn't become a series of temporary stops, one step ahead of the men who were hunting her.

Or that she didn't go to jail.

There were plenty of pretty women around, he told himself. He ought to start looking instead of focusing on one consumed by fear and a fierce need to protect her child. A woman with trouble at her heels.

Somehow, this minute, he couldn't think of a single other woman who might interest him.

Growling under his breath, he fired up the engine and decided it was time to visit the Shaver brothers, just to remind them that he was watching. He wanted no meth labs in his county.

And tonight...he might visit the Grabers, after all. If Rebecca didn't know him beyond superficialities, how could she trust him with whatever it was she was afraid to say? Building relationships, that was what his job was all about.

Daniel snorted at this weak effort to justify doing something he shouldn't, and pulled away from the curb.

THEY SAT IN the darkness on the porch steps this time. Venturing farther might have offended *Onkel* Samuel's sense of propriety. Besides, no one in the house could possibly hear them. She and Daniel were both speaking softly, even though nothing they had said was really intimate.

In the kitchen, Samuel had told Daniel in

more detail about the private investigator's visit. Then Daniel had asked if he could speak to Rebecca privately. She had tensed. Could he have learned something new about the intruder? Or about Tim? Had he violated his promise not to make inquiries?

But so far, all he'd done was listen to her talk about how deftly *Onkel* Samuel had deflected questions without actually lying, and how frightened she'd been.

"I never really saw his face."

"Just as well." Soothing, he placed a hand atop hers, which she realized had been clenched in a fist.

That touch, simple and kind, was more comforting than it should have been. She felt the strength in that hand, so much bigger than hers, and let herself return his clasp. Still, she couldn't relax, not when he, too, was a threat. She didn't dare give him even a hint about why she was such a target. But…maybe she and Matthew really were safe, now that the PI was gone. Rebecca wanted so much—too much—to believe that was so. Even if eventually she would have to surface, she was desperate for a reprieve.

"Tell me about yourself," he said unexpectedly. "And your parents. Did your mother let go of her Amish beliefs?"

Rebecca shook her head. "As little as possible.

My father didn't mind. He understood, because he'd spent enough time in various Amish settlements to have sympathy for their way of life and values. He wasn't really a modern man himself, not in the way the Amish mean it as a negative. Neither of them were interested in partying, or going out often, or fancy cars." She paused. "We did have electricity. *Mamm* accepted that."

"That's what you called her?"

She smiled into the darkness. "*Ja*. None of my friends ever realized I wasn't saying Mom like they did."

He chuckled.

"We hardly ever watched television. We read, we played games, we talked and debated. I rolled my eyes when I got to be a teenager when my parents still insisted we sit down to dinner every night as a family, but now I'm glad we had that time. We'd debate the day's news, talk about why people made the decisions they did." Rebecca fell quiet for a moment. "I don't think *Mamm* ever really understood worldly ways. She would shake her head and say, *'Auslanders,'* so bemused. Dad…" She choked up a little. "He was gentle with her, as if she was something so wondrous he couldn't believe she was his."

Daniel's hand tightened on hers, silent encouragement for her to continue.

"One of *Mamm's* favorite biblical quotes was

from John. 'My little children, let us not love in word or in tongue, but in deed and in truth.' That was her. I swear I never went out the door without her calling after me, *'Da Herr sei mit du.'*"

"The Lord be with you," Daniel murmured.

"I miss them both every day, but especially my mother. *I* became so modern, I wonder how disappointed she was be in me. She never said."

"Don't be ridiculous." This briskness was comforting, too. "I've seen you with Matthew enough to know that, like her, you love 'in deed and in truth.' And isn't that what is most important?"

"Yes." She blinked against the sting of tears in her eyes. "Of course it is." At least she knew that what mistakes she'd made had been made out of love. It had all been for Matthew, even her defense of Tim.

"Would you have gone to them, if you could?" Daniel asked suddenly. "Instead of here?"

Chilled, she said, "No. No, Tim knew them, of course. I wouldn't have wanted to expose them to his anger or even the possibility of violence." She shivered. "Instead, I've brought those troubles to my aunt and uncle and grandparents, who are even less equipped to understand something so alien to their framework of belief."

"I'm not sure that's true," Daniel said, sounding thoughtful. "Your uncle, for sure, has dealt with enough outsiders to see clearly their thinking even as he holds to his faith. Perhaps not your aunt."

"No, she's not even curious about the world outside her everyday experiences, not the way Sarah and *Onkel* Samuel can be. Even Mose," she added. "*Grossmammi…* She seems effortlessly able to forgive, to count the blessings of each day. Right now, her world has shrunk. Holding on to each moment with *Grossdaadi*, that's what matters."

"And you, and the rest of her family."

"Yes, of course. Having me home with Matthew, that's one of the blessings she counts."

"As she should."

Rebecca wished she knew more about Daniel's childhood. She would have asked, except she was very aware that they'd been out here awhile. Her uncle would soon check on them or send her aunt to do so. She felt at peace in a way she hadn't in a long time, even if the man beside her was a police officer who would disapprove of so many decisions she'd made.

Right now, she thought of him only as a man, one who seemed to share her contentment in the moment. Her eyes had adjusted to the darkness enough for her to see him tip his head up to look at the moon.

Indulging herself in his company too much, however—that could be risky. She stirred and said, "I need to get back inside before someone comes looking for me."

"I know you do." He swiveled on the porch step to face her, still holding her hand. "Rebecca…"

Suddenly he was close. So close, she could reach up and touch his jaw, feel the rasp of a day's growth of beard. She could make out the fascinating shape of his lips, which seemed softer than usual. The tempo of her heartbeat had quickened, and warmth curled in her lower abdomen. *This* was why anticipation quickened in her every time she thought of him, however foolish that was. "Yes?" she whispered.

He made a muffled sound and bent his head. Her reaction came without thought. She rested her free hand on his shoulder and lifted her face to his.

THE FIRST TOUCH of her lips jettisoned any common sense. Daniel knew he should keep this kiss gentle, noncommittal, something he could later tell himself had been meant as reassurance. It didn't happen that way.

He nipped at her intriguingly full bottom lip, savored the sweetness of apple pie, and his tongue found its way into her mouth. Her eas answer awakened his blinding need. The on her nape was silky beneath his rougher hand. His other hand slid upward from her waist toward the beckoning weight of her full breast.

It was she who ripped her mouth away, her body suddenly rigid. And then Daniel heard it, too—footsteps, the sound of the door opening so close behind them.

"Good night," she said hastily, leaped to her feet and was at the door by the time it opened.

As he stood, Daniel said his good-nights to her and Samuel, framed in the doorway. Then he strode away into the night, praying Samuel hadn't looked closely at him.

The dogs decided to accompany him when he crossed the lawn. After bending to slide between rails on the fence, he was greeted by the nicker of horses and the muted thud of giant hooves. Aroused and not thinking clearly, Daniel was grateful for the level, grazed pasture. At least he didn't have to stumble through a stand of woods. A pair of the enormous horses, appearing pale and ghostlike in the darkness, joined the dogs to accompany him all the way. Next time, if there was a next time, he ought to bring carrots and dog treats, he thought. Fortunately, all the animals seemed pleased enough the unexpected company, stopping at the the far side to watch him out of sight. arked at the next property, tucking his SUV behind Willard Kemp's barn. He had heard talk in the café about the Kemps visiting a daughter in southern Iowa, and had indeed found the house dark.

Reaching his SUV, he flattened both hands on the roof, groaned and let his head fall forward.

He had promised himself he wouldn't touch her. He'd had complete faith in his self-control. *Idiot*, he castigated himself. Rebecca was on the run from her ex-husband. She was depending on his protection. He still wasn't sure how honest she'd been with him. No, that cast his doubts in a positive light—he suspected she *hadn't* been honest. He'd known he really just wanted to see her again, but the surface plan had been valid. Build trust with her so that she *would* open up.

Amazing, the power of lust.

Maybe it wasn't Rebecca at all; maybe it had just been too long since he'd had sex. The recent, self-imposed celibacy had been a mistake.

Shaking his head, he unlocked the SUV and got in, still taking another minute before starting the engine.

Sexual deprivation was not his problem, he thought grimly. Rebecca Holt was. But, damn it, he *couldn't* go anywhere with this until the full truth came out and she and her little boy were safe to resume their lives as she chose.

Too bad all he wanted was to sneak back across the pasture and toss a pebble at her bedroom window, invite her outside and keep on kissing her.

HELD IN REBECCA'S gentle clasp, her grandfather's hand was frail, the dry skin like crepe paper. Like other members of the family, she took turns sitting with him to relieve her grandmother. Today, *Aenti* Emma had insisted *Grossmammi* come to the main house for lunch instead of picking at her food and eating almost nothing while she hovered over her husband.

Rebecca was glad of any distraction. Three days after the kiss, Daniel hadn't returned—not that she'd expected him to. She kept reliving the unaccustomed peace he had given her. And the kiss, of course.

Right now, she was glad to be useful.

Her grandparents owned a sofa with built-in recliners that overpowered the small living room and looked new. She wondered if it had been purchased after *Grossdaadi*'s health had begun to decline. Comfortably ensconced at one end with his feet up, he peeled off the face mask that had been delivering oxygen from the portable tank and smiled. "Such a good girl you are," he said. "We are so glad you came, Rebecca. We missed your *mamm* so much. With you here, when you came, it is like having her back, almost."

Sitting beside him, she returned his smile despite a sudden sting of tears. "I wish I had come sooner."

He shook his head. "Never too late."

Except, sometimes it was. Rebecca's mother had been able to see her parents when she dropped off and picked up Rebecca. That had given her an excuse to visit. Young and as insensitive as children often were, Rebecca had never understood why her mother cried every year as they drove away. "But we'll be back next year," Rebecca would say, and her mother would try to smile and say, "Of course we will," but even at that age Rebecca could tell she wasn't so sure.

"You only saw *Mamm* a couple of times after I quit coming, right?"

His expression grew sad. "*Ja.* Whoever thinks their child will die before them?"

Rebecca touched her cheek to his shoulder, so thin now. "I miss her."

"But it is good to know she is at peace. God had His reasons for taking her and your *daad* when He did. It does us no good to question those reasons. We must accept and know that however sad we feel, there was a purpose and we will see her again."

His certainty comforted her, let her almost share his faith, if only for that moment.

He shuffled off to the bathroom using his walker and, after he came back, felt well enough to sit at the kitchen table and sip half a mug of homemade chicken noodle soup before pushing it away.

When he stood again, he jerked and grabbed his shoulder. His eyes were wild, and although his lips moved, he couldn't seem to form words. Spittle dribbled from his lips.

Rebecca half carried him to the sofa, strapped the mask over his face and made sure the oxygen was flowing, then flew out the front door of the *grossdawdi haus* for help.

Two HOURS LATER, the hospital waiting room was packed with family and friends. Rebecca sat between Sarah and Mose, whose wife, Esther, was on his other side. Mose's eyes were on *Grossmammi*. She held herself stiffly, staring at nothing. Rebecca had seen her respond as each newcomer paused to say a few words, but those responses seemed to come automatically, as if she was only partly in the here and now.

"I thought we were agreed," Mose grumbled, for the fourth or fifth time.

Not even Esther said anything. The family *had* been in agreement that they would not allow

Ephraim to be hauled off to the hospital again. He had asked to die at home.

But *Grossmammi* had insisted her son run to the phone shanty and call for an ambulance. It was not her husband's time; the *Englisch* medicine could help, give him longer.

Now, Rebecca suspected she regretted her decision. She couldn't even be at his side while doctors worked over him. He'd have a tube down his throat and others going into his collapsible veins, causing enormous bruises.

The atmosphere in the room was funereal, nothing like other gatherings Rebecca had been to. The men's faces were stern, set so that they didn't reveal emotion. The women wiped at tears and chided children who squirmed and whined.

Matthew had been whispering with Abram, but now he slid from his chair and came to her. "I gotta go to the bathroom," he said.

She managed a smile as she rose to her feet. "Then let's go find one."

She'd noticed one down the hall, almost as far as the lobby, as they came in. After checking to be sure it was a small, single-toilet bathroom, she let him go in alone. Hearing water run after he flushed the toilet surprised her. Just because she insisted he wash his hands after using the toilet didn't mean he would do it when she wasn't there to see. Maybe he felt her stare through the bathroom door. *Supermom's X-ray vision*, she thought. If only.

He had just come out when she heard a man's voice from the lobby.

"I'm looking for the Grabers?"

Oh, dear God. That was *Tim*.

Rebecca grabbed for the bathroom door handle even as she reached for Matthew. They could hide inside—

But he cried, "Dad! That's Dad!" and, before she got a hand on him, raced down the wide corridor.

CHAPTER EIGHT

BONE-DEEP SCARED, Rebecca ran after Matthew.

Too late. Too late. Tim turned from the information desk and saw Matthew, who cried again, "Dad! You came!"

Tim saw her, too, his gaze first startled then searing, before he crouched and held out his arms. They closed tightly around Matthew, and Tim stood, lifting him to sit on his hip. "Of course I came," he said. "Your mother knew I would."

Fingers biting into her palms, she resisted the need to snatch Matthew out of his father's embrace. "How did you know we were here?"

"First thing I heard when I stopped for a bite to eat at some little café on the main street. 'Ephraim Graber has had another heart attack, sad to say. The whole family is gathered at the hospital.' Of course I came here." His eyes met Rebecca's. "What else would you expect?"

"This isn't a good time. My grandfather—"

"I'm here now, Rebecca. Let's go outside and

talk. I didn't come all this way to sit in a waiting room and pat your hand."

He turned, still holding Matthew. The glass doors slid open for him and he walked out to the small shady area under a portico, his son on his hip. She could do nothing but hurry after them, only distantly aware of the wall of heat outside.

"Let him down, Tim. He can go back and sit with his cousins while we talk."

Lips compressed, eyes cold, he wasn't the man she'd known. She'd seen him angry, yes, but not savagely determined. "You're both coming with me. It's time to go home. Although you'll have to change out of that ridiculous getup."

"Dad?" Matthew suddenly sounded uncertain. "We can't go now."

"You're wrong," Tim snapped, and kept walking toward the visitor-parking area.

Almost running to catch up, Rebecca didn't see another soul. Would anyone hear if she screamed? And then what? He hadn't threatened her. He had a right to see his son. What could she say? *He might have murdered his friend, but I didn't go to the police.*

"Wait!" Surely she could make him see reason. Agree to sit down with him, even to return the damn ring and wallet.

He kept walking because he knew she'd go anywhere he led as long as he had Matthew.

And he wouldn't let Matthew go. The only way she'd get him back would be to give evidence that would ensure he was arrested. And even then, she would have to fight Robert on his home territory. Robert, who could afford better lawyers, who probably socialized with some of the judges.

She heard a beep as he stopped beside a rental car. He opened the back door and tossed Matthew inside.

"Put on your seat belt."

Matthew stared at his father in shock. "But—"

Tim slammed the car door and opened the front-passenger door, then grabbed her arm. "Get in, Rebecca."

Trying to wrench herself free, she called, "Matthew, run back to the hospital."

Tim turned his head enough to snarl, "Stay where I put you." Then he dragged Rebecca toward the front seat.

She was screaming now, she knew she was. Swearing, Tim slammed her toward the front seat, and her face smashed into the top of the door frame. Pain exploded from her cheekbone and the ridge of her eyebrow throughout her entire head. She heard a car coming. Would anyone see? Stop?

Matthew was the one screaming then and she looked down to see him head-butting his father.

"Let my mom go! You're mean! I hate you! Let Mommy go!"

The slam of a car door and running footsteps, and suddenly Tim threw her aside and raced around to the other side of his rental. Reeling against the fender of the car parked beside his, she blinked against the encroaching darkness. Matthew? Where was Matthew? But he was clutching her leg, and it was Daniel running between cars and bursting into the open, right in front of Tim's car.

Which accelerated forward, going straight at Daniel. As he leaped aside, Daniel was yelling, too. He'd pulled his gun, but then his head turned toward her.

Legs like noodles, she let herself slowly slide down the side of the car. And then Daniel was there, catching her in his arms.

DANIEL CARRIED REBECCA in through the front entrance, snapping to the volunteer behind the desk to call for a gurney. Having to let that bastard drive away infuriated him, but she was more important. He'd catch up to Tim Gregory eventually and take great pleasure in snapping on the cuffs.

Matthew hovered, tears running down his face. "That was my dad. He was so mad. Why did he hurt Mommy?"

Rebecca's head rested against Daniel's shoulder. Her lashes formed dark fans against her cheeks. He couldn't tell if she was conscious or not, but rage filled him at the sight of the discoloration and swelling that had already begun.

From one direction, nurses or orderlies raced toward him with a gurney. Down the cross corridor, an Amish man appeared, then broke into a run at the sight of Daniel carrying Rebecca. *Mose*, he realized with relief.

They arrived almost simultaneously. Even as he gently laid her on the gurney, Mose was at his side.

"Rebecca?"

Her eyelids fluttered open. Daniel could tell she was struggling to focus. "Matthew?"

Her cousin took her hand. "He's fine. Right here." He bent and lifted the boy so mother and son could see each other.

"Thank God," she whispered. Her eyes closed again, then almost immediately opened, seeking him. "Daniel?"

He gripped her hand, noticing her *kapp* was gone, revealing gleaming chestnut hair gathered into a mass at her nape. "I'm not going anywhere," he told her. "I'll stay with you, and Mose will take care of Matthew."

"Thank you." She tried to smile, first at him, then at Mose. *"Denke."*

"You will be fine, Rebecca," her cousin said. "Just a headache, *ja*?"

Daniel nodded at the two attendants and said, "I'll be right behind you."

They pushed the gurney away. The last he saw, Rebecca lay heartbreakingly still, eyes closed.

Now he had things to do.

"It was her ex-husband," he told Mose. "He tried to force Matthew and Rebecca into a car." He reached out and stroked blond hair back from the boy's forehead, finding a smile. "Matthew was very brave. He fought to protect his mother."

Matthew sniffled. "He didn't *act* like my dad! Sometimes he gets grouchy, but...not like that."

"We worried when Rebecca and Matthew did not come back," Mose said.

"Any word on Ephraim?" Daniel asked.

"No." He scowled. "*Grossdaadi* should not be here."

Daniel sympathized. They had all known Ephraim was dying. It was unlike the strong woman Ruth Graber was to have permitted this.

"You will arrest that man?" Mose asked.

"That's my intention."

Mose only nodded, his mouth tight. If Tim had been Amish, would Mose have protested? Daniel wasn't sure, but thought Rebecca's cousin wasn't in a forgiving mood. With a last nod, Mose led Matthew away, holding his hand and telling him that they would come back to see his *mamm* as soon as the doctor said it was all right.

Already striding toward the emergency room, Daniel took out his phone and called Dispatch. Chances were good the bastard would bolt for an airport. The closest was St. Louis, but there were other options. If Daniel had anything to say about it, Tim Gregory wouldn't escape.

WHEN DANIEL DROVE Rebecca and Matthew to the house in his own SUV rather than the marked one owned by the police department, Samuel came out to talk to them. The ER doctor had noted that Rebecca had a crashing headache and was sick to her stomach, but he'd decided, reluctantly, to release her because she had never actually lost consciousness. He'd also been swayed by Daniel's explanation that she needed to be placed in a safe house before her ex-husband had a chance to rebound and look for her again.

"Stay put," Daniel ordered.

She might have taken offense if she didn't feel so wretched. Instead, she rolled down her window as he got out and walked around to meet her uncle, who braced a hand on the roof of the SUV and looked down at her.

"You just missed the ambulance," he said. "Ephraim is back in his bed, but not so good. The doctor said his heart was damaged too much this time. He said maybe hours, maybe days. *Mamm* wanted him home again." The relief in his voice couldn't be mistaken. Whether he would have gone toe-to-toe with his mother over his father's wishes, Rebecca didn't know, but he wouldn't have wanted to be put in that position. She knew he shared Mose's unhappiness that Ephraim had ever been taken to the hospital in the first place.

"Sarah is packing up your clothes and Matthew's things, too," he continued. "You are to go stay with Amos and Barbara Troyer. Glad to have you, Barbara told me to say."

A fleeting expression crossed Daniel's face that she didn't understand even as he nodded. Did he dislike the Troyers? She knew he and Samuel had agreed that she and Matthew should move to another household, preferably to someone not closely related to the Grabers.

The Troyers were members of Rebecca's family's church district, so they weren't complete strangers. She couldn't picture Amos but had liked Barbara, who said she and Rebecca's *mamm*, Miriam, had been *gut* friends as girls. Perhaps that was why she and her husband had agreed to hide Rebecca and Matthew.

"They know it could be dangerous?" she asked anxiously.

"*Ja*, they know what happened today. But I think Tim won't be able to find you," her uncle said.

Daniel was clearly furious that Tim hadn't been located. Coming and going from her side all afternoon and into the evening at the hospital, Daniel had been on his phone nearly constantly. He'd kept her updated, his expression grim.

Tim hadn't checked into any B and B or hotel within a three-county radius. His rental car had not been returned, or spotted by a Missouri State Highway Patrol officer or local cop. He'd disappeared, either by ditching the rental car and getting his hands on a different vehicle, or because he'd had a bolt-hole prepared. That was the theory Daniel was going with, which was why he was determined to move her and Matthew tonight.

Rebecca also had a suspicion he was afraid if he didn't, she might take off without telling him where she was going. He already knew her well enough to guess that would be her first instinct. Only…here she and Matthew had so many people determined to protect them, who cared. One of whom, inexplicably, was the county sheriff. That perplexed and worried her, even as the knowledge warmed her deep inside. Turning to him today had felt natural. The evening that they had sat close together in the dark, holding hands, had apparently switched off all her internal warnings.

Sarah hurried out of the house with her arms full, *Aenti* Emma behind her carrying more. Daniel popped the hatch so they could stow everything. *Aenti* Emma came around to the open window, looking first to the backseat.

"*Ach*, Matthew is asleep. *Gut*, *gut*, after such a day, he needs the rest."

Rebecca hoped he regained at least some of his confidence. He had been clingy and frightened since the awful scene with Tim. As furious as she was with Tim for scaring their son, she kept thinking how dumb he'd been. Matthew would never trust his father or feel the same about him again. And for...what? Had he really believed he could force them into the car and somehow get them back to San Francisco without them drawing attention or running away?

Maybe that wasn't what he'd intended, she thought queasily. What if he had the use of a house locally? An isolated one? He could have taken them there to force her to tell him where the ring and wallet were hidden. He might have intimidated Matthew into going home with him, but not her. And he couldn't have just let her go.

Maybe she'd never known him at all.

Her aunt and uncle and cousin took turns to lean in to hug her gently and murmur reassurances. Rebecca accepted them all, tears stinging her eyes. Staying with people who were no relations of hers couldn't be anything but temporary. Panic stirred, but she pushed it down. She'd feel better tomorrow. Surely she would. Then she could come up with a plan.

Right now, she wanted nothing but to lie down in bed and close her eyes.

"Tell…tell *Grossmammi* that I wish I could be with her. That I will be praying for her and *Grossdaadi*."

"She knows already," Samuel said kindly. She made herself nod, then expressed thanks that they turned aside the same way they always did. "You're family."

A moment later, Daniel was driving them away, and the family and farm she had believed would be a refuge fell behind them.

HAVING WAITED ONLY until darkness fell the following evening, Daniel drove out to Amos Troyer's place. He hoped Rebecca felt better because he was determined to get some answers out of her.

Didn't it figure that her new protectors were members of his own family. He'd seen Rebecca's surprise when he greeted her hosts as *Onkel* Amos and *Aenti* Barbara. Barbara was his father's sister. She and Amos had chosen to move their young family to Missouri with Daniel's parents, eager to find affordable land.

What mattered was that Amos and Barbara had welcomed Rebecca and Matthew generously. Even Daniel's uncle, a dour and generally humorless man, had expressed his willingness to help. When she tried to thank him, he had shaken his head and said, "With our last child gone, it will be good to have young people in the house, not so?"

The sight of strange faces had alarmed Matthew, so Daniel was elected to carry the half-awake boy upstairs in the traditional, two-story house and lay him down in a room that had once been shared by two of Daniel's cousins. Leaning heavily on Amos's arm, Rebecca had followed. In the light of the gas lamp, he had seen her pallor and wished she was leaning on him. But Barbara rushed to her, so he helped Matthew take off enough clothes to sleep comfortably in his twin bed, then tucked the covers over him. He'd murmured, "Sleep tight," before turning to the other twin bed and taking Rebecca's hand. "I'll be out to see you tomorrow night. Rest. Don't try to leap out of bed in the morning and help."

"Bossy," she mumbled.

Barbara chuckled. "We won't let her, don't worry."

There hadn't been much he could do but leave.

Tonight, Daniel parked in a tractor turnout a short ways down the road from his aunt and uncle's, slipped up their neighbor's driveway and made his way through a greenbelt, *Aenti* Barbara's orchard and at last to the kitchen door. Through the glass, he saw only Amos, apparently nursing a last cup of coffee. When he rapped lightly, his uncle rose and let him in.

"Coffee?"

"*Denke*, but no. I've had enough for one day."

"That never stops me," Amos said, deadpan, making Daniel wonder if he had a sense of humor, after all. "Rebecca said you would come for sure."

"We still haven't found her ex-husband, and I'm hoping she can help."

Amos studied him, taking his time before nodding. "If she is up."

Had she spent the day in bed? Alarmed, Daniel wondered if he'd made a mistake pushing for her to be released from the hospital.

Amos left without another word, and Daniel felt constrained to wait in the kitchen. His aunt treated him like family, but his uncle maintained more reserve. It might only be his personality, but Daniel knew him to be rigid in his beliefs. Beliefs Daniel had violated.

It was a good ten minutes before Rebecca entered the kitchen, her appearance causing him to grind his teeth. This time, her eye had escaped the damage, but otherwise she looked like she had when he'd first seen her getting off the bus. Except that this time the bruises were fresh, mounting from her cheekbone over her temple and onto her forehead. Purple and black instead of fading to yellow. Even the good side of her face was wan, and he had the feeling she wasn't focusing well.

He had half risen at the sight of her, but now forced himself to resume his seat. "Amos didn't get you up, did he?"

"Yes, but I was just lying on top of the covers, not sleeping." Moving gingerly, she sat across the table from him. "The headache is bad, but I'm not dizzy or seeing double or anything else the doctor warned me about. I count my blessings."

"How very Amish of you," he said drily.

For an instant, her gaze sharpened. "Seems like there's something *you* never mentioned."

He ignored that. "Are you taking the pain pills the doctor gave you?"

"Mostly. I'm a mother, you know. I can't expect Barbara to take over entirely."

Stubborn woman, he thought, not for the first time. "Where are they? You need one right now."

"I…" She closed her eyes. "Ask Barbara."

He came back a minute later with one in his hand, poured her some milk to protect her stomach and watched her down the pill. "Go back upstairs and lie down, Rebecca. You're not ready for this."

"No. But…will you stay for a few minutes?" She sounded timid. "Just talk to me?"

Daniel hesitated, even though he knew he'd agree—despite the risk of letting her get under his skin enough to shake his resolve. He'd come here to wring a straight story out of her.

"It's okay—" she started to say, but he shook his head.

"Of course I'll stay."

"Can we go out on the porch?" Rebecca offered a weak smile. "The dark would be soothing, I think."

"We seem to do all our talking on front porches."

He kept his hands to himself, but stayed close as she went to the living room to tell his aunt and uncle where they were going. Once they were outside, she headed toward the porch swing, then stopped.

"I think I'll sit on the steps."

He watched anxiously as she eased herself down, resting her head against an upright sup-

porting the porch roof. Sitting beside her, he
swiveled so he could keep an eye on her.

"Where's Matthew?" he asked.

"I already tucked him in. I was keeping him
company until he fell asleep."

The air felt, if not cooler, at least less stuffy
than inside. The moon was three-quarters, and
the golden squares of the kitchen and living-
room windows provided some illumination.
Fireflies darted through the night.

"How's he taking the change?" Daniel asked.

"I don't know." He heard worry in Rebecca's
voice. "You saw him yesterday. He's still the same,
not wanting to be more than two feet from me."

Silence enveloped them. Daniel braced himself.

EVEN WITH THE throbbing in her head, curiosity
had eaten at Rebecca all day. Daniel knew so
much about her that it seemed only fair to ask
him to reveal a small part of himself. It would
be different if he had always approached her as
the sheriff, but the attraction they both felt made
everything they said and did personal.

Finally she said, "You were Amish." She
couldn't deny the craving she felt to really know
him.

"Yes," he said readily, as if he'd expected her
to ask. "You know my parents, Isaac and Susan.
They're in your aunt and uncle's church."

"I remember them. I should have guessed. You look like your *daad*."

"*Ja*, so people tell me," he said in Deitsch, sounding rueful.

She laughed, then moaned. "Don't do that to me!"

His quiet chuckle felt like a touch.

She waited for the sharp pain to subside before asking, "When did you leave the faith?"

"In every important way, when I was sixteen. I stayed at home for a couple more years—we moved here from Iowa during that period—but I never accepted baptism, and my parents weren't surprised when I packed up one day and left."

"I'm assuming it has something to do with why you went into law enforcement." Before he could answer, she said, "Just tell me to butt out, if you want. It's really none of my business."

He shifted on his step, but said, "No, it's okay. Many of the Amish in the area know something of my history. Otherwise, I've kept quiet about it until recently. Away from here, all I wanted was to erase my roots."

"Starting with the accent and the tendency to say *ja* or my *daad*."

She caught his smile. He'd stretched out long legs.

"Starting with those, *ja*."

Rebecca had the startling thought that, if not

for the confession she needed to make, she could have been completely happy right now. There was something about Daniel Byler. She clasped her hands together, wondering how it would feel to be tucked against his side, his arm around her. He had kissed her, yes, but to be held lovingly, that was different.

What she ought to ask herself was how he'd look at her when he learned about the wallet and ring. Would he understand her decision?

Just for now, she shoved her worries aside, letting the tension ease from aching muscles.

Daniel started talking, gazing out over a field of hay to the woods beyond. The minute he described the impromptu party put together by a teenager who didn't think it important to deposit the day's business receipts the way his father had asked him, she knew what had happened was bad. She tensed again when he told her about the boys' ineffectual efforts to keep the thieves away from the girls. When he reached the rape, she heard the remembered rage bubbling beneath Daniel's matter-of-fact recitation. The rest was terse, but she had enough history with the Amish to read between the lines.

Finished, he let out a long breath and scrubbed a hand through his short hair. "My parents hoped I would regain my faith if we lived in a less conservative settlement. My mother sent letters far and wide, trying to find the right place. She has a distant cousin who lives near Jamestown. This settlement in Henness County was fairly new, the farmland cheap compared to Iowa. *Mamm's* cousin had heard good things about the bishop."

"Is he still here?"

"Bishop Jonas."

She blinked, picturing the man with a long white beard and a twinkle in his eye. "He does seem nice."

"He's a good man."

"But you'd seen what you'd seen, and done what you'd done."

"That pretty well sums it up."

Studying his face in profile, she said tentatively, "Was it hard? Out there, I mean? With only an eighth-grade education?"

He turned his head, eyes a dark charcoal in this light. "Yes."

He'd said all he meant to, she realized. Maybe more than he had meant to. She closed her own eyes and let herself drift.

She didn't know how long had passed when she felt a touch on her shoulder.

"Bedtime, Rebecca," Daniel said in that impossibly gentle voice. He wrapped an arm around her waist and set her on her feet, turning her toward the front door. "Sleep tight. And if you wake up hurting, take the damn pills."

A kiss on the cheek, and he ushered her inside, where Barbara took over.

Swaying, Rebecca wished for foolish things before deciding all she really *needed* was to be prone.

DRIVING HOME, DANIEL wondered how she'd softened him up when he knew she hadn't told him anything close to the truth. Did she think she could keep playing him?

He grimaced. Maybe he was a sucker for a delicate face framed by chestnut hair and a *kapp*. But at thirty-five, he had never yet allowed himself to veer from a path he considered right by a pretty face or a lush female body. Or, truthfully, by anyone or anything, unless he were to count the sight of girls he'd known all his life being raped on the cold concrete floor in front of him. The bishop and even his parents believed he had chosen the wrong path from that moment.

But, for all his sometime regrets, he knew he couldn't have done anything but fight. Or to find a different meaning in his life from that moment on. He did respect the Amish choice to live by Jesus's teachings to be harmless as doves. But he'd found enough passages in the Bible to know God had given His blessings to warriors, as well as men of peace. Most of all, he took comfort in the knowledge that God called men according to His purpose. That didn't stop him wondering, at his darkest moments, if he was only trying to justify his decisions.

But it was an old debate, and he had mostly made his peace.

Daniel's mouth tipped up when he remembered a passage from Matthew that he ought to bring to Rebecca's attention tomorrow: "Fear them not, therefore, for there is nothing covered, that shall not be revealed; and hid, that shall not be known."

Somehow, he didn't think she'd appreciate his bit of piety.

CHAPTER NINE

THE MEMORY OF Rebecca's pallid, bruised face stayed with Daniel that night, sleeping and waking, and was on his mind from the minute he got up. He'd seldom struggled more than he did that day to concentrate on his job.

He trusted that Amos or Barbara would have let him know if she had a bad turn. But did they understand the dangers of head trauma? Were they watching her closely?

He chafed at having to wait until nightfall to return to the Troyer place, but also felt dread. Had Rebecca done anything he couldn't accept? How hard would he have to push to get the truth from her? He might lose his temper if she kept defending her scumbag of an ex, the man who had brutalized her.

As he'd done last night, he parked in a tractor turnout, at last reaching the kitchen door.

When he knocked, it was Rebecca who appeared, letting him in.

"Hi," she said shyly. "I've been waiting for you."

"You look better." He studied her. "I think."

Rebecca made a face at him. "I do feel better." Apparently seeing doubt, she said, "Really. It's just…" She touched her cheek carefully. "I think it's getting more colorful."

It was, but her eyes were clear, and she didn't hold herself as if she feared an incautious movement might make her head explode.

So he nodded. "I'm glad." He glanced around the otherwise empty kitchen. "Do you want to include Amos in this discussion?"

Distress replaced the gladness he thought he'd seen when she first let him in. "Do we have to?"

"Of course not." He hesitated. "In that case, let's go outside again."

They paused on the way so he could greet his aunt and uncle, sitting in the living room. Never idle, Barbara was knitting, the needles flashing beneath the propane-powered lamp. With one finger, Amos marked his place in the bible passage he had been reading aloud, took in the uniform Daniel had worn to emphasize his purpose tonight and said only, "Nephew." Barbara smiled a greeting.

"We'll sit out front again," Daniel said, and Amos nodded.

Daniel was glad, once the front door was closed behind them, to realize he could no longer hear Amos's voice, which meant his family inside wouldn't be able to hear him and Rebecca, either.

This time she chose the glider, while Daniel remained on his feet, leaning against a porch upright.

Assuming Matthew was asleep, Daniel asked how the boy was adjusting.

"I don't know." Worry sounded in Rebecca's voice. "He's shy with Amos and Barbara, and she's really tried with him. Mostly, I think he's scared. And, of course, he misses Abram. I'm having to sit with him until he falls asleep every night."

"Seeing his father hurt his mother has changed him," he said gently.

"Yes. So stupid of Tim."

"Under stress, he seems to have poor impulse control." Daniel congratulated himself for describing inexcusable behavior so clinically.

She gave a half laugh that held no amusement. "That's truer than I knew. Matthew had seen a few outbursts, but nothing awful until yesterday."

"I'd guess Tim's stress level is cranked even higher now."

She started the glider rocking, perhaps to comfort herself. "I…suppose so."

"You need to tell me why, Rebecca." He kept his voice soft, but with no give. "Your hideout has been blown. It suggests that your ex-husband paid a lot more attention than you thought he did to your reminiscences. It's also clear he's not going to back off. If this was all about him getting Matthew back, he wouldn't have been trying to stuff you into that car. He'd have grabbed his kid and taken off."

She stared at her hands. In this light, the garish bruises were less obvious. She appeared demure, her heart-shaped face set off by her gauzy white *kapp*.

Daniel let the silence stretch, acquire a weight.

Finally Rebecca sighed and lifted her head. "No, it's not all about Matthew, although he's a big part of it. And I got to thinking about how Tim found me. I still doubt he paid any attention to what I told him about my family. But when we left to come here, I couldn't take much from the apartment."

Daniel nodded for her to continue.

"I had a box of family stuff in my closet. A bible, letters from my mother and from *Grossmammi* dating, oh, way back. The *kapp* I wore that last summer. If Tim got into the apartment..."

"I think we can assume he did."

"Yes." Her shoulders sagged. "Have you heard anything about Ephraim?"

Was she trying to distract him?

"Last I knew, his condition was unchanged. Word will spread fast when he dies."

"I suppose that's true." She pressed her lips together, then chewed on the lower one for a moment. "Why Tim wanted to find me. You won't be surprised to hear it has to do with that whole mess at G, G & S."

No, he wasn't surprised. But he had tensed, his body suddenly battle ready.

"Were you involved in any way with the company?"

"Me?" Her eyes widened. "Heavens, no! Tim didn't even talk about work, which made me feel as if I was on the sidelines of his life." Sadness infused her voice, although it had the patina of something long accepted. "He'd brag sometimes about a new project, and show off anything in print about him or the company. But when things went wrong, he closed up. Until he and Josh had to call the police, I didn't even know there *were* money troubles, just that he was worried and…angry. It wasn't until quite a bit later that I knew more than what was in the newspapers."

He raised his eyebrows. "Except for the fact that your husband was relieved, when a normal person would expect about any other reaction."

"Well, yes, but there might have been legitimate reasons for him acting that way."

He'd conceded as much the last time they talked about this. Now he was only annoyed that she kept making excuses for the creep.

Possibly reading his expression, she looked away from him, toward the moonlit pasture. She fiddled with one of the long ties dangling from her *kapp*.

"What happened is, during a meeting with our attorneys before the divorce, Tim gave me permission to take anything from the house that I wanted." She told him about deciding she wanted to keep a particular necklace, and opening a hidden safe her husband hadn't known she could get into.

Oh, hell, was all Daniel could think.

"I opened it and, well, there was something at the front. Now I wish I'd never looked, but then... It was Steven's wallet. With his driver's license and credit cards. The thing is, the police had been tracing him because he'd been *using* those credit cards." Very softly, she said, "Or someone was."

"He's dead, and your husband was encouraging the police to believe he's alive," Daniel said slowly. Having seen pictures of the two men, he immediately understood how easily Gregory could have gotten away with using the partner's ID and credit cards.

"Yes," Rebecca whispered.

"How did he know you'd seen the wallet?"

She bent her head. Her rocking picked up speed. "I was dumb. I, um…"

"You confronted him." Daniel felt sick.

She didn't want to look at him, which made him immediately suspicious. But after a moment, she said, "He walked in the door just as I was leaving. He was surprised to see me and, well, kind of hostile. A week later, when he was picking up Matthew, I begged him to tell me that he hadn't had anything to do with Steven getting hurt."

"That sounds more suicidal than dumb," he said, infuriated that she'd taken a risk so huge. *Hurt?* Really? How about *dead*? And she was *still* making excuses for this guy?

She glared at him. "He was my husband. I didn't believe—" After a few seconds, her shoulders sagged. "What I did was stupid, okay? I didn't give myself time to think through what I really should do."

Truth, Daniel thought.

"He insisted he didn't have anything to do with Steven dying, and I believed him."

More truth. So what *had* she lied about? He crossed his arms. "But he didn't deny the guy is dead."

"Not exactly. I was…pretty freaked. If Steven hadn't taken the money, where was it? And if he had…well, I guess Tim and Josh could have been frantically searching for it."

"That makes no sense," he said brutally. "Once law enforcement was involved, the two of them wouldn't have been able to recover the money without explanation. If they did explain, there would be a lot of questions. Starting with why the man who'd embezzled it didn't have the money." He frowned. "When did the police become involved?"

"A good friend of Steven's reported him missing after he didn't show up for their usual game of tennis. He went to Steven's town house, called around, found out he hadn't been at work for a couple of days."

"If Josh and Tim had had their way, they'd never have involved the cops. If anyone else within the company knew money was missing, they could have blamed Steven but said they didn't want clients to know the foundation of the firm had a giant crack." Major businesses did often keep financial disasters secret.

"I suppose I didn't think it through," Rebecca said. "All I can say is that I once loved Tim. We'd been together for nine years."

That precarious dignity of hers got to him, although he didn't want it to. Not now.

"That's a long time," she said. "And, no matter how I felt about Tim, I didn't want to see

Matthew's father go to prison. It's not like I *knew* what happened."

"You didn't go to the police."

Her chin came up. "The lead investigator grilled me right after Tim and I separated. He was so nasty I didn't *want* to cooperate with him. I know I should have. But I justified it to myself, and then… The truth is, we'd been arguing about custody. Tim backed down and said he'd allow me primary custody."

"If you kept your mouth shut." Crap.

Back to examining her hands, she said, "Matthew is everything to me. I couldn't let Robert have him. Tim and his father could afford better lawyers than I could. They're successful community leaders. I wouldn't look like much in comparison."

Frustration with the woman mingled with his fear for her. She'd danced with the devil and was now paying the consequences.

Feeling cruel, he said, "Did you give a thought to Stowe's family, waiting for news about him?"

She lifted her head for a fleeting look at him. "He doesn't have any family. He wasn't even in a relationship. If he had been…" Her throat worked. "I'd like to say I would have called the police."

Sucker that he was, he wanted to believe her.

"So then you and a bullet had a near miss," he said wryly.

"No, it was quite a while." She kept her eyes on her clasped hands. "Since we were in agreement, the divorce went through. Tim seemed… mostly like himself when I saw him the next few months. I think he believed I wouldn't say anything. He had Matthew every other weekend. I got mad once when Matthew came home upset. His grandfather had spanked him for standing up for me. Matthew didn't like the bad words Robert used about me. But I don't think anything else like that happened. Then suddenly Tim told me that Josh didn't like me knowing so much. Josh felt threatened, too, Tim said."

"Too."

"That's what he said. I thought Tim believed I'd never go to the police. Maybe if he'd never told Josh…" She trailed off.

"He and Josh were coconspirators. *You* are an ex-wife."

Sounding unhappy, she said, "Josh wasn't the only one angry at Tim. His father was, too."

"And you have primary custody because you had knowledge to hold over his head."

Her chin came up. "He offered. I didn't ask."

"Doesn't change the reality."

The chin came back down. "No."

"You know what we have to do now."

"Tell the investigator something I'm sure he already suspects?"

"You can give him someplace to start. With that focus, they'll find proof Tim was out of town when the other guy's credit cards were used. With luck, he'll have left some trail that will allow them to put him right where the card was used."

"But I *don't* believe Tim had anything to do with Steven's dying, if that's what happened." She was pleading for him to believe her. The glider action became agitated. "And it's *not* because I have some kind of lingering feelings for Tim. I don't. Right now, I'm furious. But I do know him. I believe he got sucked into something bad by Josh. Because of his father, Tim is all about impressing people, showing he's the big man—even if that means doing something he wouldn't otherwise. Only, the way things stand, it will be *Tim's* face that appears on some security camera using Steven's cards. *He'll* take the fall for Josh. I'd feel different if I really thought Tim had killed Steven."

She might as well be wearing blinders, like the harness horses that pulled the buggies. Daniel would have been disgusted except a lot of this sounded familiar. He could have been talking to one of his sisters who'd gotten herself into a similar spot. It was as if Rebecca shared the Amish reluctance to go to the law. She certainly hadn't wanted to turn to *him*.

He was willing to bet she had determined to forgive her ex-husband for any and all sins, too. The Amish believed that if a man repented of a wrong he'd committed, he should be accepted back into the faith and the community, forgiveness absolute, past actions left behind. Rebecca wanted to believe Tim really was a decent man, influenced by the truly wicked.

He shook his head. She'd spent enough time among the Amish. It wouldn't be surprising if their attitudes had worn off on her. And her mother hadn't rebelled from her childhood beliefs, not the way he'd done. She would have gently influenced her daughter to believe that forgiveness was right, that people deserved second chances.

Fine. Daniel believed the same, up to a point. And maybe Tim Gregory really wasn't the bad guy. But he'd had his second chance now, and he'd blown it. Never mind that, at the very least, he had helped cover up a death that had likely been a murder.

"He's a dangerous man, Rebecca."

"The thing is, something else happened."

"Besides you almost getting shot?"

The strain on her face found an echo in her

voice. "After the shooting, I was still lying on the sidewalk when my phone rang."

He tensed.

"It was this sort of metallic voice. He said I'd had a warning now, to keep my mouth shut. That if I went to the cops, Matthew would die."

Gripped by now-useless fear and anger, Daniel could only articulate one word. "He?"

"I'm pretty sure. Um." She didn't want to look at him anymore. "Tim wouldn't have threatened his own son. He does love Matthew. When I called him about what happened, he sounded really shocked and mad. He said he'd try to find out more and, well, make sure there wasn't a repeat."

And she'd believed him, because the son of a bitch was so trustworthy.

"Except..." She chewed on her lower lip. "When he called back, I could tell he wouldn't be able to stop Josh, if that's who was behind it."

Huh. A dose of common sense.

"I packed to take off, but that same day, I got hit by the car," she said. "There was another call. This one said, 'Lucky for us, you have a weakness.' I couldn't risk Matthew!" she cried. "I couldn't."

"It didn't occur to you that telling the truth to the investigators in San Francisco would have taken the pressure off?"

"Would it?"

"I can't see your father-in-law going the route of threatening Matthew," Daniel said slowly. "I wouldn't let your ex off the hook. Threats are cheap, and he of all people knows how to get to you."

Her mouth formed a circle of outrage. "He wouldn't! You don't know him!"

"Think about it. Would Josh really do anything to his buddy's son? He'd have risked Tim turning on him."

She was still angry, but thinking. "What if he's set up the money trail to make Tim look guilty? I don't have anything but Tim's word that points at Josh. No matter what, if I'd gone to the police and they'd made an arrest that day—and how would they have proved Josh was behind the attempts on my life?—a trial would have been months away. Would I really have survived to testify?" She glared at him. "Besides, there's still Matthew."

"With Tim under investigation, he wouldn't have had a chance of gaining custody." Daniel couldn't let himself soften. "You have good reason not to allow him visitation. No court would dispute that, under the circumstances. And Josh wouldn't have dared go after you or Matthew, not if he was trying to look like the bewildered innocent. Sounds to me like you're still trying to protect your ex."

She hesitated. "Not for his sake, but…is it so bad to want Matthew to be able to respect his father?"

Daniel shook his head. "After yesterday, I think that ship has sailed."

"I'm also afraid of Robert."

He thought that over. "You believe what you're holding over Tim is also what's keeping your father-in-law from taking you on in court."

Her hands twisted in her lap. "Yes. He belittles Tim, but he's all about status. To have his son *arrested*? I think he'd do anything to prevent that."

"But does Robert know why Tim didn't fight for custody?"

"You mean, does he know what Tim's involved in?"

"That's what I'm asking."

Her beseeching gaze met his. "I don't know. I kind of doubt it, but…I can't be sure."

"It's time to talk to the detective," Daniel said flatly.

She crossed her arms, almost hugging herself. "If I do, if I give him everything, I'm defenseless." She hesitated. "The thing is, I have—"

Losing patience, Daniel shook his head. "Tim, at least, has already come after you. You're kidding yourself if you think anything you can do protects either you or Matthew. Once the San Francisco investigator knows—"

Rebecca surged up from the glider. "You won't call that detective yet, will you? Promise me!" Tension vibrated through her. "I need to figure out what to do—"

Daniel resisted the need to push away from the railing and take her hands in his. Pull her into his arms. *This* was why he should have kept his distance from the beginning.

Body rigid, he said, "I can't make that promise. This will become a murder investigation, Rebecca, and you've left the detectives so in the dark they don't even know they should be looking for the body." He understood her turmoil, up to a point, but he couldn't let it sway him. "I have to do my job."

"Please! Just give me a day."

He made himself shake his head. "You've had too many days already."

She let out a cry that pierced him. "I trusted you!"

"You know who and what I am," he said, his jaw tight. "Have you given any thought at all about what the *right* thing is?" The question came from both sides of him: Amish and cop.

"A thousand times," she whispered. Her voice gained strength. "But, obviously, what I think

or feel or fear is irrelevant. After all, you have
to do your job."

A hand seemed to grip his throat. "I do, but
that doesn't mean—"

"All of this—" a wave of her hand encom-
passed them both "—was nothing but you doing
your job." Her stare burned. "Then go do it."

The next second, the door banged closed behind her, and he was left alone on the porch.

SHE WAS AMAZED that she was able to speak nor-
mally to Amos and Barbara once she went into
the house. Amos invited her to join them, and
she managed to sound regretful when she said
she had a headache and thought she needed to
go to bed. Not that she expected to sleep.

Wrestling with her conscience, trying to deal
with her wrenching and probably unfair sense
of betrayal, Rebecca lay awake through much
of the night. Tim's terrible behavior had built
in slow increments. In contrast, Daniel's scathing words and expression left her devastated.

It wasn't as if she'd refused to talk to Detective Estevez. She was past the point of being
able to navigate a booby-trapped maze alone.
All she'd asked was a little time to think about
what she should do once she handed over the
only thing she had to bargain with. Daniel's reaction told her the truth. He'd been nice to her,

kissed her, only so he could uncover what she was hiding. The irony was he had cut her off just when she'd been about to tell him she *had* the wallet and ring.

Of course Detective Estevez would insist on talking to her himself. She would tell him what she had, not just what she knew. It was true that Tim hadn't earned her silence. If she needed to do the right thing, that went double for him. He should come forward, accept punishment for what he'd done rather than condone threats against his own son.

For her, admitting what she knew to Estevez would be a small way of making up for her sins.

But Daniel… She wished she never had to see him again. A day—that was all she'd asked for. What difference did one day make now? He'd refused her even that. So arrogant, he thought the little woman couldn't do anything to protect herself. *Shouldn't* do anything. As if he could protect them.

Her conscience pointed out that he had come to her rescue in the hospital parking lot. Well, fine, but it was pure luck he'd been in the right place at the right time. What was he going to do, take a leave of absence to be their bodyguard? Of course not! His *job* was more important than her, that was for sure.

Anger at Daniel balled in her stomach, but

she felt at peace with her decision. Soon it would all be out of her hands. Ironically, he'd be unlikely to reach Detective Estevez tomorrow, it being a Sunday. How foolish of him not to realize. To think he could have given her the day she'd asked for, and she'd never have known how much contempt he really felt for her.

Her eyes dry but burning as she stared at the dark ceiling and listened to Matthew breathe in the other twin bed, Rebecca comforted herself that at least tomorrow she would be able to pray with a clean heart, truly give herself to God instead of holding back. The rest...she would deal with when it came.

CHAPTER TEN

DANIEL PULLED OFF the road midafternoon when his phone rang. Shorthanded today, he had gone out on patrol himself, as he often did. Truthfully, he'd had no desire to attend church. He wouldn't have been able to pay attention to a sermon or feel any of what he ought to when he was in a house of the Lord. Helping keep the roads safe for the faithful felt more important.

He'd left a message that morning for Detective Estevez in case the guy was working on a Sunday. But this wasn't Estevez. The number was unfamiliar, but local.

"Byler here," he answered.

"Sheriff." The voice was unexpected. "This is Samuel Graber. I wouldn't usually call you about what has happened, but I think it must have to do with my niece."

"You're at the phone shanty?"

"Ja."

"What happened?"

"Today was church Sunday. We were at Levi

Troyer's. Nothing wrong there, but when we got home, we found someone had broken in."

Stiffening, Daniel said, "If Emma and Sarah are already cleaning up, please stop them. I want to see exactly what was done. I can be there in ten minutes."

"*Ja*, I will tell them to wait. They itched to set everything right, you know how it is, but they will understand."

Daniel had to force himself to stay under the speed limit during the drive. Nobody had been hurt, he reminded himself, before remembering that Ephraim and Ruth might have been on the property in the *grossdawdi haus*. Surely Ruth, at least, would have heard intruders. He shuddered at the idea of the tiny old lady confronting them. But Samuel would have said if something like that had happened.

He made an effort to brake gently rather than slide to a stop in front of the Grabers' house. Samuel and his son Mose strode out to meet him immediately. Sarah sat on the front porch, but Emma wasn't in sight.

Daniel got out. "I worried all the way here about Ruth. If she heard anything—"

Samuel shook his head. "They were with us. Ephraim was too *agasinish* to stay home with the oxygen the doctor says he must have."

The word meant *contrary* or *stubborn*, and Daniel smiled.

"He did fine." And Samuel was clearly marveling that Ephraim had been able to accomplish such a thing. "Maybe *Mamm* knew best and it was not his time."

"God didn't need him yet, which is a blessing for Ruth," Daniel said automatically.

"The blessing," Mose said more grimly, "is that *Grossmammi* and *Grossdaadi* were not home when these people came."

"You're right," Daniel agreed, still appalled to think what would have happened if Ephraim hadn't stubbornly insisted on attending the service. "Did they go only into the house?"

"No, everywhere. The house, the *grossdawdi haus*, the barn, even the chicken coop. Usually, I would have been thinking it was *Englisch* teenagers, tearing the place up for fun. But they would have stolen, or written on the walls, or…" He stopped. "This has us *fernhoodled*, it does. Makes no sense."

"Show me," Daniel said.

They started with the house, and he saw immediately what Samuel meant. This wasn't pure vandalism, although things had been broken. The crocks that held sugar, flour and oats were smashed on the floor, as were other containers. The counters and floor were a mess. The refrig-

erator door stood wide open as did many of the
kitchen cabinet doors.

"They were searching for something," Daniel
said after a minute.

"*Ja*, it is like that everywhere," Samuel said.
"They had to have been here for hours. Mattresses off the beds, clothes all over the floor,
boxes upended. There are many smashed jars
in the cellar." Grief filled his voice.

Daniel understood. Cleaning up the bedrooms,
that would only be a *bodderation*, as the Amish
put it. But Samuel was thinking of the enormous
amount of work his mother, wife and daughter
had put into the canned foods—planting, weed-
ing, picking, even before the fruits and vege-
tables reached the kitchen. Because they were
taking care of their family, it had been a labor of
love, now smashed and trampled. His impression
was that Samuel and Emma were comfortable
enough financially that they could still afford to
eat well, but that wasn't the point.

Daniel skipped the *grossdawdi haus* during
his tour, guessing that Ruth had already begun to
clean up. But he saw that straw had been pulled
out of the hen's nests, tools flung everywhere in
the shed. The destruction was the worst in the
barn, as if the intruders had grown frustrated
or had recognized the impossibility of finding
whatever they sought if it was hidden here.

He stood looking around at what he knew had been an orderly space. Tack was now tossed in heaps, some pieces cut. Neatly baled and piled hay had been flung against walls, bags of grain dumped out. Thank the good Lord the horses had been out to pasture, Daniel thought.

"Even the buggies," Mose said with a gesture.

They would have driven the large family buggy to church service, but both Sarah and Emma had their own, smaller ones. In Sarah's, the velvet seat covers had been slit with knives, the filling ripped out. Side panels were torn out. This damage would be costly to fix, though Daniel guessed Harvey Stolzfus, who built and repaired buggies, would not charge Samuel.

At the sound of steel wheel rims approaching, he glanced toward the open barn door. It would be a neighbor arriving, the first of many who would help with the cleanup. No Amish man or woman, however unlikable, was ever left to face troubles alone. Everyone in the church district, and some people from beyond, would pitch in. By evening, the women would have a feast laid out on tables on the lawn, and the kitchen, barn and bedrooms would be neat as a pin.

"I'm going to call for a deputy who does fingerprinting." Seeing the two men's expressions, Daniel continued, "Not in the house. I think he can get clear impressions from the tool handles and the doors and panels in the buggies. If these men are smart, they will have worn gloves, but people aren't always smart. Or a glove could tear, the man not noticing. We can at least find out if these are known criminals."

Samuel nodded with clear reluctance. "Could this have something to do with Rebecca?"

"I can't be sure." Oh, he knew, all right, but didn't want to admit as much, not yet at least. "But I think so. These were not thieves, and they didn't commit the kind of vandalism teenagers do. Whoever they are, they think something is hidden here."

"*Fernhoodled* we are, for sure," Samuel said for the second time, shaking his head. "Glad I am they don't know where to find Rebecca."

Even September's heat had done nothing for the icy chill Daniel had felt since he'd received the phone call. "You and me both." He nodded toward the barn doors. "I'll make that call and wait for my deputy. You can go ahead with the house and the henhouse. Even the barn, except for the buggies and tools with smooth handles."

"*Denke,*" Samuel said, his disquiet undiminished. He and Mose walked out to greet whichever neighbor had arrived first, while Daniel took out his phone.

Would Rebecca be quite as *fernhoodled*? he

wondered, his molars grinding. Or would she only pretend to be?

He should have known she was still lying.

SINCE THE MOMENT they had returned from the church service and fellowship meal, Rebecca felt the weight of tomorrow's inevitable visit from Daniel. She bustled in the kitchen, unable to settle down even though she knew Amos was waiting for her to join everyone else in the living room for a Bible reading. She seemed to be the only one aware of how thick the air had felt today, as if a storm approached. She kept remembering a time when she was only eight or nine. *Grossdaadi* calling, such urgency in his voice, as he shepherded them into the cellar. She'd felt as if she'd been electrified, every tiny hair on her body standing on end.

That day the tornado bypassed the farm by half a mile. They'd been lucky. She had gone with the rest of her relatives to help another family rebuild. In the years since, she never saw mention of a tornado on the news without feeling a shiver of dread and remembering that barn, flattened, the house missing its roof. And the dead animals.

Amos and Barbara trusted in God's will and His mercy in a way she didn't quite. Perhaps Amos had chosen a particularly appropriate

Bible passage to read tonight. She would do her best to find comfort in it.

A sharp rap came on the kitchen door behind her. She jerked, then spun to face the danger.

Not danger—Daniel. But why come on Sunday evening?

Apparently her reprieve was over.

She hurried to let him in even as she heard footsteps behind her. Daniel stepped inside, nodding at her but addressing his uncle.

"Have you heard what happened at the Grabers' today?"

"Ephraim?" Amos said.

"Oh, no." Rebecca realized she had splayed a hand over her chest, as if to calm her speeding heartbeat. One thing she hadn't thought to worry about. Her grandfather had looked surprisingly sturdy at the service this morning.

"Ephraim is still fine," Daniel said. "As fine as he can be."

Amos said, "Sit down, Daniel. Rebecca, he would like coffee, I think. I will ask Barbara to take Matthew up to bed, *ja*, so he doesn't hear."

To compose herself, she focused on removing two ceramic mugs from the cupboard and pouring the coffee that was almost always on the stove.

She had just set one mug in front of Daniel at the kitchen table when Matthew flew into the kitchen, his sun-streaked hair tousled. She had the thought that soon it could be trimmed to look like the other Amish boys' hair. And how tan he'd gotten! Rebecca bent to hug him, closing her eyes for a moment at the sheer joy of holding his long, bony body close.

But anxiety filled his eyes. "Do I really have to go to bed? You'll come up to say good-night, won't you?"

"You do, and of course I will." She found a smile for him. "Say hello to Sheriff Byler."

He looked at Daniel with suspicion, which made her heart sink. He must sense her tension. But after a moment he said, "Hi. Why do I hafta go to bed?"

"Because I need to talk to your mother," Daniel said.

"And because Barbara said you must," Rebecca added sternly.

He grimaced, but went.

"Good night," Daniel called after him, but got no response.

"It's not quite dark yet," Rebecca said as she glanced out the window at the deep purple of dusk. And then she really let herself look at his face. Her apprehension became dread. He was all cop.

No, she reminded herself, he was just letting her see the truth, now that he had what he wanted from her. *This* was who he was. She fastened her gaze on Matthew's artwork decorating the front of the refrigerator and sat silent, nerves taut. Had Tim gone to the Grabers' today looking for her? What could he have said or done?

Amos reappeared and settled with a sigh on the chair beside her, facing Daniel. It was probably wishful thinking to believe he was allying himself with her.

"What is this about, nephew?"

"While you were all attending the service this morning, someone ransacked the Grabers' house, barn and outbuildings." His jaw muscles kept flickering, his gaze shifting between her and Amos.

Rebecca sat aghast, speechless.

"Even the *grossdawdi haus*. There was destruction, but none of the usual vandalism I'd expect of teenagers. Nothing stolen, so far as we can tell. It would appear they were hunting for something small, because they dumped out kitchen canisters, swept jars off the shelves in the pantry to see behind them, tipped mattresses off beds, yanked panels from the buggies, slit the seat covers. They lifted and flung hay and straw bedding. Even searched the henhouse. It must have taken hours."

Her fingernails bit into her palms and her teeth wanted to chatter. Realizing both men were now looking at her, she said, "What if *Gross-mammi* and *Grossdaadi* had stayed home?"

"The intruders might have made some excuse for being there and left. But they might not have, too. This search was ruthless, Rebecca."

"It's because of me." Of course it was.

"You have another idea?" he asked, voice hard. "Unless it's drug related, we don't have this kind of crime in Henness County."

Head spinning, she asked in an absurd last hope, "Do you think they expected Matthew and me to be there?"

"That's possible, but this wasn't just a temper tantrum because they'd been thwarted." Daniel suddenly looked weary, the lines in his face deepening. "They hoped to find something, whether you were there or not."

Shame flooded her. This wasn't how she'd wanted to make this admission, but it had to be done. A just punishment for her pettiness.

Amos said nothing. So much for being her ally. And why would he be, when Daniel was family? Daniel's connection to them was the only reason he and Barbara had taken her in.

Tears burned at the back of her eyes, but she refused to let them fall. Instead, she focused on Amos's face, which didn't help. The dry humor and occasional twinkle she'd seen in his eyes before were no longer apparent.

"I did hide something at my aunt and uncle's," she said baldly. "Something I should never have had. I thought it would keep Matthew and me safe, but…" She didn't bother finishing, although her gaze sought Daniel's.

He was looking at her, all right, with cold judgment. "The men might have taken it."

Fear sprang from nowhere, spreading with sickening speed. What if he was right? Daniel said they had flung hay bales. They might have seen the loose board beneath one of the bales, just as she had.

If the wallet and ring were gone, she wouldn't be able to make anything right.

In a voice not her own, she managed to say, "It's possible, but…I found a good hiding place."

Devastated by the trauma her family had suffered today, she couldn't worry about herself or feel crushed by Daniel's condemnation. Even if she'd told *Onkel* Samuel up front that she was hiding something as a kind of insurance, this would have been bad. Now, all she could do was confess to her aunt and uncle and cousin Sarah, to Mose and Esther who'd been so kind. They would offer forgiveness, of course, but trust once lost was rarely extended again. Except for Matthew, they were her only family. She hoped her grandparents could be left with their illusions.

Amos's stern regard had her wondering if he would ask that she and Matthew be moved again.

She said quietly, "I'm sorry, Amos. I know that's not adequate, but…I believed I was protecting Matthew. And I never thought anyone would be at risk but me."

Amos nodded, still gravely. Kindly? She hoped so. There was certainly no kindness on Daniel's face.

She made herself look at him. "Can we…go see?"

THE GASP AND small thump coming out of the darkness compelled Daniel to turn and help Rebecca, despite his lack of sympathy. Navigating the woods along the creek wasn't easy without using a flashlight, but at least he wasn't wearing skirts to midshin.

He could make out her shape, and he could tell she was still upright.

"You okay?" he whispered.

"Just—" She shook her head hard. In such moonlight as there was, he saw her *kapp's* white ties swing. She waved him forward.

He hadn't wanted to bring her. Not because he believed whoever had been watching the Grabers' farm still lurked in the woods. Any city boy would be scared witless out here the first time an owl with full wingspan dropped from the sky or a deer crashed through the undergrowth. Even so, Daniel couldn't entirely discount the possibility—thus this trek from three farms over.

No, being mad at her was his real problem.

Rebecca had tried to describe the exact location of the loose board in the barn, but since it apparently wasn't close to the stalls or any other obvious landmark, he'd had a vision of himself crawling around that huge barn until dawn. No saying she could go right to it, either, especially by flashlight, but she would have a better chance than he did.

They should be able to slip in without announcing themselves or scaring everyone. Barn doors were never locked, not with the fear of fire in these huge, old wooden structures filled with hay and straw. The long dry spell increased the risk when the next lightning storm swept through. Being able to get animals out as quickly as possible, that was what mattered. This being an Amish homestead, there wouldn't be any motion-sensitive floodlights, either.

And since, for the first time all day, he was being glass-half-full here, he should also be glad that if the horses were to trumpet a challenge and Samuel came to find out what caused the racket, unlike an *Englischer* he wouldn't shoot first.

At another snapping sound accompanied by a rustle and a tiny whimper, he reached back for Rebecca's hand. A branch had whipped toward her—not into her face, he hoped. He couldn't let her be hurt because he was sulking. Her hand felt icy cold and stiff in his, but she accepted that she needed guidance.

He made out the bulk of the barn roof at last, veering so that they would emerge behind it.

"Side door," he murmured.

She nodded and moved silently along with him. He groped his way along the stone foundation until they reached the door. He hadn't expected it to be locked any more than the main entry, and it wasn't.

As they stepped inside, a soft whicker greeted them. Big feet thumped as horses shifted in stalls.

After gently closing the door, he took the flashlight from his belt and turned it on, keeping the beam low. Rebecca went to the first stall and stroked the nose that poked over. Daniel joined her. It was worth taking a few minutes to calm the horses.

Her quiet voice came to him. "Yesterday, I started to tell you I had the wallet and ring, but you interrupted and I didn't make myself try again. Last night, I made the decision to tell Detective Estevez when you came back with your phone. You may not believe me—"

"I don't," he said shortly.

If anything, she stretched her neck to hold her head higher. There was her dignity again, fragile though it was.

He was being a jackass, he knew, and was afraid his fury was all because she hadn't trusted him, not because he didn't understand why she'd held back.

After a moment, she nodded, then said, "I need the flashlight."

He handed it over, and she swept it across the floor of the cavernous barn.

"It doesn't look anything like it did!" Her voice rose in dismay.

He kept his mouth shut, tempting though it was to say, *Gee, I wonder why?* Okay, he hadn't gotten over being mad.

After a minute she advanced toward the center of the barn, not far from a ladder that rose to the loft above.

"I think…" She crouched and began pushing loosely piled hay aside. When she reached for a burlap bag of oats, he hefted it aside before she could. He kept moving them out of her way until she gasped.

"This is it!" Her certainty seemed to diminish. "I think this is it." She directed the beam of light at a joint where two boards met, and he saw that nails were missing. He also saw her hands ball into fists. She was girding herself to find an empty space beneath the floor. "I need a hoof pick or something like that."

Daniel took his Swiss Army knife from his pocket, flipped open the longest blade and handed it to her.

He held the flashlight as she lifted the board. The wood squeaked, and then she breathed, "Oh, thank God."

Daniel had his doubts whether God would want any part in this mess, but he could be wrong. It didn't seem that anyone else cared much about Steven Stowe.

Crouched beside her, he watched as she eased a clear resealable plastic bag through the crack the knife blade held open.

The bloodred light of a ruby winked at them.

BACK IN THE SUV, Daniel set the small bag on the floor by Rebecca's feet. Without saying a word, he reached to start the engine.

Seat belt secured, Rebecca twined her fingers together on her lap and stared straight ahead. He wasn't talking to her any more than he had to. This silent treatment was worse than being berated.

He probably only saw her now as a witness

requiring protection. Just think how much he'd have to tell Detective Estevez in the morning. Triumph was probably all he felt.

But the engine didn't start, and, after a moment, his hand fell to his thigh.

"Please tell me you know how stupid it was to take those damn things." His voice wasn't quite a roar, but close.

Watch what you wish for.

"I know it was, but—" No, no, don't argue. Too late.

"But?" Frustration filled that deep voice. "Did having them keep you safe?"

She shook her head.

"Did it keep Matthew safe?"

And then she lost it. "Yes! *Yes,* a thousand times, yes. Don't you see? If I hadn't had Steven's wallet, not only would Tim have gone on fooling the police, he would have won joint custody. Which means *Robert* would have had Matthew most of that time! At least I got primary custody out of it. The rest of this... I never imagined..."

His snort of disgust cut deep.

"I had barely a minute to decide what to do when I heard Tim walk in," she defended herself.

"But you had months to decide you weren't going to the police," Daniel countered.

Rebecca swallowed. He was right. Why was she arguing? She *ought* to be contrite.

"You know my reasons. And...I'd given my word."

"To a man who conspired in a murder." Daniel just kept scowling at her. "You know you could face charges of withholding evidence."

She swallowed and nodded. That had always been one of her terrors.

If she had volunteered all this to Detective Estevez rather than having it dragged out of her, the investigator might have been more sympathetic. Daniel might have, too. She understood his abhorrence for lies. A deep core of him would always be Amish, plus he must get frustrated day in and day out with the ease with which people lied to the police. *Like I did.*

He shook his head. "Blackmail wouldn't have worked, any more than it did the first time around."

The attempts to kill her, the threat against Matthew, suggested he was right. In the end, though, it didn't matter. She couldn't keep endangering her family, and Tim no longer deserved anything from her.

"I've been scared," she said finally. "What other weapon did I have?"

"The entire San Francisco Police Department!" Daniel snapped. "Tim and Josh would have been behind bars in no time."

To her astonishment, anger swelled inside her, blistering hot. How many times did she have to say this? "You mean, *Tim* would have been. My word wouldn't be enough to provide grounds to arrest Josh, not without...without some corroborating evidence. You know that! And how long do you think Tim would have *stayed* in jail? Twenty-four hours? He'd have been out on bail before I had time to pack a suitcase. No matter how high it was set, he or his father would have paid it! And what if that detective had arrested me, too? What would have happened to Matthew?"

A moment of silence descended. Daniel flexed his fingers a couple of times on the steering wheel before finally gusting a sigh.

"You're right." His voice had softened, in a rumbly way. "I do understand why you made the choices early on."

Still stinging from the anger, Rebecca said, "But once I met you, I should have cast myself at your feet? Turned gratefully to you to get me out of this mess?"

"I would have tried, you know."

She almost believed that. He *had* tried. But even though the anger had left her with a whoosh, she shook her head.

"I do trust your intentions as a police officer, but... Thirty seconds more, and Tim would have had me in that car. You *can't* provide twenty-four-hour-a-day security for me and a six-year-old who needs to play and have at least a little bit of freedom."

"Your trust doesn't go very far, does it?"

She couldn't read his tone, but what did it matter?

After a moment, he fired up the engine and released the emergency brake. "I need to get you back. *Onkel* Amos will be waiting up for you."

A lump in her throat, her vision blurred, she nodded.

He drove in brooding silence, his brows drawn together. She averted her face so she could swipe surreptitiously at her damp cheeks.

When he finally pulled off the road, she unclicked the seat belt. "You don't have to come with me. I know the way."

Waste of breath.

"I'll see you to your door," he said shortly.

Even if they'd felt inclined, talking wasn't an option as they passed through the neighboring farmyard and sneaked behind the hay field and through Barbara's orchard. Daniel seemed to have eyes like a cat, or maybe he'd just learned this route by heart. She acquired a couple of new scratches and stubbed her toe painfully.

Only when they approached the back door,

where a light showed, did Daniel stop her with a hand on her arm.

"Rebecca…"

She didn't let herself look at him, but she didn't pull away, either.

"Are there any more secrets?"

"No."

"Whatever you think, I wanted to spend time with you, get to know you. It wasn't all about this mess you've gotten yourself into."

Rebecca gave a broken laugh. How could she believe him?

His hand dropped from her arm. "Expect me tomorrow after I talk to Estevez."

She only nodded and let herself into the house, never looking back.

CHAPTER ELEVEN

"DETECTIVE ESTEVEZ HERE, San Francisco PD. What can I do for you, Sheriff?"

Considering the caseload the guy probably had, Daniel was impressed to have gotten a call back by ten in the morning. Pacific time on a Monday morning.

Daniel gave his usual silent thanks to God. Spinning his wheels waiting would have made this day hellish. He was already suffering with remorse for his attitude last night—and because Rebecca thought he had betrayed her. He felt like he had a splinter working its way so far beneath the skin it would require a scalpel to dig it out. He'd swear it was inching toward his heart, the sharp end deadly.

Don't think that way. He couldn't in good conscience have kept her confession to himself. He was a cop. He had to believe God had called him to this job.

Leaning back in his desk chair, Daniel swiveled to look at the branch of an old oak tree through his tall casement window. The leaves were already turning colors after the exceptionally hot late summer.

"It's more what I can do for you," he said.

"That so." Estevez didn't sound impressed.

"Tim Gregory's ex-wife has taken refuge here in my county with relatives of hers. Ms. Holt has some knowledge that implicates her ex-husband in the mess she says you're investigating."

"What does she know?"

Daniel told him, including the fact that he had Steven Stowe's wallet and ring in an evidence locker.

Estevez growled, "Do you know how much time she would have saved us?"

Daniel had a good idea.

"Why the hell didn't she call me?"

"I think that's better coming from her." Into the silence, Daniel continued, "She felt her life was in danger after she had a near miss in a drive-by shooting followed by a hit-and-run accident in your city, Detective. After each incident, she received threatening phone calls." He described both, feeling a change in the quality of the silence. "Since she left Gregory, she's also dealt with pressure from his father-in-law, whom you may have encountered. Robert Gregory would like his son to have custody of Matthew."

After talking about the PI's appearance, Daniel went on to describe Tim's attempt to grab his boy and Rebecca, detailing the findings of the doctor who had treated her in the ER. "The guy has gone to ground here, unless he's reappeared in your city."

"I've spoken to him on the phone, but he claimed to be out of town on business." Estevez sounded intrigued. "Wasn't sure when he'd be getting back."

"He had a little glitch getting his hands on Ms. Holt."

"If she's decided to come forward, why use you as a go-between?"

"She's in hiding with an Amish family." He explained her family history, the fact that they didn't permit phones in the house and that she'd agreed to live plain while here. "I can take a phone to her. Anytime today, if you want."

Was her forgiveness even a remote possibility? If he extended it to her in turn? And what kind of idiot was he, to feel so much for a woman who had lied to him from their first meeting?

The detective huffed out an exasperated breath, then said, "I just pulled up reports of the hit-and-run. Doesn't appear she mentioned the drive-by when the police came after the hit-and-run."

"She took seriously the threat not to go to the cops."

Estevez grunted.

"There's something you should understand." He rubbed the back of his neck. His explanation of Amish attitudes was necessarily brief, and he expected skepticism, but at least Estevez listened. "You mind telling me if you've gotten anywhere in your investigation? I admit to having developed a dislike of Ms. Holt's exhusband."

"The forensic accountant started digging deeper after Stowe dropped entirely from the radar and we began to wonder if he hadn't been a scapegoat. One who'd been slaughtered," he added drily.

So Rebecca had succeeded in that much, Daniel thought.

"Our guy is still hip-deep in numbers and who knows what," Estevez continued. "He has pinned down a string of G, G & S's supposed projects that never really existed. In each case, there are blueprints and sketches on file. Money appears to have been paid to suppliers and workers. There are just no buildings, or at least not ones that match the plans."

"And presumably the suppliers and workers are fictional, too."

"Oh, yeah."

"I gather Stowe was the money man."

"Which was why we initially zeroed in on

him as the embezzler. Along with his disappearance, of course. But once he disappeared
from the radar, I started leaning on Gregory and
Griffen a lot harder, as well as other employees
at the company. I'll be able to get a warrant for
Gregory's house now, at least, although what
are the odds he has anything else incriminat-
ing there?"

Daniel grimaced. "Not high. Make sure you
include both safes in the warrant."

"Both?"

"She says there's one in his home office as
well as the smaller one in a walk-in closet in the
master bedroom."

"Good to know. Let's make the phone call
one o'clock my time," Estevez asked abruptly.

Daniel glanced at the wall clock. "Sure. I'll
call you once I have her available."

They signed off, leaving him apprehensive.
He was biased toward Rebecca, whether or not
she believed it, and she felt Estevez's interroga-
tion style was aggressive. Plus, the San Francisco cop had good reason to be frustrated with
her. He might even press charges because she'd
hidden critical evidence.

Daniel told himself the best course was to
step back, not stay stuck in the middle. His emo-
tional entanglement appeared one-sided now,
if it hadn't been all along. And even if she felt

anything but anger for him, Rebecca wouldn't be staying in Henness County when this was all over.

All his tension exploded. He hammered a fist on his desk, then shoved his chair back violently. Who was he kidding? Whether she appreciated it or not, he'd keep fighting for her. He couldn't stand an arm's length from her, absorbing those wide blue eyes or the generous curves beneath the theoretically plain Amish dress, the delicate lines of her face and the bruises that had yet to fade, and allow Estevez to threaten her.

He groaned and rolled his tight shoulders, then grabbed his gun from a drawer, holstered it and strode out of the office.

REBECCA REFUSED TO look at Daniel as she defended herself to Detective Estevez. Daniel's stance, while outwardly relaxed, still managed to be intimidating, so she focused on the dried bird's nest tucked beneath the eaves. Because this was daytime, Daniel had parked out of sight and ushered her behind the house where they couldn't be seen from the road.

Since he'd already told the detective everything, Estevez had barely snapped out questions that she could only answer with a "Yes" or "That's true" or an occasional "I don't know."

Now, clutching Daniel's phone to her ear, Rebecca said with what dignity she still had, "I know it seems foolish to you, but Tim will forever be the father of my son. I suppose I wanted to believe he's at least close to being the man I thought he was when I married him."

Detective Estevez grunted.

"He assured me he had nothing to do with Steven's death," she continued.

"He admitted his partner is dead?" he asked sharply.

"Well, not in so many words."

"What *did* he say?"

Very conscious of Daniel's presence despite her best effort to pretend he wasn't there, she struggled to cast her mind back. "I said something like, 'Tell me you wouldn't hurt anybody,' and he said, 'It wasn't me.' Then he said misleading the cops—" specifically, the one to whom she was speaking "—was the only way to save the company."

"He just came out and told you that."

She closed her eyes. "He was angry. We were arguing. What was he supposed to do, insist I hadn't seen Steven's wallet?"

"No one else heard him."

Stiffening, she said, "He'd just brought our son home from a visit, and Matthew had gone to his room." Detective Estevez would interview Matthew over her dead body.

"It was months before the shooting. If you're telling the truth, nobody had threatened you at this point. You expect me to believe your tender feelings for the guy you'd just dumped kept you from giving me evidence you knew was critical to our investigation?" The sneer came through.

This was the explanation she had dreaded most. She took a deep breath. "I don't expect you to understand, but Tim had been demanding joint custody of our son. He worked too many hours to be any kind of parent. I knew his father was behind it. Robert is a harsh, demanding man who never thinks Tim has performed up to his standards and tells him so frequently. He wanted control of Matthew. I suppose he thought he could mold him into the perfect grandson to replace his inadequate son."

If Tim had stolen money from his own company, she felt sure it was because he was so determined to appear wildly successful to his father.

Daniel shifted, uncrossing his arms and rolling his shoulders. She sneaked a look. To her surprise, his expression wasn't hard, as she'd seen it when he was all cop. Some small lines had formed on his forehead, and the deep blue of his eyes mesmerized her.

"When he learned I had taken the wallet, he offered to back off and let me have primary custody as long as he got reasonable visitation. I'm not proud that I understood he was offering a bargain, or that I took it. But I believed I'd lose in court. My ex-husband's family has a great deal of influence in San Francisco. My attorney thought the request for joint custody would seem reasonable to a judge. I was afraid to allow Robert to have any more access to my son than he had during the every-other weekends with Tim."

"So you abetted your husband's cover-up in what's very possibly a murder," Estevez said, making no effort to hide his contempt.

Past the lump in her throat, she said, "As I told Sheriff Byler, I do not believe Tim killed Steven. He's just…not the kind of man who'd do something like that."

"And yet, not much later, you believed he was trying to kill *you*, either to silence you or to gain undisputed custody of his son."

She found herself shaking her head. "No. I never thought it was Tim. My best guess is that Josh Griffen was behind it. Tim apparently told Josh that I'd seen Steven's wallet. Tim told me once that Josh felt threatened, that he didn't trust me to—"

"Keep your unsavory little bargain?"

Feeling sick, Rebecca bent forward. "Think whatever you like about me," she said in a shaky voice just above a whisper. "Protecting my son is the most important thing in the world to me."

The lengthy silence increased her nausea.

"I'll be out there to pick up the evidence as soon as I can arrange it. I want a face-to-face with you." His growl sounded like a threat, and she took it as one.

"Do you think I haven't told you everything? You're wrong. But I'll see you whenever you come. Goodbye, Detective Estevez." She thrust the phone at Daniel, whirled away and started walking, not caring where she ended up.

Beyond the trellised green beans in the garden, she reached the rows of raspberries, soon to be pruned, the new shoots tied up. There, she plopped down on the grass, bent her head to her knees and listened to the *rat-a-tat-tat* of a woodpecker, seemingly answered by an odd cry that sounded like "Peter, peter, peter." A bird—what had *Grossmammi* called it?

A shadow fell across her. She didn't look up.

"He was doing his job," Daniel said.

"Is that how it's done?" She didn't look up. "If so, I doubt he ever elicits genuine cooperation from a witness. You, at least, *pretended* to understand."

He crouched, bringing himself down to her level. From the corner of her eye, she saw the khaki of his trousers pulled tight over powerful thigh muscles. His bare forearm, lightly dusted with hair, was braced on his knee, his big hand dangling. Relaxed.

"Rebecca, you know he can ask for obstruction-of-justice charges to be filed against you." Suddenly his voice sounded hard. Because she'd refused to continue buying into his slick manipulation? "You should be thankful he didn't mention the possibility."

Thankful? "Let him try," she snapped, and finally did raise her head to glare at him. He wore dark glasses to hide his eyes. "Please leave. I'm not in the mood to answer any more questions."

She didn't let her glare waver. After a minute, he tipped his head and rose effortlessly to stand over her.

"I've tried to help," he said quietly. "If you want to talk, I'll be behind the barn at about eight tonight. Your choice." And he turned and walked away.

Rebecca dropped her forehead to her knees again, her arms squeezing her shins, pulling her body into the classic fetal position.

You know he can ask for obstruction-of-justice charges to be filed against you.

Fresh terror ricocheted through her body. Knowing vaguely it was a possibility was one thing, the reality another. *She* could end up going to jail instead of Tim. Given how long she'd taken to tell what she knew, would a jury think the worst of her and refuse to believe her testimony about the wallet and the things Tim had said?

She heard Daniel's voice, as if he still stood above her. *I've tried to help.*

Sure he had. Earn a woman's trust—if she's scared enough she'll crack and spit out the whole story, right? What a shame nobody had ever taught Detective Estevez the technique, she thought bitterly.

She had to go inside, but not yet.

Her stomach roiled. How could she have been so stupid? So careless with her own integrity? When she had stuffed Steven's things in her purse and walked out of the house, she'd thought she was striking a compromise between the public good and her private need to protect the man she had once loved, Matthew's father. She'd meant to stop him from misleading the police. But then she'd made the whole thing ugly by accepting Tim's custody deal.

For Matthew's sake, not hers. Wasn't it?

She pictured *Onkel* Samuel, so kind, so good, with his determination to live as his savior had asked. How would he look at her if he knew everything she'd done?

Her cheeks were wet now. When had she started to cry?

It was a long time before she could work around to thinking about the future. Hurt pride and the sting of betrayal made her want to take Matthew and run again—far, far beyond the reach of Sheriff Daniel Byler.

With puffy eyes, she watched an ant struggling to mount a blade of grass.

What right do I have to be hurt when I got myself into this mess? Rebecca asked herself harshly. Daniel was a cop; *of course* he'd felt compelled to do his job, to persuade her to tell him the truth. Even if being nice was just his technique, wasn't that better than Detective Estevez's belligerence?

Anger spiked again. Fine, but he shouldn't have kissed her. Had he imagined he'd get her into bed before her legal troubles came to a climax?

If you want to talk. To him? Oh, sure. Top of her list of things to do tonight.

DANIEL GROWLED A word that hadn't crossed his lips in three years even as his hands tightened on the steering wheel until his knuckles showed white.

Estevez would have gotten a lot further if every word he spoke wasn't tinged with contempt and aggression. Even standing several feet away, Daniel had heard enough. Making witnesses cringe was no way to persuade them to open up. A degree of empathy, understanding, were more effective.

Rebecca had accused him of *pretended* empathy and understanding.

He flinched, because he did pretend sometimes when he interviewed a suspect. With her, he had been sincere. She'd been in a tough spot, pulled too many ways. He did understand her early decisions, whatever she believed of him now. Women would kill to protect their children. In comparison, covering up someone else's crime was nothing. He also recognized that her continuing insistence that Tim Gregory really was a good guy rubbed him the wrong way for personal reasons. Keeping her mouth shut about his sins in front of her kid, that was different. The right thing to do. His own mother would have made many of the same decisions had his father done something equally bad. She would have refused to lose faith in the man she felt she knew on a fundamental level. She certainly wouldn't have gone to the police.

Daniel would have almost been grateful for the call that came in just then from Dispatch letting him know about a two-car accident on the highway, had the last thing Jennie said not been "possible fatality."

MATTHEW SPUN IN circles in the middle of the
lawn until dizziness toppled him, then stood up
and did it again. Rebecca watched helplessly.
Neither of them could go on much longer if she
couldn't find a way to distract him.

"You'll throw up," she warned, the next time
he flopped on the grass.

"Uh-uh!" He staggered to his feet and started
spinning again, his arms outstretched.

Once she'd tried catching him, but he had
struggled wildly. This frenzy wasn't like him.
Her stomach churned, just watching him.

Again he fell. This time, she sank down beside him, staring up at the sky.

"Look," she said, pointing. "There's a red-
tailed hawk. I think that smaller bird is chasing him."

"How come?"

"The hawk might have gotten too close to a
nest." Except this wasn't the right season, was
it? But Matthew wouldn't question her.

Because moms were supposed to be all-knowing,
she thought sadly. It would never occur to him
that she could be wrong about something.

She and Matthew stayed on their backs as the
long shadow from one of the apple trees reached
toward them.

"Why was Daddy so mad?" her little boy
asked in a small voice.

She'd been dreading the question but couldn't see a way out of telling him the truth.

"Your dad has been mad at me for months." She turned her head so she could watch Matthew. "I saw something to do with his business that he thought he'd hidden. He was afraid I'd tell someone."

Matthew's forehead wrinkled and he met her eyes. "What did you see?"

"Right now, I don't think you're old enough to understand. Your dad's business is pretty complicated, you know."

"That's what *he* says when I ask *anything*."

She smiled a little. "He never liked it when I asked questions, either. That's part of why your dad and I aren't married anymore. Being married, you should be partners and best friends. I felt more like something pretty he'd bought to show off to his friends."

"But you're a person, not a *thing*," he protested. "You're a *mom*."

"I am." She ruffled his hair, a lighter blond now than when they had arrived in Missouri. His face and hands were tanned, his forearms less so. The strict Amish garb protected most of his body from the sun. His sleeves, he sometimes rolled up. The hat, Rebecca had almost given up on except on church Sundays. He managed to "misplace" it about two minutes after she set it on his head.

"Back to your dad being mad," she said. "He didn't like that I brought you here to visit family. I was starting to be scared about living there in the city. You know how I got hit by that car."

"Yeah. And your face was all purple."

She touched her cheek. "I guess my face turns purple pretty easy, huh?"

"He was mean." Matthew's voice had become small again.

"Your dad loves you, but he's really angry at me, and upset with things happening at his company. I bet your grandfather especially wanted him to come get you."

Matthew suddenly didn't want to look at her. "I like *Grossdaadi* lots better than Grandpa Robert."

"Me, too."

They lay quiet for a minute.

"How come we couldn't stay with *Aenti* Emma and *Onkel* Samuel? Abram was my *friend.*"

"I know." She found his hand and squeezed. "We're sort of hiding right now, from your dad *and* your grandpa Robert. I know it's boring here, without any friends, but I can't let your dad take you. Not until we work lots of things out."

"I don't want to see him ever again!" he said

with sudden passion, rolling toward her to hug her. "I'll scream and kick if he tries to make me go with him."

Tears in her eyes, she said, "I'll be screaming and kicking, too. But…just remember that you've always loved your dad, and he loves you. I think eventually you'll want him to be your dad again."

But he buried his face against her and didn't say a word.

To her surprise, when she helped Matthew to his feet a while later, she saw Amos on the porch. He was watching them, his face shaded by his straw hat. He must have come down to the house for a cup of coffee and seen the two of them out on the grass. Otherwise, he would have used the back door, as he always did. In most Amish homes, front doors were for guests and to be used on formal occasions like weddings and funerals.

"I wish it was time for dinner," Matthew mumbled, kicking a hummock of grass.

"You're hungry already?"

He shrugged, which indicated discontent rather than a growling stomach. *We can play a game*, she thought desperately. If only they weren't both sick of the few they had. They could work on reading and writing…

Amos came down the steps and said, "If Matthew is willing, I could use his help in the barn."

Rebecca could have kissed him.

One of Amos's sons had bought a farm down the road and now grew hay on his father's acreage, in addition to the crops on his own place. Amos, she learned, had never been interested in farming. Barbara was the one to tend their large produce garden and small orchard. He built beautifully crafted cabinets in his barn workshop. Cabinetry and furniture stores in Hadburg and Byrum carried examples of his work.

"Me?" Hope in his eyes, Matthew looked up at the taciturn man.

"*Ja*, you."

Amos returned Matthew to the house after an hour, his hand resting lightly on the boy's head. "Big help he was. He swept and organized my bins of small pieces of wood."

The six-year-old grinned. "I could help more."

Amos shook his head. "I will be using saws that are dangerous to small fingers. And soon it will be dinnertime. I will have jobs for you other days."

Rebecca smiled at him. *"Denke."*

"No need for thanks," he said gruffly, and went back out the door.

She took Matthew's hand and said, "Now we need to help Barbara get dinner ready, *ja*?"

"Ja," he said with a big grin.

And me, I need to decide whether I'm willing to stomp on my pride to meet Daniel. A man she had so recently wanted to hate.

Whether she remained angry or not, Daniel was the only person she really *could* talk to. Rebecca couldn't deny that he still drew her. Was she brave enough to find out if everything he'd said and done really was about the job, or whether some of it might conceivably have been about *her*?

CHAPTER TWELVE

AT DINNER, REBECCA tried to push aside her tension and indecision. Only politeness made her lift her gaze from her plate when Barbara began to talk in her placid way.

"You know we have a grandson almost Matthew's age. His *mamm* and *daad* don't live as close as we'd like, ain't so, Amos?"

She probably already had a dozen grandkids, Rebecca couldn't help thinking.

Her husband's response was a predictable grunt. Rebecca hid a smile as he shoved a forkful of pickled beets into his mouth.

"Is he six, too?" Matthew piped up.

"No, he is five. His birthday is in November, so he couldn't start school. I've been thinking Caleb must be as bored as Matthew. So I wrote to Grace—she's my daughter—and asked if Caleb could come stay with us for a little." She beamed at them both. "Today her letter came. She is happy to have him visit. Amos is to go get him tomorrow."

"That's wonderful of you to suggest. But…

what if—" she stole a look at Matthew "—this isn't a good time for him to be here?"

"*Ach*, who would think Rebecca and Matthew were here with us?" Amos asked. "Two boys here, not only one, that is better."

Rebecca's eyes stung. "It's so kind of you to think of it."

Barbara chuckled. "It makes no trouble."

Matthew looked worried. "Does he talk like me?"

"No, but you will both learn, *ja*?"

Rebecca smiled at him. "Don't be so doubtful. Wasn't Abram learning some English? And you some Deitsch?"

"For sure you were," Barbara said. "Do you remember what I said to you this morning?"

He shook his head.

"I said, *'Setz der disch,'* and you did. You didn't say, what does that mean?"

"Abram's *mamm* always makes us set the table."

"See? You are learning to speak like we do." She nodded at his half-full plate. "Now, eat yourself full."

Matthew applied himself to his dinner. Watching him, Rebecca noticed that he was a lot less picky than he used to be. *Silver linings.* One of many, she had to believe, starting with reconnecting with her family.

AN OWL HOOTED, providing companionship of a sort for Daniel.

Of course she hadn't come out to meet him. He shouldn't have bothered to come. Rebecca had been furious at him—and hurt. Picturing her face, he shifted uncomfortably on the crude bench behind Amos's barn.

Weariness kept him leaning against the side of the barn. The woman he'd pulled from her totaled car and performed first aid on had died, leaving her baby motherless. That news had put the cap on his crappy day. Or was he doing that himself, sitting here pathetically waiting for a woman who had lied to him from day one, then was furious when he called her on it?

Tonight was noticeably darker than last night. The moon was waning, suiting his mood. He'd probably clobber his head on a tree branch or get caught in a barbed-wire fence on his way back to the car. Yeah, he was in a mood.

Daniel shoved himself to his feet—just as he heard a rustle. He grabbed the butt of his gun as he spun around.

A small gasp told him who was here even before he made her out.

"You came," he said, stunned.

"I didn't think *you* would."

"Then why did you come out here?"

"I thought I would enjoy some solitude."

"Then I'll leave you alone," he snapped.

He'd taken several steps when her low voice stopped him. "I wasn't fair today. Or Saturday."

Daniel squeezed the bridge of his nose, needing the pain to counteract the flood of relief. He took a minute before he slowly turned. "Given my oath of office, I didn't see how I could delay passing on information regarding such a serious crime. Or cooperating with a detective from another jurisdiction."

"I get that," she said wearily. "Today, Matthew spun in circles until he made himself dizzy and fell down. Lately, I feel like that's what I've been doing."

"You've dealt with a lot." She sat, and Daniel walked back toward the barn and settled a foot or two from her.

"That's no excuse." She looked at him, making him wish he could see her face better.

"When I talk to Estevez again, I'll lean on him to cut you some slack. If nothing worse comes to light, I think he'll agree. He has bigger fish to fry."

He sensed as much as saw her shiver, realizing belatedly that one of those "fish" was her ex-husband. The one she'd been protecting.

"You still don't know where he is?" Rebecca sounded timid. "Tim, I mean?"

"No." The muscles in his shoulders and neck

were in knots. "I have to admit, I didn't get much looking done today."

"I don't blame you," she whispered.

"No." He reached almost blindly and found her hand. "It wasn't just you. Right after I left here this afternoon, I was called to a major vehicular accident out on the highway. Ended up with two fatalities."

"Oh, no." Her fingers twined with his, perhaps unconsciously. "But…why you?"

"I was closest, which made me first responder." He started telling her about it but stopped before he got too graphic. "You don't need to hear this."

"I think you need to tell someone. I'd…like it to be me. It's only fair, you know."

The lump in his throat surprised him. He'd never had anyone he could talk to about the things he saw on the job. From what he'd gathered, even most married cops didn't talk to their wives about the gory or brutal or senseless stuff. Why he had this compulsion, he didn't know. He'd seen plenty of dead bodies before, and tried and failed to save lives.

After a minute, he said, "One of the drivers died almost instantly. It appears he was speeding. Don't know yet if he was drinking or why he lost control. The other driver was a woman. I tried to control her bleeding while I waited for paramedics. She died on the way to the hospital." He paused. "Her baby was in a car seat. She's fine. Her grandparents picked her up because her dad—" Hell. The guy had been twenty-three. Practically a kid, his world turned on end.

"Was too grief stricken," she said softly.

"Yeah."

"I'm sorry." Suddenly Rebecca scooted closer to him. Close enough to rest her head on his shoulder.

Afraid she'd flee if he so much as tried to put his arms around her, he savored what she did offer. They sat there for quite a while, providing and receiving comfort with the contact, no more words necessary.

AMISH RARELY TURNED to the police, but now he'd received his second call in a matter of days from Samuel. Troubled, Daniel set his phone on his desk. Rebecca's uncle had told Daniel that Noah Yoder, the next-door neighbor, had seen a man with binoculars tramping through the woods behind his place.

"He could be only a bird-watcher, but after the break-in, we are all worried." He paused. "Other people I know say that cars they didn't recognize slowed down to pass their buggies. Might be only tourists, curious, but the men in the cars stared, wanting to see every face."

"I hope you'll spread the word to have the *Leit* call if they spot someone who seems to be spying," Daniel had said. "If a car slows so men can stare, a license number would allow us to find out whether these are tourists or something more dangerous."

Hesitant, Samuel had nonetheless agreed he would tell others.

In the meantime, about all Daniel could do was make cruising the back roads in the heavily Amish areas of the county a higher priority. How much good that would do was another question. Visitors frequently came to the area to crane their necks at the Amish in their buggies.

He was still at the office trying to decide where to position the even-skimpier evening shift of deputies when his desk phone rang. Melissa Sue, one of the dispatchers and general assistants, said, "There's a gentleman here to see you, Sheriff. His name is Robert Gregory."

Now wasn't that interesting. Did that mean the senior Gregory knew everything his son was up to? Or did he believe Tim was searching only for Matthew?

"Thank you. Let him know I'll be out in a moment," Daniel said, hanging up the phone.

Robert Gregory hadn't bothered to take a seat in the small waiting room. When he heard the heavy door opening, he swung to face Daniel, raking him with an assessing look. Easily recognizable from the pictures Daniel had seen online, the man fairly crackled with impatience and intensity.

"Mr. Gregory?" Daniel held out his hand. "I'm Sheriff Byler."

"Sheriff." They shook. "I'd like to sit down with you in private."

Daniel let his eyebrows climb, but said, "Certainly." He nodded at Melissa Sue, who buzzed him back through the always-locked door. He waved Gregory ahead and into a small conference room just inside.

As soon as they had taken seats, he said, "Now, what is it you think I can do for you, Mr. Gregory?"

"I know you're aware my daughter-in-law is here illegally with my grandson," the man said tightly. "I'm asking you, as head of law enforcement in this county, to hand over the boy to me."

Daniel leaned back in his chair as if taken aback. "You might want to tell me what makes you think this woman is here."

The man failed to hide his contempt. "I know that my son and Rebecca—" he said the name with distaste "—had an encounter."

"An encounter. Interesting way to describe it."

"I'm aware my son may have behaved somewhat…impetuously. I'm not defending him."

Daniel let his voice harden. "Good, because I saw your son slam his *ex*-wife into the door frame of his rental car. She could easily have suffered brain damage or lost an eye. *Impetuous* isn't the word I'd have used."

Robert made a sharp gesture and snapped, "That's beside the point."

"No, I don't think it is. I would have arrested him for assault had my first concern not been Ms. Holt's injuries and her terrified little boy. Unfortunately, your son escaped while I was assisting her."

His eyes glittered. "So you do know where they are."

"If I did, Mr. Gregory, I wouldn't tell you. In fact—" he leaned forward, wishing his size advantage would intimidate the creep "—I need *you* to tell me where Tim is. He has to answer to the charges laid against him in this county before we can have any further discussion."

Robert snorted. "I neither know nor care where he is. I want my grandson, Sheriff. Ms. Holt did not have the legal right to take Matthew out of the state without informing the boy's father. She has not made my grandson available for court-ordered visitation. Tim has himself in a mess I want nothing to do with." His lip curled. "My concern is removing Matthew from a mother who has shown herself to be unable to care adequately for him." His eyes narrowed. "And I *do* expect cooperation from you."

What a prick. Daniel felt no guilt over thinking the word. No wonder Rebecca wanted to keep her kid out of his grandfather's hands.

"Tell me, Mr. Gregory, do you have a court order indicating your custody rights to this boy?"

Gregory glared at him. "I will certainly demand full custody once I have the boy home in San Francisco."

Daniel quirked an eyebrow. "I take it that's a no?"

"Matthew's only family is in California. You cannot possibly be taking the side of a woman who has attempted to disappear with him."

"Strange you should say that." Daniel let himself smile. "As it happens, besides his mother, young Matthew has maternal great-grandparents here in Missouri, as well as any number of aunts and uncles and cousins. It's my understanding he has been warmly received by his family."

"Amish," Robert spit.

"I find them to be good folks," Daniel said. "Law-abiding and generous."

"It might as well be a cult," the man sneered. "I will not lose my grandson to those people."

"I don't mean to be unhelpful, but it seems to

me that right now you don't have a leg to stand on, Mr. Gregory. You might be smart to go on back to California and try to figure out what your son has gotten himself mixed up in."

Robert shoved back his chair. "What would you know about it?"

Did he believe the sheriff of this small county was an ignorant hayseed? Very possibly, Daniel realized.

"I do know that your former daughter-in-law barely escaped from two attempts on her life back in your fine city. I've spoken to a Detective Estevez there. Those incidents had something to do with the troubles at G, G & S. Or with someone's desire to remove Ms. Holt from the equation so that his father—or grandfather— might have custody."

Robert shot to his feet, his face dark with fury. "You're accusing *me*…?"

"No, no, not at all." Daniel took pleasure in appearing placid. "Only letting you know any discussion of the best placement for Matthew is unlikely until some questions are answered. As I said, unless you're interested in helping us locate your son, I recommend you go on home." He, too, stood, smiling. "Although I feel sure Detective Estevez would be glad to talk to you. I have his number if—"

Robert stalked out of the conference room.

Daniel ambled after him, pleased to see that Melissa Sue had waited for his nod to electronically unlock the heavy door.

Only a few feet into the waiting room, Robert turned a burning look on Daniel. "You'll be hearing from me again."

"I'll look forward to that, Mr. Gregory."

"Pissed him off, did you?" the dispatcher said cheerfully after he left.

"I did."

"Course, he was pissed when he walked in the door," she mused.

Daniel hoped that wasn't the language she used when speaking to the fine citizens of Henness County, but he let it go. The truth was, he had *enjoyed* pissing off Robert Gregory.

THE STURDY YOUNG boy perched beside his *grossdaadi* on the driver's seat of the black buggy stared at Matthew, who stared back. Like Matthew and Amos, Caleb wore black trousers, a long-sleeved blue shirt and suspenders, all in more diminutive sizes. Unlike Matthew, he also wore a straw hat identical to his *grossdaadi's*.

When the staring contest failed to end, Barbara intervened, chuckling with delight and sweeping her grandson down while chattering away to him in Deitsch. Rebecca couldn't help thinking that Caleb Lapp was a very brave boy. From what she'd gathered, he hadn't seen his grandparents since Christmas, which was a very long time ago in the life of a five-year-old. And now he was confronted with a strange boy whom he had undoubtedly been told didn't speak his language.

But Caleb finally eyed Matthew and said, "Hi." Had he rehearsed it?

Matthew's face brightened. "Hi. Do you want to play catch? I even have a bat, if you want to hit the ball." Barbara had driven to town this morning to grocery shop, returning with a bright blue plastic bat and ball, as well as bags full of food.

Caleb transferred his gaze to his grandmother, who translated. Then he grinned at Matthew, showing a gap in his front teeth. *"Ja!"*

The two boys ran for the porch, the three adults looking after them in amazement.

"He is not a shy boy," Amos finally commented, his tone odd. "A *blabbermaul*, more like. Don't know why he hasn't lost his voice." Then he clicked his tongue, and the horse started toward the barn.

Barbara laughed. "Poor Amos, hours stuck with a *kind* who talks all the time."

Rebecca had to laugh, too. "And look at Caleb and Matthew!" They had taken the bat and ball and started around the side of the house, where the ground was flat and uninterrupted enough for baseball.

"*Brederlich* already," Barbara agreed, sounding just a little smug. Rebecca couldn't blame her. Her idea to bring Caleb for a visit had been splendid, even if Rebecca still worried about Caleb's safety.

Amos deserved a good deal of the credit. Until Rebecca had seen him spending time with Matthew, she wouldn't have been able to imagine him entertaining a five-year-old boy for several hours.

Then she laughed again. It was entirely possible he hadn't had to do a thing but nod and grunt from time to time.

Hiding her hand in her skirts, Rebecca crossed her fingers. *Please let them become best friends.*

IN PREPARATION FOR DINNER, Barbara put both boys to work snapping green beans, fetching a jar of applesauce from the cellar and setting the table. Along with bible stories after dinner, Rebecca played games with them, translating for them to their merriment since her own Pennsylvania Dutch still wasn't fluent. Even so, the games were more fun with three.

Nonetheless, all she could think about was seeing Daniel again. The last thing he'd said yesterday evening was, "Eight thirty?" She had promised to try.

After tucking the boys into the same twin bed, she went downstairs and paused in the living room doorway. "I'm going outside for a while."

Barbara and Amos smiled in understanding. Perhaps she should have told them she was meeting Daniel, but as an adult she wasn't about to bow to Amish restrictions on women, even if she had agreed to live plain to blend into their lives.

What she couldn't understand was her excitement whenever she thought about meeting Daniel.

Had she let go of her anger so easily?

She had felt betrayed most to think he had fostered the sense of intimacy between them only to extract confidences. But last night, he had turned to her in his grief. She hadn't been a witness or a suspect to him, only a woman he needed.

Outside, she strolled briefly toward the deserted country road, although not so close a passing driver would see her, before turning back and continuing toward the barn.

Just as she reached it, a dark figure stepped around the corner. "It's me," Daniel said quietly.

Relief and that same excitement filled her.

He took her arm even though her eyes had adjusted to the moonlit darkness. They sat on the bench, really only a board laid across a couple of upended stumps. She pictured Amos taking breaks out here, enjoying the quiet and solitude.

They had to stay quiet. If she was caught sneaking out to meet a man, she and Matthew might lose their current refuge.

"I haven't told your aunt and uncle I'm meeting you. They probably think I'm just enjoying some peace and quiet."

He grimaced. "Maybe tomorrow you should tell Amos that I asked you to meet me outside so nobody watching would see me near the place."

Something in her relaxed, both at the suggestion and at the knowledge that she would see Daniel again. "I'll do that."

She sat, Daniel beside her. He'd laid a flashlight down but did not turned it on.

"I do have news."

She held her breath.

"Your father-in-law marched into the station today." He told her about Robert's demands, and how he had routed him, if only for now.

"Here. He's in town, so close."

"No, I followed up. He caught a flight to San Francisco out of St. Louis earlier in the evening."

"Where he'll file for custody."

"Relax." A large hand lifted hers from her lap.

After letting him lace their fingers together, she looked down, seeing their clasped hands in moonlight, her skin paler than his even after the hours she'd spent working in *Aenti* Emma's garden and hanging out laundry. His hand engulfed hers. The bones in his wrist were so much bigger than hers, his forearm strong with muscle.

"How can I relax?"

"He won't be filing for anything, not yet. He isn't that stupid. His son is in deep trouble. You're hiding out of fear of Tim—and don't say it's not Tim, because he's part of it. I pointed out that Matthew has lots of relatives here."

"They're Amish," she said tightly. "I'm betting judges are leery of them."

"In your part of the country, probably. But Robert has a big problem right now—his son. Until that's resolved and you and Matthew are safe, there won't be any hearings."

It was a long moment before she could let herself believe he was right, before the rigidity gradually seeped out of her body.

"Hey." Daniel bumped his shoulder against hers. "Caleb make it?"

She smiled despite everything and repeated what Amos had said about his grandson being a *blabbermaul*. "Although your uncle has surprised me."

"How so?"

"Yesterday afternoon after you left, I was about to go nuts when he took Matthew for an hour to 'help' in his workshop."

"Amos?"

She couldn't help laughing at his amazement. "Matthew came back feeling really proud of himself."

"Huh." Daniel shook his head. "How are Matthew and Caleb getting along?"

"Amazing, considering they can barely talk to each other. I had no idea how much I'd miss Abram. And Mose and Esther. They treated him like one of their own."

"What's one more in that household?"

"And I doubt they're done."

"No, I think the *kinder* will just keep coming for those two," he agreed.

"Caleb is your cousin," she realized, then corrected herself. "First cousin, once-removed."

"I guess he is." The words came slowly. "I've never met him."

"I suppose you have a lot of cousins."

"Nieces and nephews, too." He sounded sad. "Some I've never even met."

"Why not?" she asked, indignant. "You're not under the *bann*."

"No, but I'm not quite part of the family, either. Two of my three sisters have married out of the area. Both were visiting in Iowa when they met their husbands. My next younger brother is still angry at me. We were close growing up."

"He thinks you rejected him."

Daniel sighed. "Yes. He had no trouble convincing himself that he's really mad because I broke with the faith, and in such a conspicuous way." His shoulders moved. "I do see *Mamm* and *Daad* and most of the family who live locally on occasion."

"Is it awkward?"

"Not as much when it's just my parents and my one sister, Rachel. Otherwise...yes."

"I'm sorry." She gave his hand a little squeeze.

"My choice," he said curtly.

"But it can still hurt."

There was a moment of silence before he nodded. "You're right."

"Do you ever wish you hadn't come back?"

He gave a short laugh lacking any humor. "You have a way of getting right down to it, don't you?"

Shrinking, she said, "I shouldn't have—"

But Daniel tugged on her hand and said, "Come here."

She barely hesitated before scooting close enough for him to put an arm around her. His willingness to tell her about his life, to share the things that hurt him, had restored her trust in him. He'd known too much about her, while remaining the cop. Now, they were achieving the give and take that put them on the same footing.

"The answer to your question is, sometimes, even if I usually think I'm right where I should be."

Reassured by what felt like honesty, she said, "They may all be conflicted about you, but it's obvious they respect you, too. *Onkel* Samuel told me you're a good man."

A smile in his voice, Daniel said, "I think he is, too. And Amos, or I wouldn't have brought you to stay here."

She sat quietly for a minute, feeling the need to remind them both of the real reason for this meeting. "You didn't magically find Tim today, did you?"

"Far as I can tell, he's vanished into thin air."

Rebecca didn't know how she could smile, but suddenly she did. "Maybe a doorway into another dimension opened."

"If so, I hope some truly hideous monsters were waiting for him, and I don't care if he *is* Matthew's father." He pressed a kiss to her head. "Read a little sci-fi, do you?"

"And fantasy. You?"

"Same. Otherwise, mostly mysteries and non-fiction." He chuckled, then turned serious. "My best guess is that he's still around, and I doubt he's here alone."

She frowned. "Why?"

"Who's buying the groceries? If he's rented a house or a cabin at a resort or a hotel room, whose name is it under?"

"The PI?" she suggested.

"His name hasn't popped up. Neither has your father-in-law's or Josh Griffen's. Which doesn't mean Josh isn't in the area, or that Robert can't come back. I've asked for help from neighboring jurisdictions, but they may not be looking as hard as I am. And, for all we know, Tim could be camping out in the woods, or in a vacant house on a dead-end road."

"I can't stay here for too much longer. It's a huge imposition."

"Have you gotten the feeling you're not welcome?" Daniel asked.

Rebecca sighed. "No, of course not. Actually, I think Barbara is enjoying having someone to talk to. Your uncle, well, he isn't very chatty."

He laughed, low and rusty. "I've noticed."

She pulled back a little to look up at him. "Do you have electricity at home?"

"I do. I got spoiled. And, yes, I even have a television."

Rebecca chuckled. "And tablet and smartphone. You're a thoroughly modern man."

"In some ways." He sobered. "I watch baseball and occasionally football. Sometimes the news. I can go days or even weeks without turning the TV on. I use the internet primarily for work-related research. Most people would find my house…bare."

Rebecca squeezed his hand. "In other words, the man may leave the Amish, but he still carries the beliefs wherever he goes?"

"And where did I go?" He made a sound in his throat. "Home, but not quite. Ambivalence in action."

"But you do what you couldn't as a boy," she said thoughtfully. "You keep the people you love safe."

CHAPTER THIRTEEN

THE NIGHT SEEMED darker as Rebecca waited for Daniel to say something. Anything.

Tim had hated her attempts to get him to talk about his feelings. He'd accused her of trying to pry him open like a tin can, determined to find out if the contents matched the label. Maybe she was just nosy, and his desire to keep a big part of himself locked down completely natural.

Even in the dark, she felt Daniel's eyes boring into hers. Suddenly, he made an inarticulate sound, and then his arms were tight around her and he was kissing her. She felt his anger and desperation along with passion, and she threw her arms around his neck and kissed him back with equal ferocity. Maybe because *she* was still angry, too. And afraid.

Moments into the kiss, he groaned and gripped her around the waist, lifting her as if she weighed nothing and setting her sideways on his thighs. Then he went back to kissing her with passionate single-mindedness. One of his hands kneaded her hip. The other cupped her breast, gently squeezing and exploring. She arched to press her breast more firmly into the hand that knew just how to touch her.

His mouth left hers to string kisses over her cheek, to nip her earlobe, taste her throat. Daniel growled when he reached the high neckline of her modest dress, then returned to her mouth. She could have gone on kissing him forever, except she ached for more and began to squirm on his lap. She wanted his hand under her skirt, sliding up. She wanted—

Daniel wrenched his mouth from hers and groaned again. She felt the vibration in his chest. More than that—his hands were shaking. *She* was shaking. For a moment he didn't move except to rest his forehead against hers. Removing his hand from her breast seemed to pain him.

"I want you," he said raggedly. "But we can't—"

"No." But she wasn't sure she'd have had the self-control to stop. Imagine the scene if Amos had come looking for her! "I told them I wouldn't be gone long."

"I'm sorry." He rubbed his nose against hers. "I shouldn't have started that. I didn't mean to."

"It was me being pushy."

"It was you reading me as if—" He stopped suddenly.

She was afraid to ask him to finish. Asking him to bare himself to her just because she felt so vulnerable wasn't reasonable. Because his job was to protect her, he had to hear about her problems. She didn't have an equal right, even if she wanted that right.

Daniel stayed silent until his chest lifted and fell with another long sigh. Somehow she wasn't surprised when he said, "You should get back inside."

Unreasonable hurt had Rebecca pulling free and jumping to her feet.

But Daniel stood, too, so close she could feel his body heat. His breath was a whisper against her cheek. "This is dangerous," he murmured. "Meeting in the dark, alone."

"You don't have to come." It hurt to say. "If you have something to tell me, you could leave a note. I can check here every morning."

He pressed a hard kiss to her mouth. "I need to see you."

The hurt dissolved. "Oh. Then..."

"Tomorrow night." He made a sound deep in his throat. "Maybe it's lucky you're dressed plain. Between your *kapp* and that dress, I'm forced to remember our circumstances."

"I wish..."

"I wish, too." His knuckles brushed her injured cheek with aching tenderness. "Go, Rebecca."

Head bobbing, she turned away. She felt

sure that he watched until she slipped inside the house and he knew she was safe.

DANIEL'S DAY STARTED with a call from Little Ike Mast.

A man had visited the Mast father-and-son horse farm, but hadn't seemed very interested in the draft horses. He claimed to have heard good things about Samuel Graber's operation, but also that Samuel was too busy right now with his niece visiting to seem interested in selling horses.

Not part of the Grabers' church district, Little Ike knew only that Samuel's place had been ransacked. That made him wonder about someone more interested in Samuel's family than in the horses he had claimed he wanted to see. "The bishop said I should call to tell you."

Little Ike hadn't liked the *Englischer*. No, not a tall man, but strong, with dark hair and eyes. Not very friendly.

Josh Griffen? "What did you say to this *Englischer*?" Daniel asked.

"That I didn't know what he was talking about. Visitors? How would I know?"

Whoever these men were, they were taking risks, letting themselves be seen. Daniel thought about checking in with Estevez, but the information didn't really add to what they knew, and he expected to hear from the detective soon, anyway.

In fact, that call came a couple hours later.

"Finally got clearance for the trip and have a reservation for Saturday morning."

They discussed logistics, then Daniel told him about the apparent hunt for Rebecca and her son.

"If the stupid woman had just come to me in the first place…" Estevez sounded as if he was grinding his teeth.

"She might be dead."

Silence. Then he said, "You know I should slap her with every charge I can think up. She's wasted so much of my goddamn time."

"I'd be happier if you didn't," Daniel said mildly.

"You're kidding."

"No. I do believe Ms. Holt has suffered remorse even as she believed the items were the only way to hold off her ex-husband and his partner. I have the impression it's the father-in-law most of all that had her panicking. Having met the guy, I can understand."

"You met him?" Estevez asked, surprised.

"Oh, yeah. He marched into the sheriff's department headquarters yesterday and demanded I hand over his grandson. All but disowned his son. Didn't care what Tim was up to, or that he'd battered Ms. Holt. When I inquired whether he had any paperwork showing legal custody, Mr. Gregory assured me that the minute he had his grandson back in the state of California, he'd go to court to get that custody. Didn't seem to have any doubt of his success."

The San Francisco detective snorted. "Guy's an asshole. He's almost enough to make me sorry for his son."

"I don't know about Tim, but the grandson is a great kid," Daniel remarked. "Funny, smart, sensitive." Well, he'd agreed that he didn't want a siren to frighten the horses. That qualified, didn't it? "Got to say, the idea of him in Robert's hands gives me a chill."

"Thus your sympathy for the kid's mother."

"I suppose so." *And, by the way, I'm falling for her. Have fallen.* Not something he intended to share. "Like she told you, if she'd immediately gone to you with the wallet, you'd have arrested Tim. But you wouldn't have had enough to arrest Griffen, too, unless Tim rolled on him. And either or both of the men would have been out on bail within twenty-four hours. Meantime, the custody issue was still on the table, slowing Ms. Holt's divorce, and Robert was maneuvering in the background."

More silence, followed by a huff that combined frustration with acceptance. "I may get pushback from my boss and from the DA."

"Introduce them to her father-in-law."

Estevez gave a bark of laughter. "There's an idea."

"How did he get to be so influential?" Daniel asked.

"Money, what else?"

"Inherited, or did he earn it?"

"A little of both, from what I know. Sounds like he's smart enough." The admission was grudging. "There are a couple of software powerhouses that wouldn't have gotten their starts without him. Face it, money trumps personality."

Daniel's turn to laugh. "Can't say I'd know. I wouldn't call anybody in Henness County rich." Although he'd tangled with a few like that when he worked in St. Louis.

"Count yourself lucky." The detective sounded sardonic. "Means you don't have to tiptoe during an investigation the way the rest of us do."

Did Estevez know how to tiptoe? He might have gotten further with Rebecca if he'd approached her with some finesse.

This mess made Daniel grateful that the crimes he typically saw were straightforward with easy-to-understand motives. He frequently pitied the people he arrested, like the Shaver

brothers. What could have led Tim Gregory and
Josh Griffen, successful by anyone's standards,
already wealthy in their early thirties, to kill a
friend and partner—or at least to cover up his
death? Daniel would never understand the greed
behind that kind of embezzlement.

Daniel ended the call with a tap of his thumb
and then leaned back in his desk chair, looking
at the clock. Counting the hours until Rebecca
would slip around the corner of the barn and
into his arms.

THAT EVENING, REBECCA resolved to be *airlich*—
honest—with her hosts, although she prayed
they wouldn't make an attempt to forbid her
from going out to meet with Daniel. Out of
gratitude for their kindness and generosity, she
would comply with most requests from them,
but not that one. If they were shocked and dis-
approving, staying with them would be tense.
But she had to see Daniel.

When she told them Daniel intended to sneak
onto the property this evening to talk to her,
Amos and Barbara looked at each other. After
a moment of silent communication, Amos nodded brusquely and didn't ask how Daniel had
set up this meeting with her in the first place.

"We would not like a daughter meeting a man

in the dark, but it is not our place to tell you what you can do. And I can see why he doesn't want anyone to see him come here."

"Thank you. I won't be long. I wish I thought he would have good news."

"*Ja*, it would be good if he could find that man," Barbara agreed.

The moment Rebecca stepped out, she felt the muggy air. The latest promised thunderstorm had bypassed them, nothing but distant rumbles late in the afternoon. She walked straight to the barn, not surprised to find Daniel there before her. He reached for her hand first thing. "I told Amos and Barbara I was meeting you," she heard herself say. Self-defense—or was it defense against self? A reminder that her time was limited and her hosts knew she was with Daniel?

"And they didn't lay down the law?" Daniel sounded surprised, even though he had been the one to suggest she be honest with Amos and Barbara.

"No. They weren't thrilled, but Amos said he had no right to tell me what to do."

"I can hear the whiff of disapproval."

Her forehead wrinkled. "No, he also said he understood you can't come here openly."

"Estevez will be here Saturday."

Her heart gave a single, unhappy kick. "Oh, joy."

"I think he's more bark than bite."

"Right."

Daniel smiled at her sarcasm. "I'll come to the back door tomorrow night so I can talk to Amos about how to sneak you to town for the meet. Not sure a big city detective would enjoy beating his way through the fields and woods to come here."

She clasped her hands together. "Okay."

"Little Ike Mast called to say a man who was more interested in Samuel Graber's visitors than his horses showed up asking questions. He pretended complete ignorance." Daniel hesitated. "His description of the man could match with Josh."

"Doesn't Detective Estevez know where Josh is?" Wonderful—she sounded semi-hysterical.

"He doesn't have grounds at this point to watch the guy. Josh may do some traveling as part of his work. And remember, Robert, Josh and Tim can all afford to fly with private charters, which makes tracking them harder. I'm surprised Robert flew commercial, now that I think about it."

"Will this ever end?"

"Hey. Come here." He held out an arm that

closed around her when she slid closer. "You know we'll get them eventually."

He was asking for another form of faith from her. Faith in law enforcement, in justice and in him. It was still a struggle for her, but she finally nodded.

"Last night," he said suddenly. "I shut down on you. It's uncomfortable to feel clear as glass."

She turned within his encircling arm to look at him. "I'm sorry. I was nosy."

"Curious," he corrected. "Curious is good."

That let her relax. "You aren't easy to read. It's me. I think... I've felt pulled both ways, too. Not as strongly as you, I'm sure, but...my mother tried to instill her values in me. I never connected my stays here with home life. I didn't know why the television was rarely on in our house, why we played games in the evening or talked or cooked instead. Why she was never comfortable chatting on the phone. After the summers here, I tried to be like all my friends, and I guess I succeeded, in a way." A smile twisted on her mouth. "I'd see Mom's disappointment. And then there was my choice of Tim."

"You've felt some culture clash, too."

Rebecca nodded against his shoulder.

When he asked, she talked about growing up, and her brief rebellious stage when she'd cut her hair spiky short and dyed it various neon colors. She wondered what he would have thought of her if they had met while he was still an earnest Amish boy—or even later, when he was struggling free of the cocoon of his faith and family.

"Mom never forbade me to do anything," Rebecca said softly. "She wanted…"

"You to have a freedom she didn't?"

"I suppose that's it. She told me so many times how proud she was of me." In his embrace, her grief found solace.

DANIEL HAD HAD guarded conversations with others who had left the faith. He'd discussed the difficult transition before. But most of the people he'd met had craved a different life, some looking back with contempt that felt too much like how many non-Amish reacted. He had always wondered if they really felt no regret. He'd never heard anyone acknowledging the inner conflict he felt every day of his life. But Rebecca made it easy for him to start talking.

"I sometimes think I'm like an immigrant to this country. Someone who knows he'll never be able to go back, but will never feel quite at home here, either."

She pulled away from him at that raw honesty so she could lay a hand on his cheek. "To the Amish, you may be a…a bridge."

He grunted. "Nice thought, but they're determined to stay apart from the world. You know that. They don't want a bridge."

"That may be where some of the tension comes from. But they do trust you, and they know if they have to cross over, the bridge is solid."

Daniel expelled a breath as if he'd been punched. He had never thought of his relationship with his family and the Amish community that way. If it was true…

He didn't like to think about his first few years after leaving all that was familiar, but when Rebecca asked more questions, memories spilled out. He'd hated feeling so stupid, stumbling when everyone else ran. Too much had been new, shocking and frightening, and he had existed in an adrenaline-fueled state that had probably shortened his lifespan.

He'd lived on the street until the weather grew too cold, then in a homeless shelter, before finding work, mindless and physical. The pay had been enough to rent a room. A social worker at the homeless shelter had steered him to educational resources, and he had begun studying for his GED.

As he continued talking, he realized he and Rebecca were still holding hands. Comfort and connection.

He told her about the classes he'd taken at a

community college that helped him pass the GED, and how he'd continued on until he had a two-year degree. Scholarships and a nearly full-time work schedule had gotten him through the final two years at the University of Missouri—St. Louis.

Even then, he had been ill prepared for the realities of policing a major city with crimes that once would have been unimaginable to him.

He talked until he was hoarse, giving no thought to whether Amos would come to check on them. When he finally fell silent, he gathered Rebecca into his arms and just held her, soaking in this closeness to another person.

After he'd left her with a gentle kiss that required every ounce of self-control he could summon, he watched until she entered the house through the back door. Then he set off through the small orchard in what was becoming a familiar trek. This time, the owl's soft *whoo* sounded like a greeting between friends.

He'd desperately wanted to kiss her as he had the night before, when he'd been so damn close to bearing her back on the bench and stripping off her undergarments, or lifting her skirts and adjusting her to straddle him. The vision was so vivid a groan escaped him. They might have gotten caught—but he was embarrassingly aware that once her snug body closed around him, he wouldn't have lasted more than a minute. It had been too long since he'd had a woman—and he had wanted this one too long, besides.

It hadn't been until later, when he was sneaking through the neighbor's dark farmyard, that he realized he hadn't had a condom with him. He'd like to think that would have stopped him…but wasn't so sure.

Tonight, an odd thought struck him. In roughly the last hour, he and Rebecca had shared much more than he ever had with any woman he'd dated. In fact, all of their hushed meetings in the dark, sitting on porch steps or the bench behind the barn, were building a stronger foundation than would the sex he craved.

And yet he still felt helpless, unable to arrest the men hunting her. Or even to be sure she would stay once she was safe. He also knew he couldn't let himself ask until she really had a choice.

GRATEFUL FOR THE slight padding provided by the horse blanket Amos had thoughtfully laid on the floor of the buggy, Rebecca started out cross-legged, skirts covering her to her stocking-clad ankles. But no position was very comfortable, and she had to keep shifting.

Even though the buggy was well sprung, it hit

a hole in the road hard enough to bounce her. Wincing, she squirmed into another position.

The drone of the metal tire rims on the paved county road and the swaying of the buggy made her drowsy. Several cars passed, but she didn't think any of them slowed to a crawl to allow someone to peer in the windows.

But the sound of increased traffic, cars and other buggies, banished her sleepiness. The dread she'd been trying to suppress poked its way free. Would Daniel stay or hand her over to Detective Estevez? Silly to be so anxious about talking to the man in person when she had already told him everything. The tightness in her chest didn't ease. Detective Estevez had become a bogeyman, as frightening as all the other ones currently populating her head.

Possibly because *he* could arrest her.

Thank goodness for Caleb, Rebecca thought for at least the hundredth time. One of Amos and Barbara's daughters had brought her children over, and Matthew had hardly noticed when his mother left.

Now, the buggy made several turns, Amos clucking once to his bay mare and saying, "Almost here," ostensibly to Barbara but loudly enough for Rebecca to hear. A minute later, the mare slowed to a walk and then stopped when Amos said, "Whoa, Jessie."

The buggy swayed some more as the two got out. The clank of a bucket and a sloshing sound suggested Amos was providing water for Jessie. Then Barbara's voice drifted to Rebecca, receding as she spoke.

"I need a few things in Miller's. And flannel and thread for a new nightgown."

Amos's answer was barely a rumble.

Rebecca got to her hands and knees, afraid to lift her head in case someone walked by.

Not a minute later, what sounded like a truck came slowly down the alley, stopping right beside Amos's buggy. She had to believe it was Daniel, as planned, not Tim or Josh or one of their confederates. If she was wrong…she'd scream and struggle.

"Rebecca," said a quiet voice.

She rose to a crouch and opened the door, scrambling ungracefully out and into the backseat of the black SUV with tinted windows. The door slammed shut, and no more than a few seconds later Daniel drove them away. He turned right out of the alley to avoid the main shopping street, then kept going.

Detective Estevez swiveled in the passenger seat and looked sourly at her. "Interesting getup."

That stiffened her spine. "My family is Amish. I'm living plain."

One of his heavy eyebrows lifted as he surveyed her with dark eyes. "You're full of surprises, Ms. Holt. I sure never expected to have to travel halfway across the country to see you again."

Her cheeks heated. "Staying in the city didn't seem to be smart."

"So Sheriff Byler tells me. I wish *you* had."

"I should have come to you," she made herself say. "But I didn't think I'd live long enough to testify in any trial."

"The sheriff here suggested you might be more afraid of the senior Mr. Gregory."

"I never thought it was Robert trying to kill me. Just that if anything happened to me, he would swoop in and claim my son." Discovering her arms were wrapped as tightly around herself as she could manage, Rebecca tried to make herself loosen them. Under that sour gaze, she failed.

"All right," the detective said, still irritable but less aggressive. "We need to cover some of the same ground again. Let's start at the beginning."

First, he turned on a recorder and asked her to acknowledge that she knew she was being recorded and had given her permission.

Her eyes met Daniel's in the rearview mirror. She drew strength from his presence.

The real beginning, she knew now, had been months before she'd discovered the wallet, when Tim became so tense and angry, so secretive. But what Detective Estevez needed to hear…

"Tim had told me to take a look and decide what I wanted from the house," she said, grateful that she sounded almost composed. "So I let myself in…"

DANIEL FRETTED FOR what remained of the day. He'd told Rebecca to expect him tomorrow night, but not tonight. He didn't want to stretch his uncle's tolerance. But he had underestimated how stressful Rebecca would find today's meeting—and maybe the uncomfortable trip to and from town on the hard floor of the buggy.

What was she thinking? She had to be going a little crazy. He wished suddenly that they'd talked more about the future instead of concentrating on the past. He knew why he had—he saw her future here, with him, and had been afraid to find out she didn't. She'd said nothing to make him think she would do something dumb like take off or try to contact her ex, but he'd be reassured to hear that from her.

Sneak out there tonight? No, Rebecca wouldn't know to meet him. Anyway, he thought he'd like to see her face when they discussed the meeting with Estevez and where they'd go next.

He considered openly stopping by for once. Amos and Barbara *were* family. Why would anybody pay attention? While he was out, he'd make other stops, as was his habit. Just to remind people that he was willing to help…or, in a few cases, that he was keeping an eye on them. One of his deputies had reported seeing some traffic coming and going from the Shaver brothers' place, not a good sign.

But he was shaking his head even before he'd consciously made a decision. No. He couldn't risk drawing any attention at all to her location.

Go after dark and knock on the kitchen door again, then. Sit down with her *and* Amos.

With luck, she'd walk him out when he left and he could sneak a kiss to sustain him.

CHAPTER FOURTEEN

REBECCA WAS JUST tiptoeing out of the bedroom after tucking the boys in when she saw Amos at the head of the stairs.

"Asleep?" he asked in a low voice.

"Caleb is," she whispered.

He nodded. "You are needed downstairs."

What on earth? She hurried after him.

Not until they reached the main floor did he say, "My nephew is here, wanting to speak to us."

Her pulse rate rocketed. What could have happened?

She almost ran for the kitchen, brushing by Amos on the way. It was an anticlimax to find Daniel sitting at the table polishing off a piece of apple pie swimming in cream while Barbara unnecessarily wiped kitchen counters and chattered about what her daughter had told her about the boys' doings today.

They were surmounting the language difference with astonishing speed. Matthew, Rebecca was beginning to think, had already picked up more Deitsch from the Grabers, and especially Abram and Mose, than she'd realized. "Hi" had been the extent of Caleb's English when he'd first arrived, but increasingly he mixed English words and phrases into his Deitsch. However the two boys accomplished it, they seemed to understand each other.

Matthew still needed a hug or just the knowledge his mom was there, but the clinginess had passed. Rebecca was grateful for his resilience. If only she could feel as strong.

Seeing Amos and Rebecca, Barbara exclaimed, "*Ach*, here they are! You need to talk, *ja*? I will go back to my knitting."

"You're welcome if you'd like to stay," Daniel said unexpectedly. "I have nothing to say you can't hear."

Amos raised an eyebrow but, as was his way, wordlessly pulled up a chair to the table. He nodded his thanks to his wife for the cup of coffee she poured. Rebecca found herself directly across the table from Daniel.

They all stared at him until he scraped his plate clean and sighed. He smiled at his aunt. "I should steal you away. My cooking is nowhere near as good as yours."

Rebecca's fingers bit into her palms. Was he trying to torture her? "Why are you here?" she burst out.

Amos gave her a reproving look, which she ignored. Daniel focused on her, his expression calm.

"I wanted to tell you that Estevez and I talked after we dropped you off, and he says he, er, appreciated your cooperation and won't be filing charges."

Her breath whooshed out of her. At the same time, she couldn't help saying, "*Appreciated?* Detective Estevez?"

Daniel grinned. "He may have expressed it more begrudgingly than that."

Amos and Barbara stared at her as she laughed, which suggested she didn't sound quite sane. She couldn't decide if her relief was even proportional, given that someone who wanted to kill her was still on the loose.

Daniel just waited her out, his gaze steady. If they'd been alone, she felt sure he would have at least taken her hand.

"Thank you," she said. "I mean, for coming here to tell me."

"I also wanted to find out how you're holding up." He hesitated. "You've had all the control taken out of your hands, with nothing to do but wait."

It was as if he'd bulldozed a barricade holding back a toxic brew of emotion. "I keep wanting to *do* something! This is my mess, and now I'm

completely helpless, waiting to be bailed out."
She glared at him, even though none of it was
Daniel's fault. "I *hate* feeling like this."

"I understand." His mouth twisted. "I wish I
could suggest a way for you to help, but I don't
know what that would be."

She looked down at her hands. "I could…
take off. Make sure they know I'm not here
anymore."

"With Matthew?" Daniel's voice sounded as
if it had been run over a grater.

"Well…no, I couldn't do that to him. But if
he could stay here—" she flicked an apologetic
glance at Amos and Barbara "—I could lead
them away." Yep, great idea.

He groaned. "How would they know to chase
after you?"

"I could call from someplace like a bus or
train station, where departures are being an-
nounced over a PA system. If he heard it in the
background…" Seeing Daniel's expression, she
mumbled, "It was…just a middle-of-the-night
scheme. I know it's stupid. It's just…"

Amos surprised her by setting a big, work-
roughened hand over her knotted fingers. "We
have thought of you like a daughter, Rebecca.
Stay as long as you must. You and one small
boy make no trouble."

Through the blur of tears she saw Barbara smiling encouragement.

Rebecca sniffed. "Two small boys and a woman like me can make a whole lot of trouble."

"The good kind," Barbara said. "Enjoying you all, we are."

"Is common sense all that's stopped you from embarking on this great plan?" Daniel asked, his blue eyes penetrating, his voice almost harsh.

She couldn't look away from him. "I couldn't really have left Matthew and—" *you* "—everybody who cares about me."

"I'm one of those people, you know," he said quietly.

The floodgates opened. She mumbled, "I do know," and buried her face in her hands. She didn't see him move, but suddenly he had circled the table, pulled out the chair next to hers and wrapped his arms around her, right there in front of Amos and Barbara.

Rebecca let herself cry on his uniform shirt for only a minute, then gave herself another minute to steep in the pleasure of being held close. His smell was mingled sweat, a hint of aftershave. Man. His arms were so strong, his shoulders reassuringly broad. She hated to look up, because now she'd be blotchy and puffy and she'd have to see how shocked his aunt and uncle were, but finally she had to.

"It's just me, you know," she said in a soggy voice, "Matthew seems really happy." She smiled shakily at Barbara. "Thanks to your brilliant idea. It's just… I hate knowing I've brought danger to all of you. I never meant—"

Amos stirred. "Here, you have our nephew to keep you safe."

She did. The miracle was, despite the fact that she felt trapped, she did believe in Daniel.

"Yes," she whispered, but wasn't sure he was convinced.

MORNING BROUGHT THE usual distractions from the minute Daniel walked into headquarters. Plus, a deputy had called in sick, leaving them shorthanded at a time when they could ill afford it. Lucky he hadn't planned to take this Sunday off, Daniel thought, since he'd be replacing his absent deputy.

He hadn't driven two miles during his patrol when a voice crackled through his radio. "Found a buggy. Nobody in it. Horse seems upset."

After a quick glance in the rearview mirror, Daniel braked. "You've searched in case the driver got thrown out?"

"Drove back a ways," Deputy Sloan responded. "Nothing."

This couldn't be good. He could only pray whatever had happened was unrelated to the reports of men studying the faces of Amish traveling the roads. Today was the "off" Sunday for the Amish, who used it for visiting instead of church.

"Location?" he asked.

"Westwood Road, 'bout half a mile this side of the river bridge."

The Thompson River took a curve into Henness County, the banks sandy in that stretch. Fishermen could often be seen in their waders, lines cast. Westwood Road narrowed to cross a rusting steel bridge preferred by the Amish to the busier and more modern bridge to the south.

"On my way."

On cresting a gentle hill, he saw two buggies ahead, as well as a sheriff's department vehicle. Daniel parked behind his deputy and got out to find an Amish couple he knew only slightly, the man soothing a sweating, wild-eyed bay gelding hitched to a small, open buggy, while the woman had stayed in their own buggy. The deputy was almost in the ditch, keeping a wary distance from the horse. If this had been a busier road, the scene would have been considerably more chaotic. If the horse had run in a panic out in front of a car...

He shook off the image.

"Paul Glick?" Daniel ventured.

"*Ja.*" The man, perhaps forty, was unusually

dark-haired and dark-eyed for the Amish. "You are Sheriff Byler, not so?"

"I am. Do you know whose buggy this is?"

"*Ja*, Anna Lantz lives with her husband and children on Sandy Creek Road." His accent was stronger than most. "Her *mamm* and *daad* live near my wife and me, half a mile over the river. She and her oldest boy, I saw them when they left her parents' to go home, maybe half an hour ago." His head turned, his eyes sweeping the woods on one side and the overgrown pasture on the other. "Where could she be?"

"Let me call this in and make sure she and her son weren't transported to the hospital."

Dispatch checked; no Amish woman had arrived at the hospital in Byrum or as an emergency at the medical clinic in Hadburg, although if an *Englischer*, local or tourist, had found her or her boy in distress, they could still be in transit. But would even an anxious or suddenly ill mother simply abandon her horse and buggy without at least turning them into the next lane?

Daniel returned to Paul Glick. "How old is the boy who was with her?"

"Luke is five, I think. Just too young to start school."

Daniel didn't like being proved right. The dread felt like a too-tight band around his rib cage. "What does Anna look like?"

Paul stared at him like he was *ab im kopf*—off in the head, for sure. But seeing something in Daniel's expression, he said, "She is a pretty woman. Even after two children, she is thin. Her hair is…" He hesitated, obviously floundering.

"A red-brown," his wife called. Daniel had assumed she was too far away to be able to hear them talk. "Wavy, sometimes curling out from under her *kapp*."

His deputy had been shading his eyes and looking back down the road. "I think I see something," he said suddenly, and jogged along the shoulder.

"She has blue eyes," the wife added.

In other words, she met the basic description of Rebecca Holt.

"Her boy?"

"Blond, like his *daad*."

The dread coalesced into naked fear.

Seeing that Sloan was jogging back, something in his hand, Daniel said, "Excuse me a minute," and walked to meet him.

"A bonnet," the young deputy said, holding it out. "One strap is torn off. I didn't see this from the car."

It was black, the kind of bonnet any respectable Amish woman wore when out in public. Picturing rough hands ripping it from her head, Daniel said tensely, "Start canvassing. Go back as far as the river. Let's hope we find some people who were outside and noticed passing vehicles. I'll bring in help."

He allowed Paul Glick to unhitch Anna Lantz's mare and tie her to his buggy. He would detour to take the horse home, he promised, before he and his wife continued into town. Daniel walked a few feet away and made his calls to bring in every possible deputy and volunteer.

Knowing how much he had to do, he still stood beside his car for a minute, paralyzed with fear for Rebecca. The Lantz home wasn't a mile from Amos and Barbara's. That suggested the hunt was closing in. Daniel wanted her out of there.

Not Matthew, at least not yet. One more Amish boy would pass unnoticed, once his mother wasn't in the picture. The kid today wouldn't have been grabbed, and probably not the woman alone, either. It was the combination that had put them in danger.

We'll never find them in time. No wonder Rebecca hadn't wanted to give up her bargaining chips.

And that was when he had a lightbulb moment.

He couldn't get away himself, so he called a deputy whose shift hadn't yet started. After that, he drove to the Lantz home, passing Paul's buggy on the way.

Out in a field, two men seemed to be inspecting the enormous bales of hay, but both turned to look when the marked police car drove up the driveway. As he came to a stop, one of the two strode across the field toward him. Out of the corner of his eye, Daniel saw that a heavy, older woman had stepped out onto the porch with a toddler on her hip.

Being the bearer of bad news was a part of the job Daniel couldn't push onto others, but he hated it nonetheless.

The man, no older than Daniel himself, had wheat-colored hair and beard. Daniel took a few steps to meet him. "Eli Lantz?"

Worry filled the blue eyes. "*Ja*, I'm Eli."

"Mr. Lantz, one of my deputies found your wife's horse and buggy abandoned on the road this side of the river. Paul Glick and his wife came along. He's bringing the horse to you. You can retrieve the buggy later." After Daniel's one crime-scene technician had gone over it. "He says Anna had your son Luke with her."

Eli nodded, his gaze straying to the woman and child on the porch. "The little one stayed home."

"I've received no word from emergency services, and the hospital and medical clinic have both promised to let me know if an Amish woman or child is brought in by anyone. Failing that—" he hesitated "—I have to worry that Anna and your boy have been abducted."

Eli called, *"Mamm!"*

The older woman hurried from the porch.

Soon the other man was approaching, as well.

Daniel explained the situation again to all of them, then asked Eli to go to the nearest phone shanty and check for messages. The families nearby always shared an answering machine as well as the phone.

"Ja, ja," he said, and ran. But only minutes later he returned, shaking his head. "No messages at all."

"Keep checking every once in a while," he advised.

Daniel didn't want to tell them the possible connection to Rebecca and Matthew yet. The implications were too ominous. What would happen when Tim or Josh saw that the wrong mother and son had been snatched? She'd all too likely seen the faces of her abductors. And the boy was old enough to be able to describe their captors. These men weren't likely to guess the Amish wouldn't go to the police if she and the boy were immediately released, uninjured.

Were those bastards cold-blooded enough to

murder a young mother and child inadvertently caught up in their hunt for Rebecca?

REBECCA MASHED POTATOES while Barbara took sourdough biscuits from the oven. As they prepared the midday meal, Caleb and Matthew contentedly sat at the table drawing pictures and giggling at each other's efforts.

Both women turned in surprise when Amos walked in the back door. He had gone out to feed their two horses only a minute ago.

"Rebecca," he said, expression grave, "*komm.* I must speak to you."

Alarmed, she followed him to the living room without argument.

"Harvey Zook's boy, Mark, just ran over." His accent had thickened, making the "just" more of a "chust." "A sheriff's deputy came to his house, says Daniel asked him to pick you up. Wants you to pack a change of clothes and sneak with Mark back to the sheriff's office. Says he needs you to do something, and that maybe you not being near Matthew right now would be good."

She listened to this speech, heart drumming. The Zooks' farm was probably half a mile down the road. "Something happened. This Mark doesn't know what?"

"No, but my nephew would not ask this without reason."

Even through her panic, she noted his calm faith in Daniel. A bridge, indeed. "No," she said. "I mean, yes. Okay." She drew a steadying breath. "I'll go pack some things into my duffel. Where's Mark?"

"The barn. He came in the back, so he would not be seen."

She ran upstairs, stuffed another of her plain dresses into the duffel, as well as the limited wardrobe with which she'd begun her journey.

Matthew took the news well. He held her only a little longer than usual when she hugged him. Then she hugged Barbara and hustled out the back door with Amos before she burst into tears.

IT WAS A *huge* relief to crawl out of the police car. Of course, she'd had to lie on the backseat, behind the grill. The car rode a whole lot better than the buggy, and moved faster, too, but the upholstery stank, an awful mix of cleansers and something really gross. She found herself staring at stains, too.

Annoyingly, the young deputy refused to tell her *why* he had been sent to pick her up. Maybe he didn't know. When he helped her out and she discovered he had pulled right up to the back door of the sheriff's department, she asked, "Do people throw up in your backseat?"

He flushed, making him look about sixteen. "Uh…yes, ma'am. I've even had drunks, uh…" He thought better of what he'd almost said, but Rebecca could fill in the rest. She desperately wanted to scrub herself, head to foot.

He did allow her to detour into a restroom and wash her face with a paper towel, then her hands. She almost went back out, but instead locked herself in a stall and changed to her alternate dress and apron. She needed to stay plain until she knew what Daniel needed, but at least she felt almost clean now.

She was tying her apron when a knock came on the door.

"Ma'am? Are you all right?"

She jammed the clothes she'd just shed in the duffel bag, zipped it and opened the door. "No, I didn't squeeze through that tiny window and make a getaway," she said drily.

He blushed again. "I didn't mean…uh… I never thought…"

How on earth did this poor boy ever make an arrest? Or did he believe she *was* Amish and therefore had delicate sensibilities?

He handed her over with obvious relief to a receptionist, who introduced herself as Melissa Sue and ushered her into a conference room.

"Sheriff says he'll get here when he can. He doesn't want anyone to see you, so if you don't mind..." She looked uncomfortable.

"Don't stick my head out?"

"Something like that."

She did bring Rebecca a can of pop and a small bag of peanuts in case she was hungry, then left her alone.

DANIEL HAD DRIVEN back to the scene of the abduction, where he started knocking on doors himself. Even the make of the vehicle would give them something to go on. Nobody had had reason to note a license-plate number, and out-of-state plates were commonplace around here because of tourism, but there might have been something distinctive about the vehicle—a bumper sticker, damage from an accident. Anything.

What they got was nothing. Not a single person along the road had happened to be working in a field close enough to notice traffic.

"Ach," said one Amish woman with a shrug, "cars pass all the time, and buggies, too. If someone doesn't turn up to our house..."

Finally he let everyone know he was returning to the station. Anna and Luke Lantz had only one hope: Rebecca.

He found her stashed in one of the small conference rooms. Hand on the knob, he paused for a minute, looking through the wire-mesh window. She sat at one end of the table with a book open in front of her, but she wasn't reading. Instead, she gazed straight ahead, toward a wall that held nothing but a blank whiteboard.

Her head turned when she heard the door opening. Worried blue eyes met his.

"Sorry to put you through that," he said. "I know you had to hike cross-country again, but I didn't want a deputy seen stopping too close to Amos's."

The sound she made was something like *pfft.* "It was nothing. As your uncle said, you wouldn't have sent for me without good reason."

"He said that?" Maybe he shouldn't be surprised, but Daniel was.

Rebecca smiled and nodded, although the smile disappeared too quickly, her eyes searching his face. "You don't look good. What happened?"

"An Amish woman and boy were abducted this morning," he said bluntly. He went on to explain about the buggy and horse abandoned on a road and that Anna Lantz at least superficially resembled Rebecca, as her boy did Matthew. "Her bonnet had been ripped off—we found it in the ditch—probably so that whoever grabbed her could see her face better."

"Oh, dear God," Rebecca whispered.

"Nobody saw what happened. That stretch of road isn't in sight of any house. A few people along the road have noticed slow cars lately, but figured tourists were out looking for Amish or were just lost. So far, we haven't found a trace."

She stiffened, anger transforming her face as she thought about the woman and boy who had been taken in place of her and her son.

"You brought me here to call Tim."

He should have expected her to make that leap, and knew she would have offered if he hadn't thought to ask.

"Yes."

CHAPTER FIFTEEN

DANIEL WISHED THERE was a plan C, one that didn't put Rebecca right in the bull's-eye. The very blackmail he suggested hadn't worked to hold off her enemies, but he prayed it would save two lives.

Fortunately, he'd already purchased a cheap phone loaded with minutes, and his intention was to persuade Amos to let her carry it. He'd meant to give it to her this evening.

He bounded upstairs to get the phone, grateful he had charged it last night, knowing that Rebecca would have no way to do so at the Troyers'.

After handing it to her, he drew up the chair beside her. "I won't ask you to put the phone on speaker, because he'd be able to tell and wonder who else was listening."

Not even blinking, she nodded.

He bent forward to kiss her cheek. "You know his number?"

"Yes. But what if he isn't carrying his cell?"

"He was until not long ago. Estevez spoke to

him. Tim was evasive about his whereabouts, implied he was away on business."

"Wait. Can't you use the GPS in his phone to find him?"

"Estevez is getting a warrant to do that. Griffen's phone, too."

They talked for a minute about what she should say. Then she took a deep breath, murmured, "Okay," more to herself than him and dialed.

Looking tense, she waited through the rings followed by a message Daniel could hear. "Call me."

"This is Rebecca. I have something important to tell you. You need to call me. The number is—"

Daniel slid a piece of paper with a phone number written on it in front of her.

She read it aloud and ended the call. Her hand shook as she set down the phone. "He didn't answer," she said unnecessarily. "Should I try Josh?"

He took a hand that was ice-cold into his, rubbing to try to restore her circulation. "No. Now we wait."

"Do you think he knows Detective Estevez came here?"

"I doubt it, but even if he does he can't know you've already handed over that damn wallet, if that's what you're thinking."

Rebecca nodded, her gaze staying fixed on the phone. They waited in near silence, Daniel willing Gregory to have heard the ring, to be checking his messages.

Not even five minutes had passed when the phone rang. Rebecca jerked. "It's him."

"Okay." He laid his hand on her back, moving it in gentle circles. "You can do this."

HIS STEADY VOICE and gaze, his confidence—confidence in *her*—had a calming effect. She wouldn't let him down—or Anna and Luke Lantz.

Rebecca fixed her eyes on Daniel's as she answered. "Tim."

"You know I didn't mean to hurt you when I was helping you into the car, don't you?" Contrition and sincerity rang in Tim's voice. "I lost my temper and screwed up again. But, damn it, Rebecca, all I want is to see my son!"

"Really?" She spoke coldly. "Somehow, I doubt that's all you want."

"Where are you?"

"You think I'm going to tell you?" She hoped her laugh was as jagged as broken glass.

"If you'll just hand over the things you took from me, let me see you and Matthew, give him a hug."

She might have been touched if she didn't remember all too clearly what had happened outside the hospital.

"Here's the deal," she said crisply. "An Amish woman was kidnapped this morning along with her son. I'm told she looks like me, and her son is about Matthew's age and coloring."

"I don't know what you're—"

"I think you do."

Daniel nodded encouragement.

"Why would I—" Tim tried.

Rebecca interrupted again without compunction. "If she and her son are not released, alive and well, in the next hour, I will hand over Steven's ring and wallet to the police. The county sheriff has already been in touch with Detective Estevez after your attempt to force Matthew and me into your car. He doesn't know the whole story, but he will if Anna Lantz and her son aren't released."

"But I don't know anything about them!" Panic infused her ex-husband's voice.

"Find out," she said flatly. "I will promise that, if they are uninjured, they won't go to the law. The Amish don't, except in the case of serious crimes." Like kidnapping, but she didn't say that. "Whoever took her doesn't need to worry if she or her little boy saw faces."

"How can you accuse me—"

"One hour, Tim." She ended the call, dropped the phone and let out a shuddering breath.

"Well done." Daniel's big, warm hand moved up to her nape. When she let her head fall forward, he kneaded until she had to stifle a moan. His hands moved on, working her shoulders, until she felt so limp she wasn't sure she could lift her head at all.

But at last, with a sigh, she made herself straighten and, to her regret, Daniel's hands left her.

"Do you think it will work?" she asked—no, begged.

"I think what you just did is Anna's and Luke's best chance."

Only chance was what he meant. Fear curling in her stomach, she said, "What if Tim was telling the truth when he claimed not to know anything about them?"

"He'll call his partner and deliver the message."

She shivered. "This is a nightmare. It's completely insane! These are businessmen. Pictures of them make it into the newspaper when they attend a charity event. How can they be willing to kidnap and maybe even kill to protect…what?"

"My guess is that they stumbled into this. One or both got an idea of how they could short the third partner, maybe keep salaries down company-wide while padding their own income, just by tallying up some extra expenses. It could be Josh was the one doing the financial tricks, but Tim found out and he let him in. More likely, the two of them dreamed it up. It might have even seemed harmless. It was their own company, after all."

"Not quite. They were all equal partners, which means Steven owned a third."

Daniel probably had other things he should be doing—he'd silenced his phone twice in the last five minutes—but he didn't make any move to leave. Instead, he asked, "Did Tim like Stowe?"

"Originally, he must have. But by the time we were married...no. Steven did come off as arrogant, although I used to wonder if that wasn't a cover for major insecurities. He had a lousy childhood. And, yes, he did make sure everyone noticed his Harvard ring, and that they knew he was the money man for G, G & S. I had the feeling he and Tim had a sort of mutual-resentment thing going. Tim because Steven was an Ivy League grad, Steven because he thought Tim had grown up privileged and spoiled."

"And Josh?"

She hesitated. "Tim implied that both of them found Steven irritating, but that's secondhand. We socialized more with Josh than Steven, but I never felt like I really knew Josh. Steven and

I would talk sometimes, but if only Josh was over, the minute we finished dinner he and Tim would close themselves in his office or the media room."

"The media room." Daniel had a bemused expression.

She made a face. "It scared me. I knew how to turn the TV on and put in a DVD when I let Matthew watch something, but I was afraid to push buttons. Tim would come scowling to say, 'How many times have I explained how to use the remotes?' But there were at least four of them, with all those buttons." She gave herself a shake. "It doesn't matter."

They both knew what *did* matter now.

"I wonder," Daniel said, "if one component of the embezzlement was putting something over on Steven. He was supposed to be the financial genius, and he didn't even notice all the fake expenditures?"

Oh, yes, she could see that. Their secret pleasure, because in their eyes they were proving themselves smarter than Mr. Harvard.

Daniel's phone rang again. This time, after a glance, he said, "I should take this call."

"Go." She flapped her hand toward the door.

He smiled, kissed her lightly and went. He was already talking on the phone by the time the door swung slowly shut behind him. A minute later, he popped back in to dump some change on the table.

"Last door on the left is the break room. Get yourself something to eat or another soda."

And then she was left to watch the second hand jerk slowly around the big wall clock. And pray.

Dear Lord, don't let an innocent woman and child suffer in my place.

THE CALL DANIEL had hoped for came fifty-seven minutes after Rebecca had spoken to Tim Gregory.

"Daniel, we have something here you've been looking for," said Ben Slater, Byrum police chief. "An Amish woman and kid. They're shaken, but not badly hurt so far as we can tell."

Daniel murmured a silent thank-you to the Lord. "I'll drive over and pick them up. You have them at the station?"

"I do."

"Where were they found?"

"They were dumped out of a van on the outskirts of town. Nobody was close enough to get a license plate, even though half a dozen people saw the van brake just before two people came tumbling out. One witness told me she'd seen someone throw a cat and kittens out of a car once, and this was just like that. Mrs. Lantz's apron was caught in the door and ripped and she's moving a little stiffly. The boy skinned his hands when he hit the pavement, but we've cleaned him up."

"Thanks, Ben. I don't have to tell you what a relief this is."

"Is there more going on than you've told me?"

Daniel didn't hesitate. He quickly summed up recent events, leaving out only his personal involvement with Rebecca.

"Well, damn," Ben said.

They signed off, and Daniel bounded down the stairs. He went first to tell Melissa Sue to call off the search, that the Lantzes had been found, then opened the door of the conference room.

If Rebecca had moved since he had left her, he couldn't tell. Her book lay closed on the table. But when she saw his jubilant smile, she sagged.

"They're safe?"

"They are. Thanks to you." He circled the table to draw her out of her chair into a hug, not caring whether anyone passing in the hall saw. He shared what Slater had told him, and said, "I'm going to pick them up and take them directly home unless they need any medical attention."

She let out a shuddery breath. "Oh, thank God."

"Your phone call worked, sweetheart."

"But we're no closer to catching Tim or Josh."

"I'm hoping Anna can tell me something that will help. How many men she saw and who. If she has any idea where they were held."

"I did say—"

"That they wouldn't be charged with kidnapping Anna and her son, and they won't. Even without your promise, I can't imagine she would be willing to testify in court."

"No." Rebecca sank back into the chair.

He frowned. "I hate to leave you stuck here, but I don't see an alternative."

"No, I suppose I can't go anywhere until after dark."

Oh, crap. Had he given her the impression she'd be returning to his aunt and uncle's? Daniel grimaced.

"Rebecca, at this point, I'd rather you keep some distance from Matthew, and the Amish in general."

"But…"

"I'd rather keep you closer." Would she trust him enough to go along with his plan? He had to say it. "I want you to stay with me for now."

She gaped, finally managing to say, "You mean…your house?"

"Yes. I have plenty of room, and there's no reason anyone would suspect you're there." He shook his head when she appeared ready to object. "I need to get going. We can talk about it when I come back. Yes, I know Amos won't approve, and probably your uncle won't, either. But you'll be safe. Anna's kidnapping tells us these scumbags will do anything to get their hands on *you*. I doubt it will occur to them that you'd leave Matthew behind. He should be safe with Amos and Barbara. For all anyone but their church members know, they have two grandsons visiting."

"Yes, but—"

Daniel smiled. "Store up your arguments for later."

She blinked a couple of times. "Okay. You're right. Go."

"If you need anything—"

"I'll ask the woman out front."

"Melissa Sue." And, damn, he wanted to kiss her before he left, but with an inarticulate sound he made himself leave Rebecca in that bare conference room and jog out the back to his SUV.

DANIEL COULD AGREE that Anna Lantz was a pretty woman, but with a pleasantly rounded face she didn't look much like Rebecca, whose features were delicate. Anna's hair was closer to auburn than Rebecca's chestnut, too, and far curlier. Any of the men who knew Rebecca wouldn't have mistaken this woman for her, which meant her abductors had been hired muscle.

Shy with him and obviously overwhelmed by events, Anna hesitated to get into a police car, but finally did so. Daniel fastened her son's seat belt in back, the mother craning her neck to watch. She managed her own, but awkwardly. Not all Amish had ridden in cars. Anna might not have been rebellious enough to have *Englisch* friends during her running-around years, and perhaps as an adult, she'd never had need of a taxi or a ride from an *Englisch* neighbor.

Learning that they hadn't eaten since morning, he detoured into the drive-through of a burger place, and soon Luke was slurping happily on a milk shake in the backseat while Anna devoured a burger in the front. She didn't say a word until she'd finished it.

Then, voice soft, she asked if her husband knew what had happened.

Daniel stuck to English so the boy wouldn't be able to understand. "Yes, I talked to him and your mother-in-law after your horse and buggy were found abandoned. I know he's scared."

"Colleen—my horse—was she hurt?" Anna asked anxiously.

"No, pretty upset, but Paul Glick came along.

He got her calmed down and then took her to your place."

"So nice," she murmured.

"I sent a deputy out to let Eli know you two had been found. Your family will be glad to see you."

With a half-hour drive, Daniel was able to let her finish her fries and float, and to see young Luke had fallen asleep, before he started questioning her.

"Ja," she said, "I saw faces, but I didn't know those men. Two of them, there were. Outsiders. They talked different, not like *Englisch* here." She produced descriptions that could have fit half the male Caucasian population between thirty and fifty years old. She had no idea where she had been held, only that it was a bare bedroom with a boarded-up window.

The room had to be pretty bare indeed if it seemed so by Amish standards. They often had nice furniture, but didn't put up wallpaper or decorations. This bedroom hadn't been dirty, but wasn't clean by her exacting standards, either, he gathered from her wrinkled nose. The floors were wood but scratched and scuffed, the old chenille bedspread threadbare.

Twice, she had had to knock and ask for her and Luke to use a bathroom, which had been right beside the bedroom where they were held.

Fixtures were clean but stained, linoleum old and cracked. No window. Yes, she said, it was one of the same men who had taken her from the buggy who escorted her back and forth.

Then she said, "Another man came, maybe an hour after we were locked in that room? All he did was stare at us. Then he left."

"Can you tell me what he looked like? How old he was?"

"Older than Eli," she decided. "Your age?"

"I'm thirty-five," he told her.

"*Ja*, something like that." She described the man's brown hair—much darker than Daniel's—and brown eyes. He was shorter than her Eli, she was sure, but more muscular. "And mad! Even after he slammed the door, I heard him yelling at the other men. I covered Luke's ears." She gave Daniel a perplexed look. "Why was he mad? Why did they do this, if we weren't what the man wanted?"

So he told her the basics—that a young woman and her son, relatives of a local Amish family, had been hiding here in Henness County from those men. That Anna looked enough like this other woman, and Luke enough like the woman's son, that they had been abducted by mistake.

"They let us go, at least," she said, giving a small nod as if satisfied that "those" men had behaved decently in the end. Daniel didn't have the heart to tell her Rebecca's threat had bought her release.

Her entire family and likely most of the members of her church district swarmed his vehicle the minute he pulled in. Tears ran down Eli's cheeks as he enveloped his wife and son in his arms. An older woman who had to be Anna's mother hugged Daniel and kissed his cheek before saying, *"Denke. Denke."*

He wasn't allowed to leave until he'd had a cup of coffee and a slab of shoofly pie. A huge meal was being laid out as he made his excuses. Enough food to feed a family of ten was thrust on him. Thanking the Lantzes, promising to return the dishes, he finally escaped. At least he wouldn't have to worry about what he'd feed Rebecca tonight.

FROM HER POSITION crouched on the floorboard of Daniel's own SUV, Rebecca heard the garage door rolling down. The lighting dimmed. Wow, she was getting good at this.

"You can get up." Daniel turned in his seat to watch as she squirmed out from behind his seat. "I wasn't sure what you'd brought, so I picked up some clothes for you. I'm going to get out and turn my back while you change." Seeing her surprise, he said, "This is a detached garage. We have to cross the yard to the kitchen door. I don't want a neighbor or anyone else to catch a glimpse of an Amish woman entering my house."

"Oh." She blushed. "No, that would be bad."

His smile made her tingle. "I'm not trying to protect my reputation. I just don't want even a hint to get out that you might be here."

"No. Of course not."

While she was peeking in the plastic bag he handed over, Daniel got out. Rebecca found he'd bought an airy cotton skirt, a scoop-necked peach T-shirt and flip-flops. Cool, pretty and he'd guessed her sizes perfectly, which was interesting.

She hurried to change, one eye on his broad back, then set the athletic shoes she'd been wearing into the bag, followed by her stockings and the neatly folded dress and apron. On top she laid her *kapp*. It would feel odd not to wear it. After a moment's thought, she pulled pins to let her hair down from the distinctly Amish style and dropped them in the bag, too.

When she got out, Daniel surveyed her, a glint in his eyes. "Good" was all he said, but not all he wanted to say, she thought.

She brought her clothes, and he opened the rear hatch to grab her duffel, which he slung over his shoulder, and a large bag filled with plastic containers. Food given in thanks from the Lantz family and friends, he told her.

His lawn, like most this summer, was brown, crackling underfoot, the leaves on two sheltering trees in the yard turning autumn colors. The house was a white two-story with an enclosed back porch. He let them directly into the kitchen, with its aging cabinets painted yellow and a black-and-white checkerboard floor.

"Place could use some work," he said, glancing around as he set the food on the counter. "I keep telling myself I'll get to it."

If he'd bought this house immediately upon returning to Hadburg, he had been here for three years. Remodeling wouldn't be much of a priority for a single man, though, Rebecca supposed. One whose family probably never came to see him here.

"Let me put the food away," he continued, "and then I'll show you your bedroom."

On their way, she caught glimpses of a living room that held a sofa, recliner, television and not much else, and a dining room. Upstairs, he said, "We'll have to share a bathroom, since the only other one is a half bath downstairs. There are four bedrooms, but only one of them is set up for guests." He opened the wood-paneled door and showed her inside.

The room was prettier than she might have expected. The wallpaper, sprays of flowers against a white background, must already have been here when he bought the house. Sheer curtains framed a tall casement window that also had a roller shade. A beautiful old quilt in a churn dash pattern covered the antique wood bed. The other two pieces of furniture were antiques, too: a bedside table and an armoire notable for its simplicity.

Sounding stiff, he said, "There's no closet, so…" He gestured toward the armoire. "It has some drawers inside. And hangers, too."

"I don't have that much." After a moment, she set her plastic bag on the bed, stroked the quilt, then said, "This is really nice. Thank you."

He dropped the duffel bag on the bed, too, then retreated to the doorway. Strangely, she was reluctant to face him. Maybe it was knowing they were alone in the house. And that there was a bed, right here.

"My room is just across the hall." He cleared his throat. "In case you need me during the night."

She did. But she was afraid of the force of that need. Finally, she turned to see that he hadn't moved. He was watching her, his eyes darkened to navy.

"You look different," he said quietly. "Like I imagined you, but…not quite."

What a strange thing to say. "How you imagined me?"

He shook his head. "It's disorienting. I knew

you weren't Amish, but seeing you like this…
surprises me."

Did he mean that she looked wrong now? "I
appreciate the clothes. I only have a couple other
outfits. What I set out with."

He nodded, his gaze unwavering.

Why was this so awkward? He'd held her,
he'd kissed her passionately, and now he was
keeping his distance.

Because of the bed, she realized. She wasn't
the only one aware that they were alone in the
house, and in a bedroom. He wouldn't want her
to think he had any expectations.

Daniel gave himself a shake. "Take your time.
I'll go see about heating some of that food for
dinner." He backed into the hall, raking her with
one last, sweeping, somehow incredulous look
before disappearing.

She let out a tiny whimper and sat on the edge
of the bed—although she had to hop up to get
onto it. Then she pressed a hand to her throat and
waited for her racing pulse to slow before she
even *thought* about going downstairs to join him.

CHAPTER SIXTEEN

"IT'S PROBABLY OKAY if you watch TV tomorrow," Daniel told Rebecca as he helped himself to a third piece of corn bread.

She blinked. "What would I watch during the day?"

Truthfully, he had no idea. "CNN? Doesn't it run news all the time?"

"I don't know."

"There are talk shows." He was sure about that. And soap operas, which he knew about even though he had never watched one. Come to think of it, Rebecca's life could be used as a script for one. "Keep the volume down. Same for the radio. Just in case somebody comes to the door, we don't want anyone outside to be able to hear it."

Her confusion suggested it hadn't occurred to her to turn on anything electronic. Such habits had been broken in recent weeks, he supposed, if she'd ever adopted them at all.

When he looked at her, he kept seeing double. The frame of her *kapp*, hiding much of her heavy mass of hair, the plain-colored dress and apron, only hinting at curves. And here she sat now in the knit shirt that clung to her breasts and bared the wings of her collarbone and a creamy chest as well as a hint of cleavage. Even her slim, pale arms looked sexy to him. And she'd found something to tie her hair with, because she'd gathered it into a high ponytail that spilled below her shoulders. She wore a bra now, which was a relief and a disappointment, all at once. After changing in the car, her nipples had poked the thin fabric of the shirt and her breasts had swayed when she moved. Of course, he'd known she didn't wear one when she was dressed plain, but it hadn't been so obvious. That first glimpse, when she'd stepped from the car... Daniel hoped she hadn't noticed the effect she had on him.

Even now, eating at the kitchen table, he found keeping his eyes on her face took increasing effort. Thinking about her safety was the best distraction he could come up with.

"Don't walk in front of windows." He frowned, foreseeing problems. "You'd better not lower the shade in your bedroom, even at night. I'm sorry. We can switch rooms, if you want. I wake up early, anyway. I won't mind the sun coming in."

Her lips curved. "Me, I've been sleeping in until ten or eleven every morning at your aunt and uncle's."

He laughed, relaxing. "Right. I suppose *Aenti* Barbara has you out collecting eggs at six a.m."

"She does." Her forehead crinkled. "I worry about her having to keep up with everything, and now taking care of the boys, too."

Daniel hadn't thought about it because Amish women were such hard workers. His aunt had raised four children without much help—but she was in her late fifties or even sixty now, and he'd seen that she got to her feet more slowly than she used to, sometimes pressing a hand to her back as if it ached.

"I'll go by my parents' tomorrow," he said. "Ask them to spread the word quietly that Barbara could use some help." He could stop tonight, after he'd sneaked in to talk to Amos, but he knew he wouldn't. He could already taste his eagerness to get back to Rebecca, and he hadn't even left yet.

Worry showed on her face. "That would be nice, as long as nobody talks about who Matthew is."

"You know they won't."

After a minute, she nodded.

"I'll leave the drapes closed in the living room." He rarely opened the curtains here in the kitchen. They were thin enough not to shut out much light, but he doubted anyone could see in.

"I'll be careful."

"I know you're going to be bored," he said.

"Oh, Daniel. You worry too much. It will be quiet and peaceful! I haven't been sleeping well, so I might even take a nap tomorrow."

"If you do, sleep in my bed. I won't open my blinds in the morning."

Some emotions shimmered through her eyes. Her teeth closed on her lower lip, but she only nodded. Daniel wondered if she was thinking that his sheets might carry his scent, just as he was enjoying the picture of her in his bed.

He glanced irritably at the window, not wanting to leave, but seeing that darkness was falling. "Once we clean the kitchen, I'll run out to tell Amos what's happening."

Her gaze followed his. "Go now. I can take care of the kitchen." Her smile flickered. "It'll keep me from getting bored."

"I have books—"

"Shoo."

Daniel laughed. "At least you didn't say 'get lost.'"

Her smile faded. So quietly he could only just hear her, she murmured, "I would never say that."

His heart skipped a beat. All he could do was give a single, jerky nod before he went out the back door, checking to be sure it would lock behind him before he closed it.

WHILE HE WAS GONE, Rebecca indulged herself by exploring. He did own a smallish flat-screen TV, but no DVD player. CDs were something else again, but the collection was unexpected. Classical and jazz. She pulled out a number of CDs with crayon-bright covers, all featuring music from other parts of the world.

The two bookcases in the living room were packed with fiction, including sci-fi and mysteries, and an eclectic mix of nonfiction. Whatever had interested him at any given moment, she suspected.

The dining room lacked even a table. He must eat all his meals in the kitchen.

Tucked beneath the stairs was a half bath and a closet, and he was obviously using a small additional room as a home office. The tablet was the one modern note, left out on one of those acre-wide oak desks that businesses had jettisoned half a century ago. A filing cabinet sat beside the desk, and another bookcase dominated the back wall. This one held mostly nonfiction, including a shelf of home repair and how-to books.

She had noticed the wood floors on this level gleamed. Had he refinished them himself? It made her sad to think he'd have to do all the work on his own. If he were Amish, family, friends and neighbors would turn out for a work frolic.

Among them would be all the skills needed. The women would prepare a feast while the men tore out old cabinets and replaced them with new, reroofed, repaired the sagging fence, stripped molding and painted.

Rebecca started to get mad. Had his family ever even *seen* his house?

Don't judge when you don't know, she reminded herself, but his loneliness spoke for itself.

Upstairs, she opened the two closed doors. One room served for storage, holding boxes, a bathroom vanity cloaked in thick plastic and some unused or unwanted furniture. The fourth room, a small bedroom, was completely empty, lacking even curtains, although these walls were papered with ivy twining into patterns.

Really, this house was too big for him. An ache took up residence beneath her breastbone as she realized he must, even if unconsciously, want to marry and have children.

When Rebecca got to his bedroom, she didn't let herself go beyond the doorway. Not that she thought it held any secrets. His room had a large antique armoire like hers, as well as an oak dresser. The queen-size bed had no headboard. It was covered by a log cabin quilt that was, presumably, Amish, as no print fabrics had been used. If the room had ever been wallpapcrcd, he'd steamed it off, just as a good Amish man would, since wallpaper was unacceptably decorative. The walls in here were now painted a warm cream color that contrasted with the refinished wood molding. The room was pleasing and plain. Only the digital clock, the lamp beside the bed and the overhead light showed he had embraced any part of being "modern."

His parents would say he hadn't kept up the faith, but Rebecca wondered.

If she lived here, she'd add some art, but not much. In retrospect, she realized that living in the house Tim had built for them had felt like wearing a too-tight garment. Always a little uncomfortable, even though most of the time she suppressed the awareness. Her parents' house hadn't been as old as this one, but the simplicity of the decor made it almost plain. Her father hadn't minded. He had loved *Mamm* so much and had studied the Amish enough to understand what would feel right to her. She allowed electricity; he didn't expect art on every wall.

I was so foolish, she thought sadly, absorbing this house, taking in a full breath that felt clean.

CHANCES WERE GOOD Rebecca had already gone to bed. He should hope she had, removing temptation. But he couldn't quell anticipation he hardly recognized, living alone as long as he had. These feelings were too powerful. Not since he was a child had he had someone to come home to. Someone who was *his*, who would be waiting with eagerness to match his own.

But Rebecca wasn't his. He couldn't be sure how she felt about him. He hadn't liked wondering how she saw his house, after living in such luxury with her husband. When he'd showed her around, it had suddenly appeared even shabbier than usual, and he'd had to say something about meaning to remodel, as a kind of apology.

Turning the last corner, he saw that the same lights were on in the house as when he'd left, which didn't mean she had stayed up, only that she was using common sense.

His talk with himself hadn't lessened the hungry anticipation that had him leaping out of his SUV once he was in the garage and covering the distance to the back door with long strides. Stupid as it was, he had a vision of her jumping to her feet the minute she saw him, stepping into his arms as if she couldn't do anything else.

The kitchen was bright and empty, and spotlessly clean. But as he closed and locked the door, he heard quick, light footsteps. Her face lit up at the sight of him, but he also saw nerves and shyness and a whole lot more on her expressive face.

"Daniel! That was quick."

"Was it?" He glanced at the clock above the kitchen table. "I was gone an hour and a half."

"I didn't know if you had other things to do." She stayed a good ten feet from him. "Did you see Matthew?"

His pleasure was dampened by knowing she had met him so eagerly because he would bring news of her son. But he understood and sympathized.

"I did. I gave him a hug from you, and told him you weren't far away, and were thinking about him all the time."

Her eyes filled with tears, but she wiped them with the back of her hand and smiled, too. "Thank you. You knew the right thing to say. He already likes you, you know. You'll make a good father." Her gaze shied from his. "I mean, when you're ready. Um, to have your own kids."

He was ready. Not something he could say, so he only nodded.

"Barbara said he'd been good, and he only worried about when his *mamm* would come back. Amos took the boys to a pond on Rudy Bontrager's place just up the road. They swam and splashed him, he said."

"Oh." Eyes brimming with emotion, she laid a hand on her chest. But then she said, "Do you want coffee? Or something to eat? That rhubarb cobbler, maybe?"

Daniel laughed and shook his head. "I was stuffed before I left, and coffee would just keep me awake. Let's go sit down."

They went to the living room, where he saw his stereo was on, an open CD case lying beside it. She'd been listening to music.

She sank onto one end of the sofa and waited until he lowered himself into the recliner. "What did Amos say?"

"He wasn't happy I hadn't taken you to another family, but he understood." Actually, he had lectured Daniel, saying that, while Rebecca was not a *maidal*, she was a good woman, modest and knowing right from wrong. Daniel took offense at the suggestion that *he* didn't know right from wrong. He and his uncle had gone at it, shouting until his aunt rushed into the kitchen to remind them that there were *kinder* in the house. He thought he wasn't the only one to be ashamed, then.

"He didn't really understand, did he?" Rebecca said unhappily, obviously having read more on Daniel's face than he had meant her to see. "I suppose he's shocked."

He tipped the recliner forward, resting his elbows on his knees. "Not that, I think. Just… struggling with the reminder that you aren't really Amish."

She nodded after a moment, her gaze fastened on his. "Like you."

"What?" He sat up.

"Isn't that what you were telling me? Earlier, I mean, after I changed into this." She waved at herself.

"No!" Wasn't it? "The first couple of times I saw you, when I thought you *were* Amish, I was…disappointed." A mild word for what he'd felt, out of the blue. "When you admitted you weren't, that you were dressing plain only to hide—"

"And out of respect for my family," she interrupted.

Daniel nodded. "To be respectful, too. When I found out you weren't Amish, and were not married, either, I was relieved, because something about you called to me even before I knew you."

She had quit moving, maybe even breathing. They stared at each other. That was more honesty than he'd intended to give, but it was something he had needed to say.

Finally she drew a shuddery breath. "I…felt the same."

His heart began to hammer.

"I didn't want to," she said softly. "You scared me. You saw too much. I told myself you could help, but…the danger seemed too great."

"You thought I'd hurt you?"

Rebecca's ponytail swayed when she shook her head. "See right through me." She tried to smile. "Be able to tell when I was lying."

"Mostly, I could. You're not a good liar."

She made a face.

"It frustrated me that you kept withholding things."

"I'm sorry, but…I was pulled so many ways."

What he wanted to know was whether she could imagine a life here, with him, rather than returning to the city. But he couldn't ask that yet. "You never said how your parents died."

"A drunk driver. *Mamm* was gone right away. Dad…lingered for a day, but never regained consciousness. It was so hard to lose them. I wasn't ready."

This time he didn't fight temptation. He rose and went to her, sitting beside her on the sofa so he could take her hand in his. "Is anyone ever?"

She grimaced. "Probably not. But it hurt, knowing Matthew wouldn't remember them, that they'd never be there again when I had questions. Not having any other family…"

"But you did," he said gently.

Rebecca nodded. "Then…well, I was married, and the gulf seemed too great to cross. I let my grandparents know *Mamm* had died. Ever since I got over being an awful teenager, I had written them regularly. *Grossmammi* was good about writing back."

He smiled, moving his thumb gently across her palm. "The Amish are excellent correspondents."

"It's true." She looked painfully vulnerable when she met his eyes. "Have you heard anything about my grandfather?"

Daniel didn't like to tell her, but knew he had to. "He's failing. *Onkel* Amos said he was told it won't be more than a day or two now."

"Oh," she breathed, stricken. "Do you think—"

He shook his head. "You know it's not safe. He has family around him, and the joy of having gotten to know you again. He's had weeks longer than the doctors expected."

"Yes. I suppose…" Rebecca ducked her head, probably to hide tears.

Daniel tugged her toward him. "Come here."

As she laid her cheek against his shoulder, her body held no tension, as if she were trusting herself to him. Even though it would be easy to let himself become aroused, Daniel felt such contentment he didn't want to move, to lose the tickle of her hair on his throat and chin, her scent.

"Something I've wondered." *Obsessed about* was more like it. "Were you happy in your marriage until the problems at work came up?"

Daniel wasn't sure he really wanted to know. He wished he hadn't asked when she pulled away so she could see his face.

"Only at the beginning." A different kind of sadness clung to her now. "I believed marriage was forever. I didn't let myself acknowledge how disappointed I was. Tim put in such long hours. He was excited about building the company, and I was excited for him, but it was lonely. Especially since he never really talked about decisions he made or any of the important stuff. He had Josh and Steven for that. He never let me feel we were in it together. I wish I'd worked longer before I had Matthew." Rebecca sighed. "The end result is, here I am, thirty-one years old, and I only had my own classroom for a year. Getting my foot in the door now won't be easy."

"Maybe in San Francisco," he said, trying to sound casual, "if you're determined to go back there. But it's not like that in a lot of rural areas. Last year, a fifth-grade teacher here in Hadburg had to quit suddenly, and the school district ended up using substitutes all year. Shiny new grads don't want to come here. It's not so different from my problems replacing a deputy. To young people especially, life here looks backward. And the pay doesn't equal what's offered in a city."

She asked a few questions, and he took the opportunity to tell her that the county had three school districts with a total of eight schools, which didn't sound all that impressive. Still, he hoped for enthusiastic interest, but her response was noncommittal. That made him decide it was time to end the evening before he let himself do something foolish. He wanted her in his bed—but if the idea of staying in Missouri wasn't on her radar, he needed to protect himself.

If that was still possible.

THE NEXT MORNING, Daniel sat in his squad car studying a house that had been for sale for months. Backing on a creek, the property was good, eighty acres with a small woodlot and old fruit trees. The house wasn't much—dating from the 1940s, at a guess, with probably no more than two bedrooms. The place would take work—the fields were overgrown, blackberries claiming large swaths of land, and even from here he could tell that if the roof on the barn wasn't replaced soon, the whole structure would be lost. Amish were no strangers to hard work, and this would be ideal for a young family wanting to farm. The problem, as Daniel had heard it, was that the owners wanted too much money.

This house had been next on his list of empty homes that were potential hideouts for the men he sought. Ever since Tim Gregory's assault on Rebecca in the hospital parking lot, deputies had been visiting properties like this. Ben Slater had his men doing the same in Byrum, as did the chief in River Grove, although Daniel didn't think Griffen and Gregory would have gone to ground anywhere near neighbors who would be likely to notice their comings and goings.

With real estate moving slowly in northeastern Missouri, Daniel doubted local agents had shown this house in some time. Still, squatting here would be a risk. If the owner had been approached about a short-term rental, he would be crazy not to have grabbed it. Daniel had tried calling the man, who now lived in Virginia, but hadn't gotten a return call.

He lowered his window and listened, hearing nothing but birdsong. After a minute, he got out and walked toward the house, but with each step his uneasiness grew. He rested his hand on the butt of his gun. There was no reason to think he wasn't alone here, but he'd learned to listen to his instincts. Besides, what he saw lined up with Anna Lantz's description of where she had been held.

If he hadn't been listening so hard, he might not have heard a squeak as if a porch board were protesting. Going completely still, Daniel let his eyes rove. The sun off the front windows hadn't let him see until now that shades had been drawn, giving the house a secretive look that didn't fit with it being for sale.

One of the barn doors stood open, although the interior was too shadowy for him to tell if a car might be parked there. What he knew was that he felt exposed, certain that somebody was watching him.

Given his department's staffing issues, deputies all patrolled alone.

He eased one foot back, then the next. He could wait the ten or fifteen minutes it would take for backup to arrive.

At a flash of movement in the corner of his eye, a glint of sun off metal, he spun to face the woods and started to draw. That was the moment an engine roared to life.

A white van exploded out of the barn, its driver barreling right for him. He got off one shot before he had to dive out of the way, landing hard on what had been lawn. Even as he rolled, he saw the van swerving at him.

His next shot went through the windshield, but he knew he hadn't hit the driver. Another roll and he got his feet under him enough to leap away—but not before the driver's-side mirror struck his shoulder, sending him flying.

Even as he jumped to his feet and lifted his Glock, the van turned onto the road. He ran down the driveway, hearing the squeal of brakes. A car door slammed. Then the van took off again.

By the time he reached the road, the vehicle was receding. Too far away for him to shoot out a tire.

But he'd taken in most of the license-plate number—and he'd seen the driver's face.

A LITTLE AFTER seven that evening, Daniel let himself in the back door. Unless Rebecca was imagining things, he was moving stiffly as he turned to lock.

She waited until she saw his face, heavily lined with weariness and something else. Her heart cramped.

"You're hurt." She gripped the large spoon in her hand tightly.

"Nothing major." He came to her and nudged her hand back over the stove. "You're dripping on the floor."

"Tell me."

A shadow crossed his face. "Some SOB tried to run me down. Clipped my shoulder. I picked up a few bruises and scrapes."

Some SOB?

"Was it…about something else?"

His eyebrows rose. "Besides you, you mean?"

She bobbed her head.

"No, it definitely had to do with you."

When she moaned, Daniel took the spoon away from her, turned off the burner and steered her to a seat at the kitchen table. Then he pulled up a chair himself, his knees touching hers.

"You know we've been hunting for your ex and Josh." He went on to tell her about realizing the house he was walking toward could be the one in which Anna Lantz and her son had been held. And the wrongness of the shades drawn and the barn door left standing open, followed by a sound that didn't belong if the house was empty.

"You saw the driver," she said finally.

He could tell what she was asking. "Nobody I recognize, but I'll know him the next time I see him." He told her that he'd called in deputies and searched the house, finding evidence that at least two men had been staying there, perhaps more. One of the deputies had taken pictures of the bedrooms and bathroom with his phone and driven to the Lantz farm so Anna could see them.

"She made a positive ID." His eyes, that unusual, deep blue, never left Rebecca's face. "The kitchen was stocked. When they saw me out front, they must have packed fast and run, but we found a few things. A razor and two toothbrushes left in the bathroom, a few scraps of paper." Daniel paused. "One of them had a phone number. Josh Griffen's cell number."

"But…nothing leading to Tim?"

His expression darkened. "Because he couldn't possibly be involved?"

Her temper flared, but she waited it out because he was right. She did keep trying to stick her head in the sand. "No," she said at last. "I know he is."

Daniel's eyes searched hers. "I'm sorry for jumping on you. I don't like thinking you're still—"

"Still what?" she whispered.

"Holding on to any love or regret, I guess."

Her heart drummed at his intensity. She couldn't look away from him. "How can there not be regret after a divorce? You start out so filled with hope. And…we have a child together. I can't walk away and never see him again, however much I wish I could."

"Do you really want to let him influence Matthew?"

She didn't, but… "I think Matthew needs to have some kind of relationship with him. Matthew needs to see that his father has good qualities."

Daniel bent his head suddenly and rubbed a hand over his face and through his hair, leaving it ruffled. "I'm being a jerk. This is hard for me."

"Being attracted to a divorced woman with a kid?" Okay, her temper was still simmering.

His head came up sharply, his eyes pinning her again. "Not knowing how you feel about him." His voice became huskier. "Or me."

CHAPTER SEVENTEEN

"I DON'T KNOW how *you* feel!" Rebecca cried.

"I want you."

"That's not…" Her throat clogged.

"Enough?" One side of his mouth tipped up in an odd smile. "I want you to tell me you won't leave when this is all over. That you'll…give me a chance."

The feelings swelled in her until her chest actually hurt. "You've…forgiven me?"

"Forgiven you?" His face cleared. "You mean for not being truthful."

"Yes."

"Of course I have," he said, in a voice filled with tenderness. "No, that's not right. Forgiveness isn't necessary. I understand why you were afraid to tell me everything."

She couldn't cry. Not at a moment like this. *I will not.* "Thank you for saying that."

"Will you?" He took her head. "Give me a chance? Consider staying?"

She had to blink hard. "Yes. Of course I

will." A smile trembled on her lips. "I'd be crazy not to."

Just like that, they were grinning foolishly at each other. A chance. He was giving *her* a chance. What more could she ask?

DANIEL'S MOOD SOARED. Perhaps he shouldn't read so much into so few words, but he let himself believe she had meant them.

He ate the stew she had produced from what she'd found in his cupboards, and more pie given by Anna Lantz's family. He and Rebecca talked while they ate, but not about anything important. These words didn't seem to matter. The warmth in her eyes, the occasional shyness, the color that tinted her cheeks—those things spoke to him. He felt young and in love. That might sound naive by modern standards. Standards that might be hers, although he thought not. They fit so well because they had both lived with the confusion of not quite belonging where they'd found themselves.

Rebecca insisted on putting away leftovers and cleaning the kitchen while he sat at the table drinking a cup of coffee. He tried to object—he had spent enough years taking care of himself to shake the belief that the kitchen was strictly a woman's domain. Her ex-husband hadn't wanted her to have any life outside the home. Daniel knew better than to make that mistake. She wasn't Amish, and neither was he anymore. As he watched her move around the kitchen with a dancer's grace, he conducted an internal battle.

Would she come to his bed if he asked? A part of him thought it would be wrong to ask. He should wait until she wasn't dependent on him to keep her safe.

But his gaze lingered on the sway of her hips before moving to her long, slender neck, bared when her ponytail swung. He had mentally stripped her a hundred times, and he did it again now, imagining how her breasts would fill his hands, how her legs would wrap around his waist, and how the strong hands she was now drying on a dish towel would knead his shoulders and back.

Suddenly he realized she had quit moving and was watching *him*. Her eyes were dilated, her lips parted. Without thinking, he shoved back the chair and took the few steps he needed to reach her.

"You're so beautiful," he said roughly. "I don't think you know."

She shook her head in instant denial. "No more than plenty of other women."

"In my eyes, that's not so. But it isn't just your lips—" he rubbed his thumb over them "—or your eyes or..." He was the one to shake his head this time. "It's the way you carry yourself. The softness I see on your face when you look at your son, the determination to protect the people you love, the shame you can't hide when you think you wronged someone. The way you guard yourself, even as your eyes give you away." He bent his head until their foreheads touched. "Emotions so open. You've…troubled me from the minute I saw you."

Now dampness shimmered in her eyes. "You've troubled me, too. I couldn't understand why I was so sure I could trust you. Why, when I should stay away from you, I was so happy every time I saw you."

"Yes," he murmured, and kissed her.

REBECCA COULD NO more have prevented herself from responding than she could have stopped loving Matthew. Daniel's passion for her was compelling enough, but the tenderness in his every touch had brought so much to life in her. There was no need for her to ask herself whether she trusted him completely.

She had fallen in love with him so quickly, so hard, she had to believe she wasn't wrong about him.

His lips brushed hers, his tongue dampened them; he nipped and teased, and she did all the same to him. She wrapped her arms around his neck, bringing her body in full contact with his, muscular and solid. His hands roved, warm and strong. He explored every dip and hollow, his fingertips lingering on the bumps of her vertebrae. He kneaded her butt as he lifted her higher against him. She wanted more. His tongue in her mouth, his—

Daniel groaned and deepened the kiss. Suddenly, her back was against something hard. Startled, she realized he had walked her backward. By some instinct, she wrapped one leg around his. Her rubber flip-flop dropped to the floor, and he growled something as both his hands gripped the backs of her thighs.

"Your shoulder."

"Don't care," he muttered. His hard length pressed between her thighs as he pinned her to the wall and kissed her deeply with a driving passion that made her melt. She tried to rock her hips and couldn't, but, oh, he felt so good. Her fingers had slid into his hair, feeling its heavy silk as she sucked on his tongue.

An indescribable sound vibrated from his chest. When he went completely still, Rebecca almost whimpered.

He rubbed his bristly jaw over her cheek. "Rebecca." His voice was guttural. "If you're not ready…"

For an answer, she closed her teeth on his earlobe.

Another of those raw sounds escaped him. "Then hold on tight."

She already was, her legs locked around his hips.

He carried her out of the kitchen and up the stairs, pausing twice along the way to kiss her again with ravening hunger.

In his bedroom, they undressed each other. He removed his belt first, laying it with the holster and gun on the bedside table. After that, he let her undo one button on his shirt at a time. Despite their growing urgency, neither was hasty. Once she'd tossed the short-sleeved shirt aside, she squeezed the muscles between his neck and shoulders, stroked the powerful planes of his chest dusted with hair a shade darker than that on his head, kissed the horrible bruise that capped one shoulder. His muscles jerked at her every touch.

He tested the weight of her breasts, flattened a hand on her stomach before his fingers slid beneath the waistband of the skirt. Rebecca bent her head and watched him tug the skirt over her hips, letting it fall to pool at her bare feet. She was even paler than she'd been when they came to Missouri, except for tanned forearms and face. The contrast looked odd to her, but nothing in his rapt expression suggested he was disappointed. When finally he looked up, his eyes were pure heat, the blue at the center of a flame, while dark color ran across his cheekbones.

"You're the most beautiful thing I've ever seen."

He was the most beautiful thing she had ever seen, broad shoulders, sleek muscles, the arrow of hair disappearing beneath his uniform pants.

Embarrassed at the compliment, she said, "Where's the Amish in you?"

He nuzzled her face. "Amish boys dream about naked girls, too, you know. But this isn't like that."

"I'm glad," she whispered shakily.

For an instant, they looked at each other, naked in a way that went far beyond unclothed bodies.

And then he reached behind her and unclipped her bra. Even as his mouth found her breast, he swung her up and laid her down on his bed. The pull on her breast had her arching and crying out, grabbing his head to keep him close. She didn't want to let him go when he sat up—until she saw him untying and then tossing away his shoes, stripping off his socks and unzipping his pants.

Then he muttered something beneath his breath and took out his wallet, removing a small packet from it.

Oh, heavens—she hadn't given a thought to birth control. Truthfully, she hadn't done anything she could call thinking since his mouth first closed over hers.

"You've been carrying one?"

The eyes that met hers were almost black with intensity. "I came so close to making love to you that night behind the barn."

She might have been annoyed that he had assumed she was willing…except he was right. It wouldn't have occurred to her to stop him.

"Later, I realized I didn't have a condom with me. I bought some right away." One side of his mouth curved. "In case."

Rebecca felt her cheeks warming as he stripped out of his trousers and knit boxers. So silly—but she'd seen only one other naked man in her life. And this one was…magnificent. Despite the shyness, she couldn't resist reaching out to touch. He watched with that burning gaze as she tentatively stroked him and even imagined kissing him there, something she had never dreamed of doing with Tim.

Daniel's fingers suddenly closed around her wrist. "No more," he said roughly. "I need to be inside you."

He had her panties off so fast she didn't see them go flying. He was beside her, above her, stroking until she needed something so desperately. She tried in every way she knew to tell him without words. She didn't even have a moment of apprehension when he found his place between her thighs and pressed slowly inside her, watching her the entire time. His teeth were set, the skin stretched tight across his cheekbones, the dark hunger in his eyes as powerful as what he was doing to her body.

She didn't last long, but he didn't, either. She didn't quite scream…but close. The raw sound Daniel made might have been ripped from his throat.

He rolled to one side then, leaving a chill that was psychological rather than real—but then he gathered her back into his arms and settled her with her head on his shoulder.

DANIEL DIDN'T LET himself wonder whether she'd prefer not to cuddle in the aftermath, given that they were both sweat-slick from the furious lovemaking and the heat that rose to the second story on September nights. He needed to keep her close.

He was shaken in a way he hadn't expected. Sex was fun—forbidden fun, a long-suppressed voice would whisper in his head. But this, what he and Rebecca had just done, was something more. Something out of his control, as Rebecca had been from their first eye contact.

He stayed silent because he didn't know what to say. What seemed extraordinary to him might not to her. Feeling like an uncertain boy didn't sit well with him. But this silence could be damaging. What was she thinking?

She stirred. "Say something."

Did that mean she felt as vulnerable? Daniel wondered. "I'm still speechless."

"You don't look down on me because I said yes, do you?"

"What?" He rolled again, so that he was above her with his weight on his elbows. "How can you think that?"

"*Grossmammi* would think I behaved like an *Englischer*, making myself cheap."

Was she joking? But her eyes were dark and serious, her teeth closed on her lower lip.

"I think your grandmother would be angry at me, not you," he said honestly. "I know I should have waited until you didn't need me to keep you safe."

"You don't think…I came to bed with you so you'd keep helping me?"

"No." He pressed a soft kiss on her mouth. "You don't hide what you feel that well."

Rebecca wrinkled her nose, altering the mood. "I'll have to practice."

"Don't." His voice lowered. "I like seeing your emotions passing through your eyes."

"Oh." She lifted a hand to cup his cheek. "I've never felt like this before."

That was all the reassurance he needed. "I haven't, either." There was a wet smack of skin separating when he lifted himself off her. Daniel laughed. "The shower isn't huge, but I think we could share it."

"Please," she said.

Of course, they got sweaty again not long after taking the cool shower, but the experience was so pleasurable, even joyous, Daniel was happy to start all over again. In fact…he was so happy, he felt as if the hollow inside him had been filled to overflowing.

REBECCA WALKED DANIEL to the back door before work the next morning. She'd put on the same skirt with a camisole from her duffel bag, explaining she'd die of heatstroke in the clothes she set out from San Francisco with.

"Do you think you could buy me a pair of shorts?" she asked, sounding hopeful.

Imagining how they would expose a luscious length of her legs, he said, "Sure." He loved her bare toes—and that he could tell she hadn't put on a bra this morning. Her hair was still wet from a morning shower, too. It was hard to tear his gaze from the droplets shimmering on her neck.

Of course, he couldn't exactly buy shorts for a woman at Miller's General Store without giving away a whole lot, but he wouldn't mind taking the time to drive to Byrum.

Determined to do some research today and call or email Estevez, Daniel had his tablet tucked under his arm. The situation had become frustrating. What had happened with the warrant? He wanted to get his hands on Josh and Tim both and wring the identities of their confederates out of them, too—especially the one who'd tried to run him down.

Seeing her glance at the tablet, he said, "I'm sorry I can't leave it so you can go online today."

Her head tilted like a bird's. "Why are you so worried I'll be bored?"

Her question poked at his deepest core of insecurity. If she thought Hadburg was dull, she'd want to leave. Going with her…that would be like trying to transplant a deep-rooted tree. She understood that; he didn't think she'd ask it of him, but that didn't mean she'd be content here.

"I don't know," he lied.

Rebecca went on tiptoe and kissed his jaw. "You have everything here I need to entertain myself." Her lips flirted with a tiny, mischievous smile. "I think I'll start browsing those books on remodeling. It might be fun to learn to tile or who knows what else."

Because she meant to stay, to work on the house with him? He hoped the insecurity was gone, once and for all.

"Okay." He kissed her goodbye and drove to work, parking in back.

The first couple of hours were consumed by administrative necessities. Scheduling for the next week, always a juggling act. Given the current tension, he denied a request for leave. Worked on a budget request asking for some improved technology he intended to submit to the county council, even though he knew it would be denied. All the while, he kept an eye on the clock.

At nine in the morning West Coast time, he called Estevez.

"Just walked in the door. I was going to call you first thing," the detective claimed. "Warrant came through yesterday for Tim and Josh, denied for Gregory senior." He didn't sound surprised, as Daniel wasn't. "We pinged their phones. We got nothing on Griffen's phone. I did a little leg work. Turns out both Gregorys are here in the city."

"You talked to Robert?"

"Damn straight I did. I got an icy reception. He said his only interest is in his grandson, that he's 'pursuing legal remedies.' Tim was home, said he wouldn't talk to me again without his attorney being present, but a blind man would have known he's falling apart. I told him he's wanted for assault in Missouri. He tried to claim that's ridiculous, his ex-wife's bruises were the result of an accident and she's accusing him maliciously, but he's scared shitless."

"You think he'll crack."

"Oh, yeah. My gut feeling is he got in over his head. He's furious with Ms. Holt, but the possibility of being implicated in the abduction of an innocent woman and child has him shaking in his boots. I told him to be smart and stay put. That taking off, and especially setting foot in Missouri right now, would not look good to investigators, prosecutors or the judge and jury when he appears in court."

"You'll know if he takes off?"

"If he flies commercial. I'll try to keep an eye on him, but you know how overextended we are."

It was a sad truth in any jurisdiction.

"When do you intend to pull him in for an interview?"

"This afternoon. I'll call you after."

They signed off, Daniel wishing he could feel relief. Josh Griffen, likely still here in the county, was the dangerous one. He was willing to bet the partnership between Josh and Tim was irreparably broken. Tim had gotten greedy, and then panicked and tried to cover up what he'd done. But Josh had killed and was willing to kill again to save his own skin.

Knowing it was Rebecca whom Josh intended to kill sent rage running like an electric current beneath Daniel's skin. He had to find the son of a bitch.

THUNDER GRUMBLED IN the distance, increasing Rebecca's sense of unease. She didn't understand herself. Daniel had worked yesterday, too, leaving her alone, and she hadn't felt the tiny hairs on her nape prickling, hadn't been so aware of how quiet the house was, hadn't been unwilling to play music to fill that quiet.

He'd mentioned not having a landline, but she hadn't expected the lack of a phone to scrape at her nerves. Daniel had tossed the one she'd used to call Tim into a Dumpster, saying it wasn't safe for her to keep using. She wished she'd thought to ask him to replace it, but she hadn't expected this uneasy awareness that she had no way to call him for help, or for him to let her know if anything happened.

She did read, but kept imagining small sounds. Or maybe the house was settling, as old houses did. Each time she heard a noise, she'd walk a circuit through the downstairs, peeking through blinds or around curtains in a way that wouldn't show if anyone was watching the house. It was dumb to have let her imagination run wild. Tim and Josh couldn't possibly know she was here. Besides the woods in back, there wasn't a good place for a watcher to hide, either.

But instinct said *something* was going to happen.

And all she could do was wait and listen as the storm drew closer.

THEY NEEDED RAIN, but did it have to be today? Answering the internal line on his desk phone, Daniel stood at the window in his office looking at the ominous clouds filling the sky to the north.

"What's up?"

Melissa Sue said, "Bert at the corner store called. He says some young guys are hanging out in the parking lot hassling customers. He's losing business. He sounded mad."

Daniel sighed. "I'll walk over."

Forget what he'd been thinking about the storm. With some luck, he decided, the skies would open up and soak the little jackasses. A lightning bolt somewhere in their vicinity wouldn't be a bad thing, either, so long as nobody was hurt. He looked up at the sky as he turned the corner. *How about it, God?* he asked, while acknowledging that He had more important things to do. *If this is my purpose, then He trusts me to do my job,* he reminded himself.

His jaw tightened when he recognized Billy Shaver at the center of the cluster of young men, pants hanging low, cigarettes dangling from several of their mouths. Damon wasn't with them—maybe he'd acquired a little sense. A woman had pulled up to get gas in front, but two of the boys circled her car, slapping hands on the roof, hood and trunk. She jerked in fear with each ring of metal, afraid to get out. Daniel couldn't figure out why terrorizing a woman on her own could possibly be fun.

The boys saw him approaching and retreated to their pack. The woman seized the chance to drive away without filling her tank. Daniel saw Bert, the stocky store owner, standing behind the glass doors, arms crossed, glowering.

Not boys, Daniel told himself. Not this group. He knew them all. They were troublemakers, none younger than eighteen. At least two, including Billy, were over twenty-one. Old enough to know better. An Amish man of their age would have committed to his church, be marrying and starting a family, working hard at his profession.

He knew they'd seen him across the parking lot, but Daniel turned when he heard the fast clop of horses' hooves on pavement and the hum of wheels. Not much reason for Amish to be passing down this road.

It was Samuel Graber who reined in the horse at the curb beside Daniel. This couldn't be chance. "Amos says Rebecca is with you. *Mamm* sent me to find you, to say that Ephraim has died peacefully, and at home, God be thanked. If she can come, the funeral—" He stopped midsentence, his gaze going past Daniel, who swung around in alarm.

Oh, damn. He hadn't seen Billy break away from the group, or heard his approach.

"The sheriff has hisself an Amish girlfriend," Billy taunted. "She putting out, Sheriff?"

Ignoring the rest of the crowd, which was growing brave enough to swagger forward, too, and arrange themselves behind Billy, Daniel skewered the punk with a hard stare. "You don't know what you're talking about. Back off. You and your buddies."

Hate flickered in Billy's brown eyes. "We're just being friendly. Curious, you might say. This the lady some men want to find? You ought to be more careful, *Sheriff.*"

Temper filled Daniel, as dangerous as the storm but slow moving, too. He had always been able to control it. He took out his phone, wishing he'd called sooner for backup. He hoped Bert had made the call for him.

But he kept his voice calm in hopes of preventing an escalation. "I've tried to work with you, Billy. Give you a fair chance. But that's not what you want, is it?"

"Fair chance?" Billy snarled. "That what you call it? Riding my ass, sticking your nose in my business?" He spit a glob of something brown in Daniel's direction, then told Daniel where he could put his fair chances.

Would Samuel's presence make any difference? The horse was shifting uneasily, hooves clattering and harness creaking. Samuel stayed silent.

Daniel looked from one to another hostile face. "You boys need to go home. This is your warning. You have no reason to be here. I can arrest you for trespassing if you don't get moving, *now.*" He made sure they heard the steel.

Billy didn't even blink. Daniel didn't dare look away. He felt as if he was engaging in a staring contest with a venomous cottonmouth.

A couple of the others were backing away, and a guy right beside Billy said, "Hey, man, what are you doing?"

Billy shrugged insolently. "Must be the girlfriend that has the *sheriff* so hot and bothered. I'm going." He started to turn away, then, with the speed of a striking snake, he lashed out, sending Daniel's phone flying. He took off running, followed by the others.

Daniel growled something Samuel would find abhorrent, but let them go. He could track them down later. It was the threat that mattered.

This the lady some men want to find? You ought to be more careful.

If Billy knew who to call…

The horse danced, Samuel murmuring reassurance. Even so, the buggy rocked forward and back—and Daniel saw his phone just before a steel wheel rim rolled over it with a *crunch*.

Daniel's decision to arrest the punk set, concrete hard.

And then she really looked at his face, and she still couldn't ... What was wrong?

"You don't know me and I trick the car the old house tonight?" and ...

... to be in ... our ... A ... ...

CHAPTER EIGHTEEN

THUNDER RATTLED THE window glass. Rebecca cringed. No more than a second later, the shocking flash of light momentarily blinded her. Rain hammered on the roof and enveloped the house in gray sheets. The light was murky, even if it was only five thirty and sunset was almost two hours away.

With her ears still ringing, she wasn't positive she'd heard the car engine, but then the door rattled and Daniel walked in. He was drenched—hair plastered to his head, uniform to his body.

Stopping just inside, he said, "Would you mind getting me a towel? I don't want to drip all the way through the house."

Rebecca ran upstairs and brought a couple of towels. Daniel was already stripping. She watched as he tossed the shirt to one side in the tiny mudroom that also held a stacked washer and dryer. The chill she'd felt all day lessened at the pleasure of seeing that muscular body as he scrubbed himself with the first towel, ending up with his hair poking every which way.

And then she really looked at his face, and the chill returned. "What's wrong?"

"You mean, what new and fresh disaster do I have to report?"

She nodded.

"I have to move you again. A conversation I had with your uncle was overheard by an ex-con who hates me."

"But he couldn't know—"

"He does." Definitely grim. "He instantly associated you with 'the lady some men want to find.'"

She dropped into a straight-backed kitchen chair. "Right now?"

He unbuckled his belt and dropped his holster and gun on one end of the counter, then stripped off his shoes, socks and soggy pants, leaving him in nothing but shorts. "By morning. With this weather, I have to stay available. Creeks and river were so low, we shouldn't have any flooding, but there'll be car accidents and fires. I need to change, get out my rain gear and go back to headquarters."

Leaving her here, alone. But she could only nod because, of course, he had to do his job.

"You'll have to come with me," he added. "I hate to stick you in that conference room again, but you'll be safest there. If you don't have something warmer to put on, I'll find you a sweat-shirt. I have an extra rain slicker, too."

Not alone. *Thank you.*

Thunder rolled, but not overhead. The lightning flash wasn't as immediate or as bright. And…had the rain let up a little, too?

"The pisser is, I lost my phone," Daniel grumbled. "Should have stopped for a new one, but I was too worried about you. I'll have the police radio once I get back to the station, but—" His expression changed, the compassion as powerful as a touch, and somehow she knew what he would say.

"Samuel drove to town to let me know your grandfather died, Rebecca. Peacefully, he said." Daniel padded across the kitchen to her and crouched beside the chair, laying a cold hand over hers. "I'm sorry."

Tears threatened, but she held them back. She bobbed her head. "It was coming."

"Yes." His blue eyes searched hers. "Samuel sounded almost relieved. His *daad* went the way he should, at home, his family around him. It would have been harder on all of them if Ephraim had died that night at the hospital."

"Hooked up to all those machines." She still wanted to cry, but Daniel was right.

"You okay?"

She pulled herself together. "Yes. Go change."

After another, thorough scan of her face, he rose. "I need to take a quick shower. Then we can go." He grabbed his gun and took it with him.

Rebecca followed him upstairs and went into the guest room to dig through her duffel bag. Fortunately, she had jeans and athletic shoes. T-shirt, with a hoodie over it, she decided, pulling out what she needed.

She heard the shower across the hall and indulged herself in the sensual memory of showering with Daniel before she sighed, stepped out of the skirt and reached for the jeans.

More thunder, and the rain was still coming down, but she went still, listening. Was that a car? Maybe a deputy coming to get Daniel because he couldn't call?

Quickly fastening the jeans, she sidled until she was beside the window and dared to take a peek. The sedan that blocked the garage was silver, not sheriff's department green and white. And a dark-colored SUV was coming up the driveway, going fast. It veered to cross the lawn, disappearing around the front of the house. Car doors opened and men climbed out, carrying rifles.

Heart drumming, she tore across the hall. The bathroom door opened just as she reached it and Daniel walked out.

"There are men with guns outside," she gasped. "They're surrounding the house."

Daniel said a word she'd never heard him use. He ran to the bedroom, eased the shade aside and swore again. A second later, he had a big, evil-looking weapon in his hand.

"Look in my closet," he said. "There's a gun safe. I have a backup handgun and ammunition in there." He told her the combination, which she dialed with a shaking hand.

The smaller gun was already loaded but only held six bullets, he told her.

"I need to call—" He gritted his teeth. "No phone. That punk did it on purpose."

Rebecca didn't ask for explanation. "Your tablet?"

"Kitchen."

She vaguely recalled seeing him set it down.

They were completely isolated.

Glass shattered downstairs.

"The bathroom is the safest place for you," he told her with unnatural calm, gaze steady. "Sit down in the tub. It's cast iron, and will stop bullets. I'll identify myself if I open the door. If somebody else tries to come in, shoot them. Aim for the torso. It's hard to miss at close range."

"What about you?"

Even as she asked, he pulled on a vest, fastening it with Velcro tape. She'd seen those before, black with POLICE in white across the back. Thank God he had one here, only...it didn't seem to protect enough of his big body.

A voice came up the stairs and she knew her chance of scuttling into the bathroom had been lost. "Rebecca, you know what I want." Josh. "Hand it over, and we'll go away."

Sure they would. But when her lips parted, Daniel shook his head. So softly she barely heard, he said, "They can't be sure you're here."

Oh.

Daniel stood just inside his bedroom door, where he could see the hall and staircase. He raised his voice. "You're armed and you've broken into a police officer's home. If you thought you were in trouble before, it was nothing."

A shot rang out. He didn't even flinch, although she heard wood splinter and plastic crumble. Daniel leaned forward and fired. One, two.

Swearing came from down below.

He looked at her with those eerily calm eyes and whispered, "Lie down behind the bed."

She did, her head at the foot of the bed where she would see approaching feet. And then she waited.

HE SHOULD HAVE gotten her stowed in the bathroom quicker.

But—shit. He had a ladder in the garage. If they found it, they could climb the side of the house and come in through one of the windows. There were at least four of them, one of him. And no way for him to call for help.

He peered around the door frame and saw the top of a head. This time, he deliberately aimed high as he took a shot.

After hearing an obscene word and a clatter on the stairs, Daniel raised his voice. "Last warning."

He faced the knowledge that he might have to kill, something he'd avoided in his career so far. Fighting back was one thing. Taking warning shots. But killing another human being? Even cops with no religious faith struggled after having to commit that act. For him, it could be soul destroying.

His jaw tightened as he pushed the devastating realization away. To keep Rebecca safe, he'd do whatever these men forced him into. Even as a boy, he hadn't been able to turn the other cheek. Now, the weight of the gun in his hand told him what he had become.

A barrage of gunfire had him stepping back.

Then he thrust his hand around the door frame and opened fire blindly.

"Daniel?"

He glanced over his shoulder and saw that Rebecca had risen to her knees to look out the window. Damn it, she knew better.

"There's a horse and buggy coming."

"What?"

In a voice filled with fear, she said, "I think it's *Onkel* Samuel."

Had he come to apologize for betraying Rebecca's location today? Or had he heard something? *Please God*, he prayed, *don't let them kill such a good man, and in front of Rebecca.*

Some cursing and a flurry of voices came from below. Rebecca, who had stayed on her knees beside the window, said, "There's another buggy behind him. And…another turning in."

Samuel, he realized suddenly, would never have driven out here to say a few words, not when doing so would confirm Rebecca's presence.

Gripping his Glock in both hands, Daniel stole another look down the hall and saw nothing.

"What's happening?" he asked, unable to risk crossing to the window.

"They're driving onto the lawn. Oh, Daniel." Emotion swelled in her voice, because she knew a miracle was being performed right in front of her. "More are coming. The men are parking the buggies and just sitting there. I can't see the gunmen, but…" Her voice broke. "There must be a dozen buggies now. They've formed a line, and they're blocking the driveway. It's as if…"

"They're saying, *Kill us all, or know anything you do is being witnessed.*"

Her "yes" came out soggy.

Daniel heard a siren. And then…that had to be a second.

He let himself look at the woman he loved, who looked back, her eyes brimming with both emotions and tears. And then he continued to do his job. He slipped into the hall, keeping his back to the wall, and edged toward the staircase. He couldn't relax until he knew Rebecca was truly safe.

"It was Mike Bontrager heard," Samuel explained.

Daniel listened, stunned. He had yet to allow Rebecca to emerge from the house and make herself vulnerable. Until police cleared the area, they couldn't be positive a sniper hadn't set up to pick her off if she appeared framed in a window or stepped outside. And, yes, he knew how unlikely that was, and that he was being absurdly overprotective.

"Mike heard that Billy make a call, thinking himself alone. He told someone where he could find Rebecca and that he had taken care of your phone."

Mike was the teenage son of Eli Bontrager, the harness maker who had lost so much in the fire this summer. Daniel knew Mike to be enjoying his *Rumspringa* with his gang, but was still a good kid. He'd know who Billy was, and about his prison term.

By good luck, Mike had seen Samuel, who had still been in town informing others about Ephraim. Mike had used his cell phone to call several Amish businesses as Samuel rounded up what other Amish men he could find.

"We thought those men wouldn't do anything bad if they knew they were being watched," he said in his stolid way. "Mike and his friend David went to your police station. We were afraid the deputies working might be too far away, or too busy with something bad to come, but they must have driven very fast."

In fact, the two deputies who had arrived on the heels of the last Amish buggy had been joined in the next ten minutes by an off-duty deputy, followed almost immediately by officers from the Byrum police department, including Ben Slater, who was currently listening to one of his officers talking and gesturing toward the woods.

Three of the intruders now sat in police cars,

hands cuffed behind their backs, heads hanging.
Two of the four men had bolted for the woods,
but one had gotten hung up on a barbed-wire
fence almost immediately. Daniel recognized
him as the driver of the van that had nearly run
him down. No wondered he'd tried to escape.
Only Josh Griffen had made it to the cover of
the trees.

Floodlights had been set up in the back, and
deputies and two more late-arriving Byrum police officers were situated along the back roads
where Griffen would emerge if he made it that
far.

Shortly after the police cars arrived and the
first two intruders surrendered, the Amish had
nodded to Daniel and, one by one, circled their
buggies, trotting down the driveway and returning to town. They had done what they were
called to do and didn't want to be mixed up any
more with the law than they had to be.

He knew all those faces, some stern, some
usually smiling. Reuben Gingerich, Harvey
Stolzfus, Yonnie Miller, Isaac Bontrager, even
the humorless minister, Amos King. And among
them was Daniel's *daad*, whose eyes had smiled
as he bent his head to his son.

Only Samuel remained, apparently feeling
obligated to explain their presence.

"We'd be dead if you hadn't come." Daniel

choked up as he thanked the man who had acted
so decisively to rescue his niece, and done so
without violating any of his principles. "I might
have had to shoot to kill. You saved me from
that."

Samuel looked gravely down at him. "I will
pray you never have to do such a thing."

One of Daniel's deputies called for him, and
Samuel looked at the house. "You will bring
Rebecca to us?"

It was more an order than a request. Her family would not permit her to stay with him. Re-
bellion rose in Daniel, joining his burning need
to go back into the house and just hold her. Yet
he also felt driven to do his job with dignity. Rebecca would understand, he told himself.

Now he said, "I'll bring her to see you."

Samuel's eyes narrowed at an answer that
wasn't what he wanted to hear, but he finally
nodded. "Then I must go. Emma and *Mamm*
will be worrying, me being gone so long."

Daniel backed away, watching as the buggy
swung in a U-turn. Then he walked across the
wet grass to join Ben.

The rain had passed, he was surprised to realize. When he tipped his head back, he saw a
few scattered stars between shredded clouds.
A very faint rumble and flash of light in the
distance told him the storm had moved south.

"Thanks for coming," he said, holding out his hand.

Ben shook it. "Hell of a thing. What those creeps did was downright crazy."

"My place is isolated enough, they must have thought they could get in, kill us both and get out quick. My guess is they were prepared to kill any deputy who showed up, too."

"You got lucky with that Amish kid not only hearing what he did, but acting on it. From what I've learned, that's not usual."

"No." He hesitated. "It's Rebecca's connection to them. Everyone who knows her situation has joined to protect her."

"And you," Ben said shrewdly.

"Maybe." Something to think about. Had he held himself apart unnecessarily, thinking he wasn't welcome when he might have been?

Ben's phone rang. Eyes meeting Daniel's, he answered immediately. "Yeah?" After a moment, he said, "Good work. Yeah, hold on a second." He lowered the phone. "Griffen walked out of the woods with his hands up."

Relief profound, he said, "Tell them to go ahead to the jail. I'll follow in a few minutes to interrogate all four of these guys."

"Good. See you there."

The cars started to clear out, including the ones transporting the prisoners. Daniel walked back to the house, pausing to release the deputy standing guard on the front porch, and went inside.

Rebecca jumped up from the sofa, her face anxious. "Is it—"

"Over? Yes. Griffen was just arrested."

"Thank God," she whispered, and rushed into his arms.

He probably held her too tightly, but he couldn't seem to loosen his grip. He rubbed his cheek against her hair. So much emotion welled inside him that his rib cage hurt.

"I made so many mistakes," he finally said. "I think you'd have died tonight if we hadn't been lucky. So lucky."

Rebecca shook her head vehemently, lifting her chin so she could see him. "What are you talking about? How could you possibly have predicted something so insane?"

"Griffen couldn't stop. He should never have come to Missouri. The ring and wallet connected to Tim, not him. But he decided you were a threat and couldn't stop. Maybe his ego wouldn't let him."

"I think he always felt he had to prove himself. He and Tim were friends, but..."

"Josh resented Tim for having the advantages he didn't."

"Yes. And maybe Steven for overcoming even

more obstacles and becoming a man who was satisfied with what he'd made of himself."

Daniel shook his head. So much of that made no real sense to him, even if he understood it intellectually. Money or what college a man attended had nothing to do with what made him worthy of respect from friends and family. Now Griffen would be stripped of such outward signs of success when his time came to be judged.

Rebecca shivered. "When they first showed up, I was so afraid Tim was one of them."

He didn't allow himself to think that she was again being protective of her ex-husband. "That would have been hard," he agreed, instead. "When he told you on the phone he hadn't had any part in the abduction of Anna Lantz and her son, it was probably true. Stealing money, trying to get out of trouble—those he would do, but not more."

"Yes, except…" Doubt tightened her voice. "If he'd gotten me into the car that day at the hospital, where did he intend to take me?"

He didn't want to make excuses for her ex-husband, but the fact that he had gone home to face Josh—and Robert—softened Daniel's anger. "Probably to talk to Josh," he said, "but I wonder if he understood what his friend was capable of doing."

"On one level, I think he did. He hinted once

that Josh was the real threat to me. He might have even been trying to serve as a buffer. He was just…"

Weak. She didn't want to say it, and Daniel didn't blame her. It would be hard on a boy to know what his father was really like, but she could shield Matthew only so far. She must know that.

"I didn't mean to leave you in here alone for so long."

"I understood." She laid her head on his chest, showing trust and acceptance that threatened to break his control.

"I have to go to Byrum to interview all four men. It's better if I talk to them before they have too much time to think about how they can get out of this."

Her fingers bit into his back, but then she straightened, making an effort to hide her tension. "That's your job."

"On my way, I can drop you at my aunt and uncle's. You can see Matthew, stay the night."

Tears filled her eyes. "You wouldn't mind?"

He would, because he wanted her here, waiting for him when he got home, but leaving her alone now wasn't an option. And…Samuel was right.

Hiding his reluctance, he said, "Of course not."

"Should I pack everything?" she asked, sounding…he wasn't quite sure. "I mean, to stay?"

Neither his family nor hers would find it acceptable for her to remain here with him now. Letting her go was something he had to do. He could court her, take her out to dinner, for drives. Think of things they could do that would include Matthew.

"You probably should."

She gave a jerky nod and whirled away.

"I love you," he said to her back, surprising himself.

She didn't move.

His heart clenched. It was too soon. He'd presumed too much.

And then she turned back, smiling and crying both. "I love you, too. I do, Daniel."

Somehow, he was across the room, kissing her. She tasted of salt but happiness, too. He tried to let her know everything he felt: passion, desperation, tenderness.

When he could make himself release her lips, he said, "We can't offend our families." But to make himself wish her a polite good-night in front of his *onkel* Amos or Samuel… Daniel didn't know how he would be able to do that.

"I know." Rebecca sounded equally sad.

"I'll come to see you every day. We can be

like other courting couples." Minus the courting
buggy, he thought. And those couples hadn't already made love, didn't have to take a step back.

"Date." She smiled, if tremulously.

"I should get to know Matthew."

"He already likes you, but…that would be
good."

Daniel took a deep breath. "That's what we
should do. But I want you here, with me. Will
you marry me?"

Again her eyes flooded with tears. "Of course
I will!"

"Soon?"

"Tomorrow, if you can arrange it."

He laughed. "Not that soon. There's Ephraim's
funeral, for one. And we should be married in
my church, which means talking to my pastor.
Our families will want to be there. Matthew
should have a chance to get used to the idea. I
can survive a few weeks."

"I'm not sure I can. Oh." She swiped her tears
on his shirtfront.

Even though he ought to hurry, they kissed
and made plans and kissed some more. And
when she said, "Poor Tim," he only nodded his
understanding. The Lord's Prayer, made before
every meal throughout his youth, said, "Forgive
us our trespasses, as we forgive those who tres-
pass against us."

And on this night, they had certainly been delivered from evil.

Yes, he could forgive and help a man who had been led into temptation to remain important to his son.

"I love you," Daniel said again, before giving her a nudge. "Leave your *Englisch* clothes here. You won't need them where you're going."

Soon he would have a wife and family. He searched inside but could no longer find the fear that he would never quite belong anyplace, with anyone.

They held hands all the way to the Troyers'. Witnessing Rebecca's reunion with her son moved him more than he'd expected. Matthew even flung his arms around Daniel and whispered, "You brought my mommy back."

That made it not so hard to say a quiet goodbye and drive away.

What were a few weeks out of a lifetime?

* * * * *

Get 2 Free Books,

<u>Plus</u> 2 Free Gifts—

just for trying the Reader Service!

Get 2 Free Books,
Plus 2 Free Gifts —
just for trying the Reader Service!

HARLEQUIN *Presents*

YES! Please send me 2 FREE Harlequin Presents® novels and my 2 FREE gifts (gifts are worth about $10 retail). After receiving them, if I don't wish to receive any more books, I can return the shipping statement marked "cancel." If I don't cancel, I will receive 6 brand-new novels every month and be billed just $4.55 each for the regular-print edition or $5.55 each for the larger-print edition in the U.S., or $5.49 each for the regular-print edition or $5.99 each for the larger-print edition in Canada. That's a saving of at least 11% off the cover price! It's quite a bargain! Shipping and handling is just 50¢ per book in the U.S. and 75¢ per book in Canada.* I understand that accepting the 2 free books and gifts places me under no obligation to buy anything. I can always return a shipment and cancel at any time. Even if I never buy another book, the 2 free books and gifts are mine to keep forever.

Please check one: ☐ Harlequin Presents® Regular-Print   ☐ Harlequin Presents® Larger-Print
                     (106/306 HDN GLP6)   (176/376 HDN GLP7)

Name   (PLEASE PRINT)

Address   Apt. #

City   State/Prov.   Zip/Postal Code

Signature (if under 18, a parent or guardian must sign)

Mail to the **Reader Service:**
IN U.S.A.: P.O. Box 1867, Buffalo, NY 14240-1867
IN CANADA: P.O. Box 611, Fort Erie, Ontario L2A 9Z9

Want to try two free books from another series? Call 1-800-873-8635 or visit www.ReaderService.com.

* Terms and prices subject to change without notice. Prices do not include applicable taxes. Sales tax applicable in N.Y. Canadian residents will be charged applicable taxes. Offer not valid in Quebec. This offer is limited to one order per household. Books received may not be as shown. Not valid for current subscribers to Harlequin Presents books. All orders subject to credit approval. Credit or debit balances in a customer's account(s) may be offset by any other outstanding balance owed by or to the customer. Please allow 4 to 6 weeks for delivery. Offer available while quantities last.

> **Your Privacy**—The Reader Service is committed to protecting your privacy. Our Privacy Policy is available online at www.ReaderService.com or upon request from the Reader Service.
>
> We make a portion of our mailing list available to reputable third parties that offer products we believe may interest you. If you prefer that we not exchange your name with third parties, or if you wish to clarify or modify your communication preferences, please visit us at www.ReaderService.com/consumerschoice or write to us at Reader Service Preference Service, P.O. Box 9062, Buffalo, NY 14240-9062. Include your complete name and address.

HP17R

Get 2 Free Books,

Plus 2 Free Gifts—

just for trying the Reader Service!

HARLEQUIN®
HEARTWARMING™

Get 2 Free Books,
Plus 2 Free Gifts —
just for trying the
Reader Service!